Insanely Deadly

Holly Copella

To my grandmother, Myrtle "Nannie" Morris.
Thank you for introducing me to the horror genre.

ACKNOWLEDGMENTS

Copella Books
Cover Artist: Yvonrz
SelfPubBookCovers.com/Yvonrz
Printed by CreateSpace, An Amazon.com Company

PUBLISHER'S NOTE

Chapter One

*W*inter Harbor Island, a small island found just off the coast of Maine, was a renowned summer hotspot for those with wealth and influence. Its limited vacation homes and a single luxury hotel along the sandy shore made it desired by those seeking serenity and isolation. Just one mile inland was the small town of Winter Harbor, a close-knit community of small-town people who knew their neighbors--and their neighbor's business. Mostly every family in town had lived in Winter Harbor for generations. Despite the harsh winters, locals cherished their town and celebrated the end of the summer season. They could once again reclaim their quiet lives free from wealthy tourists. Further inland was miles of desired farmland and majestic woodlands. On the far side of the island, was the less scenic port, which was heavily populated with fishing boats and occupied by mostly locals.

The crisp, clear night was an obvious reminder that tourist season had ended. The full moon brightened the lush fields and thick forest. The night was peaceful and romantic. A ball of fire suddenly shot through the dark skies and disappeared into the nearby woods. A newer model sedan skidded to a halt on the back road. Dennis Albright, a neatly dressed businessman in his early thirties, got out of the car and looked at the glow within the woods.

"What the hell--?"

Dennis hurried into the woods while following the glow. He stopped near charred vegetation and stared at the smoldering meteor within the small crater. Dennis grabbed a stick, stepped carefully into the crater, and poked the meteor. He placed his hand above the baseball-sized rock. When he was certain it produced no heat, he picked it up and studied it. He suddenly yelped and dropped the meteor. A small gash on his palm bled freely. He subconsciously sucked the blood from his hand, shook it, and more gently picked up the rock, avoiding the sharp edge. His boyish grin returned.

✝

A moderately expensive home was nestled in the middle of nowhere and surrounded by mostly farmland and woods. The nearest neighboring house was barely visible beyond the field. Dennis' sedan pulled up to the well-lit house. Dennis got out of the car, grinned at the meteor he held, and then looked at the gash on his hand. It was now red and swollen. His rare find was overshadowed by the reality that he would need to visit the doctor for a course of antibiotics. Dennis headed into the house, shut the door behind him, and paused within the foyer.

"Pam! Pam, wait until you see what I found," he called out while studying the meteor more closely in the light. "You won't believe it."

"I'm upstairs, dear," Pam called back. Her tone turned seductive. "And wait until you see what I have for you!"

Dennis grinned with a lustful realization, placed the meteor on the hall table, and hurried up the stairs. As he reached the top of the stairs, a masked intruder suddenly appeared and struck him on the head with a tire iron. Dennis fell backwards down the stairs and roughly hit the bottom. The intruder descended the stairs and leaned over Dennis' lifeless body. A young, attractive woman in a sexy, white satin nightgown, Pam Albright, appeared at the top of the stairs. The intruder removed his mask to reveal a handsome man in his mid-thirties, Brian Fitch. Brian looked up at her and appeared pleased.

"He's dead," Brian informed her while grinning.

Pam appeared relieved and slowly walked down the stairs. "What do we do now?"

Brian hurried up the stairs, met her halfway, and kissed her quickly on the lips. "Just like we planned it. Give me fifteen minutes to get back to the tavern and establish my alibi before you report an intruder," he said with enthusiasm. "When Sheriff Palmer and his lackeys arrive, you'll tell them you heard a scuffle, and they'll think Dennis surprised an intruder."

Pam nodded with apprehension.

He smiled reassuringly and caressed her face. "Relax, baby. It'll all work out, I promise. I'll leave the door open."

Brian kissed her again with more passion. She uncertainly returned the kiss. He glanced over her in the sexy nightgown, groaned lustfully, and then hurried down the stairs and out the door. He left the door open as promised. Pam wrenched her fingers together and stared at Dennis' lifeless body at the bottom of the stairs. It didn't seem as easy as it sounded during the planning stages. She composed herself and hurried back up the steps.

✝

*P*am paced the bedroom and nervously looked at the clock and then her watch. It had only been ten minutes, but it seemed an eternity. She heard movement from downstairs. Had Brian forgotten something and returned? Pam fidgeted with concern and hurried from the bedroom. She cautiously walked along the upstairs hallway and paused at the top of the stairs. She didn't want to look at her dead husband again, but she forced herself to look at the foyer below. Dennis' body was gone! All that remained was a small pool of blood where his body once lie. Alarm swept through her, and, for a moment, she was frozen with fear. She gathered her courage and uncertainly scanned the lower level from her position at the top of the stairs. The front door was now closed. Concern that Dennis may have left the house to get the sheriff suddenly swept over her. She had to be certain.

"Dennis?" she called out with a soft quiver in her voice.

There was no response. Pam slowly walked down the stairs in her bare feet and stopped to stare at the blood soaking into the light colored carpet. It was going to leave a nasty stain. She didn't know why she was worrying about that right now. She carefully stepped over the pool of blood and again looked around.

"Dennis--*baby*?

She heard what sounded like someone rummaging through one of the kitchen cupboards. She uncertainly walked along the hall and approached the kitchen. Pam paused in the archway and stared at the glaring, bloody handprint on the once white island counter. The kitchen appeared empty. Where could he have gone? Her eyes strayed to the partially closed laundry room door near the back entrance. He could be in the laundry room tending to his head injury. She nervously walked across the kitchen toward the laundry room and appeared frightened at what she might find. He was supposed to be dead. How had he survived?

"Dennis?"

She slowly approached the partially open door and uncertainly reached to push it open. She suddenly felt the presence of someone behind her. Pam hesitated then quickly turned to see Dennis standing behind her with blood streaking his face from the gash on his forehead just above his eye. He had a glazed over look in his eyes. His condition and the fact that he was alive surprised her. She twitched with fear.

"Oh, my God, Dennis!" He couldn't have known she was involved. If he saw anything, he saw an intruder in a mask. She was safe. Now she had to act the part of the concerned wife. Actually, she was almost relieved he wasn't dead. "What happened?"

He reached for her with his bloody hand. She now felt sorry for him and for what she'd been an accomplice to. She hurried for the nearby telephone on the wall.

"We need to call Doc right away."

Dennis placed his hand on her shoulder. She glanced back at him. He suddenly bared his teeth with a snarl, lunged for her neck, and tore into her flesh with his teeth. Pam screamed with terror and agony as she forcibly pushed him away, tearing her flesh. He had a large chunk of her flesh between his teeth. Pam screamed while clutching her bleeding neck and stared at her flesh in his mouth. As he attempted to grab her again, she stumbled along the kitchen in an attempt to escape, but she was bleeding profusely. Dennis casually followed her while chewing on her flesh as blood ran down his chin. Pam fell to the floor and weakly tried to pull herself to the laundry room door. She heard him snarl behind her. As she looked back, Dennis dove on top of her. She screamed as his bloodstained teeth came at her face.

t

*T*he charming log cabin style, one-story country tavern was located on the lightly traveled back road to town. Being the tavern was one of the least expensive bars on the island; its parking lot was always filled with cars and trucks. The tavern was where most locals ended up in the evenings for social hour and entertainment. The sound of live music pulsated from the building. The tavern interior was tastefully rustic with local flare. Wood and nautical decor was the motif of choice. Local men and women line danced to the loud, upbeat country music. Nearly every table was filled and the bar was crowded, as it was most evenings. Scantily dressed waitresses served beer to the rowdy locals. Other patrons played pool and darts toward the back.

One woman in particular appeared to be the focus of the young men's attention. Lee Braxton was a well-dressed, blonde twenty-something with clothing that suggested wealth and high maintenance. She flirted with the men then carelessly brushed them off. She kept company with a less attractive woman of the same age, Stacy Wendt, whom no one seemed to notice. Stacy wasn't nearly as outgoing as her popular friend was. If the truth were known, Stacy would enjoy the company of nearly every man Lee brushed off nightly. Lee was extremely particular with the men she dated. Stacy wasn't nearly as particular. She just wanted a decent guy--any decent guy would do. Brian stood alongside Lee at the bar and admired her beauty and expensive clothing. Lee wasn't the least interested in him. Stacy, on the other hand, would have loved just one night with the handsome man.

"When are you going to go out with me, Lee?" Brian asked while wearing a cheap grin on his face. "A guy can only take so much of your teasing."

"Now how would that look, me dating the town stud?"

"Town stud, huh?" Brian seemed pleased with his newly found status. "When did I win that title?"

"Name five women in this bar you haven't propositioned," she said simply.

Stacy knew she was one.

Brian looked casually around without even noticing Stacy, frowned, and then looked back at Lee. "I don't like this game. Let's play something else."

Lee rolled her eyes and attempted to ignore him. Stacy couldn't take her eyes off him. She couldn't understand why Lee didn't jump at the chance to be with Brian. If it hadn't been for the rumor that he was already involved with another woman, Stacy would make her move tonight. She used a similar excuse every night. Most evenings, she couldn't even summon up the courage to speak to him.

The tavern door opened to reveal a lanky man in his late twenties, Desmond Hobart, followed by a woman in her early twenties, Jetta Cross. Several heads turned as they entered. Brian felt compelled to stare at Jetta as well. Jetta was a natural beauty with flowing dark hair, piercing green eyes, and a commanding presence. Nearly everyone she passed greeted her. Jetta was naturally friendly to almost everyone she met. Unlike with Lee, if men found Jetta attractive, she was the last to notice it. Lee sneered with disgust and watched her pass. It was obvious she despised Jetta for stealing the attention that rightfully belonged to her. Brian noticed Lee's loathe for the attractive woman and seized the opportunity to torment her.

"I'll bet you're wondering what she's got that you don't," Brian teased with a grin.

"There's nothing Jetta Cross has that I want," Lee scoffed with detest and immediately became defensive. "She's best friends with that computer nerd, Desmond. He follows her around like some little lost puppy. She baby-sits her militant father's deranged lunatic friend while her father is off in some third world shit hole blowing things up. She doesn't date, and she never puts out. What the hell is the attraction? Why do the men around town fawn over her like she's generic royalty? I just don't get it."

"Don't get all jealous, Lee. There's always a market for 'cheap and easy'," Brian said with a chuckle. "It's actually funny that she doesn't even know she's competing with you."

Lee turned to face Brian with obvious irritation at his comment then smirked. "Well, I suppose Jetta and I do have one thing in common," she scoffed while giving him a disgusted, quick once over. "Neither of us will ever touch you."

Lee turned and walked away from the bar. Stacy watched with surprise as her friend stormed off. That sealed any shot she had with Brian tonight. Stacy attempted a weak smile at Brian then hurried after her friend.

"Bitch," Brian scoffed softly under his breath.

Lee didn't matter anyway. He would soon have his payday with the recently widowed Pam Albright. Lee would be his alibi tonight. She would vouch to his presence around the time Pam reported an intruder in her house. It was all going to work out. He just needed to play it cool a little while longer.

Jetta and Desmond crossed the crowded tavern and approached the pool tables in the back. Desmond glanced at the two men playing a game of pool at one of the two tables. The first man, Tyler Kroll, was the lounge bartender at the Winter Harbor Hotel. The hotel employed many of Winter Harbor's residents, although a vast majority were laid off after the summer season. Tyler was personable and pleasing to the eyes, but his ego tended to ruin the entire package. His prestigious position at the hotel made him very popular, especially among the women in town. Rumor had it he made more in tips on a Friday evening during the summer then most men made in one week at their regular jobs.

Bishop Kane was Carter Braxton's assistant. Carter owned the Winter Harbor Hotel and was also Lee's father. Bishop was a ruggedly handsome, serious looking man in his mid-thirties. His clean-cut, business casual appearance conveyed a certain style without suggesting wealth. Jetta thought he looked more like a hit man for the mob than a personal assistant. He was a hard man to read and mostly kept to himself. Despite his good looks, most of the women in town avoided him. He was fairly intimidating, which was why Jetta enjoyed getting under his skin, a trait she definitely acquired from her father. Desmond clearly felt uncomfortable around both men and remained close to Jetta. She was his security blanket. Being Jetta's best friend granted him a certain amount of respect; respect he probably wouldn't have gotten otherwise.

"This was a bad idea," Desmond softly said to her while fidgeting.

"We came here to play pool, not let your co-workers intimidate you," she told him firmly.

"I wouldn't exactly call them my co-workers," he replied then muttered, "more like my tormentors."

"Command respect, Desmond. Own the room."

"I'm trying, Jetta, but I'm suffocating from all the testosterone," Desmond muttered.

Jetta groaned softly and forced Desmond to a table near the back and past the men playing pool. Desmond lacked Jetta's self-confidence. Most of the town lacked Jetta's self-confidence. Jetta was the daughter of Admiral Quinn Cross, one of the most respected officers this side of, well, anywhere. Some could argue that Jetta was just riding on her father's reputation among the town residents, but those who knew her would agree that she was her father's daughter in every facet.

Tyler saw Jetta and Desmond as they approached one of the back tables and grinned his delight to see her. "Hey, Jetta," he said enthusiastically.

"Tyler--" Jetta's disinterest in Desmond's co-worker was evident. It wasn't as if there was anything wrong with him or with the way he treated her. She just didn't like the way he tormented her best friend both in and out of work.

"When are you going to leave your *girlfriend* at home and hang out with a real man?" Tyler gave her a lustful once over then grinned.

"Desmond and I make a nicer couple than you and your boyfriend." Jetta indicated Bishop.

Bishop glared at Jetta without humor to her comment.

"No need to give me that dirty look, Bishop," she teased. "I naturally assume you're the dominant male in this couple."

"You know, one day Carter will grow tired of chasing you," Tyler scoffed, "and then it'll be open season on your ass."

Bishop prepared to make his next shot and allowed his eyes to stray to Jetta's backside. She caught his look but focused her attention on Tyler.

"Maybe I'll let Carter catch me," she teased. "Then your friend there will work for me, and I'll sick him on your ass."

"As if that would happen," Tyler snorted.

"Might be fun testing Bishop's loyalties," Jetta teased while smiling deviously. "Care to find out?"

Tyler and Jetta exchanged icy stares. Jetta could maintain an emotionless stare for hours if necessary. There was no way Tyler was winning this one.

He looked at Bishop and tried to act casual, although he was clearly no match for her. "Let's check out the bar scene."

"Finish the game or forfeit, Tyler," Bishop retorted with little emotion.

Bishop was an equal opportunity bad boy. Even those he allowed in his circle weren't immune to his bittersweet personality.

"Fine--"

Tyler slapped a twenty-dollar bill on the pool table and headed for the bar. Bishop casually collected the money and handed Jetta his pool stick.

"We should play pool more often," Bishop remarked with a grin then joined Tyler at the bar.

There were times Jetta was convinced Bishop was on her side, but he usually found a way to crush that theory. Jetta looked at Desmond and smiled. She was pleased with herself.

"And that's how you own a room."

"No, that's how *you* own a room," Desmond informed her. "I'm not you. I don't have a hardcore Navy Seal team watching my back."

Jetta appeared humored by the comment and leaned on her pool stick. "You actually think no one messes with me because they fear my father?"

Desmond glared at her and raised his brows in silent comment.

She shook her head and frowned with disgust. "You think you know someone--"

Jetta racked the pool balls then prepared to break. Desmond leaned on his pool stick and watched her break, but his attention strayed to the area surrounding the bar. Jetta was about to make another shot, noted his gaze and the lost puppy dog look in his eyes, and shook her head.

"Get it out of your head."

"What?" he suddenly asked while attempting to look innocent.

Jetta made her shot and straightened. She glanced at the bar area. Lee was seen flirting with another man while Stacy stood nearby and watched in silent envy. Jetta looked back at Desmond and raised her brows.

"You can't afford her," she simply stated.

"What about a lease with option to buy?"

Jetta laughed softly. "The price is still too high." She approached Desmond and placed her hand on his shoulder while looking into his eyes. "You know I love you, Desmond. Please, whatever you do, don't let her make a fool of you by asking her out. She's going to rip out your heart, tap dance on it, and flush it down the toilet."

He frowned and looked away. "I know she'll reject me in the cruelest possible way," he announced. "I've seen her do it before to, well, every guy who's ever asked her out." Desmond looked at Jetta with despair in his eyes. "I just can't stop thinking about her. She's just--so hot."

"Yeah, and she's dying to burn you."

"I wish your father was here," he remarked with a defeated sigh. Because his own father died when he was little, the admiral was the closest thing Desmond had to a father. "He always has great advice when it comes to women."

Jetta stared at him and appeared almost stunned. Had she heard him correctly? Her father had great advice when it came to women? Who was he kidding? Her father hadn't even dated since her mother died--and that was almost ten years ago. It was no wonder the admiral liked Desmond. He was a great ass kisser.

"You want to talk to my father? Okay, here's my father." She straightened, threw her shoulders back, and pointed her finger at him while giving him a firm stare. "Stop your whining and grow a pair, boy! You want to be a doormat all your life? You want respect; you have to earn it. Now go out there and get laid!"

Several patrons near the back of the bar looked at them and appeared surprised by her words and the gruffness of her tone.

Desmond stared at Jetta with his mouth hanging open then slowly shook his head with disbelief. "Okay, that was almost frightening." He suddenly grinned. "Now do Hunter."

Chapter Two

$\mathcal{I}$solated on the beach furthest from the tourist area was the perfect little beach house along the island coast. The wood and glass house was obviously custom designed with multi-level decks and wind chimes of varying sizes. It was a little past midnight. Several outside lights were on, but the inside was nearly dark except for the kitchen light. A jeep pulled up to the house. Jetta got out of the jeep looking exhausted and approached the main door facing Millers Road. She stopped several feet away and stared at the partially opened door with surprise and possible concern. Why was the door open? She assessed the situation before cautiously approaching.

Jetta entered the living room and turned on the lights. The quaint living room was in desperate need of a woman's touch, something Jetta obviously lacked. Old military photos, military swords, and framed medals hung on the walls. On the exquisitely hand-carved fireplace mantel, where some expensive family heirloom should be, there was a twelve-inch mortar shell casing proudly displayed instead. The house was quiet with no one around. Jetta heard a faint scratching sound coming from the kitchen. She uncertainly approached the archway to the brightly lit kitchen. Double French doors led out to the beachside deck. The scratching sound was louder now. She looked around the empty kitchen then saw a man's bare feet on the floor sticking out from behind the island counter, which was also the source of the repetitive scratching sound.

"Hunter?"

A man in his early fifties popped out from behind the island counter with a scrub brush in his hand. He wore only a tee shirt and shorts. Hunter stared at her a moment with a look of surprise on his face then appeared enthusiastic.

"Jetta? I'm so glad to see you!" He set his brush down, hurried to her, and pulled her into his arms. "It's been so long!"

Jetta returned the warm embrace and smiled gently. "Yes, it's been nearly four hours."

Hunter pulled away and stared at her with obvious concern. "Did my reality button get stuck on pause again?"

"Just a little, but I think it's adorable that you're so glad to see me."

John Hunter was non-impressive and average in almost every aspect. Nothing about him stuck out in one's mind, and he was easily dismissed as harmless. He was possibly the most misunderstood man on the entire island. Once a highly decorated Navy Seal, Hunter was forced into retirement after returning home from a mission that nearly claimed his life. That was the story Quinn and Jetta decided to share with the residents of Winter Harbor. Apart from Desmond, no one in Winter Harbor could possibly understand Hunter's post-coma, traumatic existence.

Hunter's anxiety was evident as he stared at Jetta. "Am I on the island?"

"Yes, we're on the island," she replied then smiled warmly. "You're at Admiral Cross' beach house, remember?"

The distant look in his eyes conveyed that he did not. "Are we under attack?"

"No, not tonight, Hunter." Jetta eyed the excessively clean floor alongside the island counter then looked at him and appeared curious but casual. "Did you shoot someone?"

He uncertainly looked at the kitchen floor, considered the question, and then looked back at her while frowning. "I'm guessing I probably didn't."

"So you can stop cleaning up the imaginary blood, right?"

"I probably could." His look conveyed distress as his body twitched. He felt compelled to ask her the question most on his mind. "Exactly how many *bodies* do you see?"

Jetta stared at his serious look, took a deep breath, and slowly glanced across the spotless kitchen. She looked back at him, offered a sympathetic smile, and shook her head.

"None?" Hunter asked with surprise. He uncertainly looked around the kitchen and scratched his brow while staring at the dead terrorist lying face down in a pool of blood alongside the refrigerator.

He was a large, brawny man dressed in blood-soaked military attire. Hunter thought it would be a relief if he didn't have to clean up the blood beneath the refrigerator. He always found that to be a difficult task. He looked back at Jetta and gave a slight nod toward the dead man by the refrigerator. "Are you sure you don't see *that* one?" he asked softly, indicating what was left of the terrorist.

Jetta took his hands in hers and stared into his eyes. "Close your eyes, Hunter."

Hunter frowned and shut his eyes. He knew what he saw, and that terrorist was the real thing. That one had been a particularly tough bastard to kill. Jetta's little mind games weren't going to work this time. She couldn't just make that son-of-a-bitch disappear with her 'reset button' bullshit.

"Hit the reset button and open your eyes."

He silently laughed at her. She was, after all, only a naïve child, which was why he humored her. She was going to look pretty foolish when he proved her wrong this time. He took a deep breath and opened his eyes. To his surprise, the dead terrorist was gone. The kitchen was again spotless. How did she pull that off? Ironically, she had even managed to spontaneously transform from a child to a young woman right before his eyes. Hunter stared a moment longer, clutched his head, and groaned softly. It wasn't her; it was him! He tried hard to make sense of what had just happened, but he couldn't.

"Why do I do this, Jetta? Why do I act so crazy?"

Hunter collapsed onto one of the stools as his proud shoulders sagged with defeat. Jetta sat on the stool next to him and took his hand in hers.

"You're not crazy. You have shrapnel pressing against your brain that sometimes causes a rift between the past and present. It'll all come back to you in the morning."

He gently caressed her hand and avoided looking at her. She had to hate him. Although he couldn't remember any specific incidents, he knew this had happened before.

"Are you tired of me?"

"Are you kidding? I love you, Hunter," she said cheerfully. "You're a hero, and don't you ever forget that."

He looked at her with surprise. "I am?"

He wondered where the admiral's daughter got her intel. He didn't remember any such incident. Thankfully, she was on their side. He'd get no pleasure from interrogating her.

"Yes, you saved your entire unit, remember? You saved my father too," she announced with a broad smile. "And when your reality button gets stuck on pause, I'll always be here to unstick you. You can count on me."

Hunter appeared relieved and hugged her. She was always so good to him. Maybe he could get her to help clean up the blood on the kitchen floor. He was sure she would help. A thought then occurred to him. He pulled away and appeared curious.

"Is Caroline coming home soon?"

Jetta shifted and appeared uncomfortable. "Not tonight," she replied gently. "You should probably go to bed without her."

A strange realization swept over him and all emotion drained from his face. "She's not coming back, is she?"

"No, Hunter," she said softly. "She moved away a long time ago."

Hunter sadly nodded then stood with exhaustion. He really needed to finish cleaning up the blood. The admiral would be upset with the state of his kitchen. But then--? Hunter looked across the spotless kitchen. There was no blood, was there? He looked at Jetta with the concern evident in his eyes.

"You won't leave me, will you?"

"You're stuck with me forever." She stood and kissed him on the cheek. "Stop fighting the war and go to bed. That's an order, Captain."

Hunter smiled with a nod and headed for the back hallway past the refrigerator. He paused just before the hallway and again looked alongside the refrigerator. He had to make sure the terrorist was really gone before heading to bed. Jetta watched him leave and sank back onto the stool. Growing up, Hunter was the uncle she never had. She hated seeing him that way--even if it was usually just temporary. When he got lost in his own mind, he usually found his way back. She feared, one day though, he wouldn't be able to find his way back, and the thought frightened her.

Chapter Three

The town of Winter Harbor was quiet and relaxed for the early fall morning. The old-fashioned, white church with elegant bell tower landmarked the town square. Beyond town square was the high school. The quaint homes along Main Street were reminiscing of Old New England. Their craftsmanship and detailed woodwork added to the charm of the little town. Cobblestone sidewalks and white, picket fences lined the clean streets. In the opposite direction, the town diner was the happening place in the early morning hours. The sheriff's patrol cruiser was always parked outside the diner early each morning. Sheriff Palmer walked out of the diner and headed for his patrol car with his usual, extra-large coffee-to-go.

Sheriff Palmer was a physically fit man in his mid-thirties. His boyish good looks were often overshadowed by his 'rule with an iron fist' attitude. In his sheriff's uniform and gun holster on his hip, he looked the part of a western day gunslinger, and, at times, he lived up to that persona. Brian nearly collided with Sheriff Palmer on the sidewalk. The sheriff was quick to save his coffee from spilling and possibly ruining his mood for the remainder of the day. Sheriff Palmer was addicted to his coffee, and there was no mercy on anyone who parted him from it. Brian appeared unusually cheerful for the early hour.

"What's the fine for running down the sheriff on the sidewalk?" he teased.

16

"Same as every other fine--a cup of coffee," Palmer replied. It sounded like a joke, but it actually wasn't. Rumor had it Sheriff Palmer had never paid for coffee since taking office.

"It's like a ghost town around here," Brian commented as he looked around while shaking his head. "Just last week we were tripping over tourists."

"Yeah, well, it's great for business, but I don't miss them," Palmer replied. "I can finally get around to some fishing, if they left any for us locals."

"Pretty quiet then, huh?" Brian appeared curious and almost concerned. "Nothing *exciting* happening?"

"Other than a drunk and disorderly whizzing in Mrs. Cooper's flower bed last night, it's been perfectly quiet," Palmer was pleased to report.

Brian suddenly appeared tense then masked his concern with his usual grin. "I'll owe you that coffee. Good day, Sheriff."

As Brian hurried away, Sheriff Palmer stared after him with a curious look. The sheriff was smarter then he looked, which most people often didn't give him enough credit. He raised his brows and appeared deep in thought.

"Whose wife have you been banging?" Palmer muttered softly then grinned at the thought while sipping his coffee.

As Palmer turned toward his cruiser, an eighteen-year-old boy, Tanner, ran into him. His coffee flew from his hand and fell to the sidewalk. Tanner appeared startled and stared at the sheriff while out of breath.

"I'm so sorry, Sheriff," Tanner announced then indicated the school in the distance. "I'm late for class!"

Tanner ran into town, leaving Sheriff Palmer staring helplessly at his spilled coffee on the sidewalk. He looked after Winter Harbor High's star running back.

"You're on my list, Tanner!" he yelled after him. Palmer shook spilled coffee from his hand and appeared disgusted. "Glad you're not the damned quarterback, or we'd be in trouble tomorrow night," he muttered.

Sheriff Palmer's day was officially ruined. The diner waitress, Stella, hurried out from the diner and handed him another cup of coffee. He looked at the coffee in her hand, grinned at Stella, and accepted the coffee-to-go.

"You're the best, Stella."

Stella smiled in response. She was obviously smitten with the handsome sheriff, despite being ten years his senior. As long as Sheriff Palmer remained a freelance bachelor, many women in town fantasized their 'happily ever after' with him. Stella was no exception. She knew he'd ultimately end up with someone much younger and with fewer curves, but it was a lovely fantasy all the same.

†

*D*ennis Albright's house appeared unusually quiet in the early morning. Brian's car pulled up to the house alongside the sedan. Brian slowly got out of his car, looked at Dennis' sedan, and uncertainly approached the porch. He paused before the door, appeared tense, and then knocked softly. There was no response. Something was wrong. Brian slowly opened the door and peered inside. He looked at the bloodstain at the bottom of the stairs then appeared curious and mildly concerned. He heard movement just down the hall.

"Pam?"

There was still no response. Brian walked along the hallway and approached the nearby study. As he entered, he saw Pam standing before the window in her sexy, white nightgown while staring outside into the morning sunshine. Brian admired the silhouette of her naked body as the sun shone through her nightgown, and he entertained a dirty thought or two. He dismissed his dirty thoughts.

"What happened to Dennis? Why did you alter the plan?" He approached Pam from behind. She didn't respond. "You aren't having second thoughts about us now that you're rich, are you? You know I'm crazy about you."

Brian pulled the hair back from her shoulder and lowered his mouth to her neck. He immediately noticed the chunk of missing flesh and the large amount of dried blood along her shoulder. Brian suddenly appeared horrified and took a step back.

"Pam--?"

Pam turned to reveal part of her face was missing. Her flesh was gray and her eyes were lifeless. Brian gasped with horror and took a quick step back. Zombie Pam lunged for him and tackled him to the desk. They fell against the desk with a thump as objects crashed to the floor. He cried out and easily threw her off him. Brian jumped to his feet and backed away while staring at her as she approached with a snarl.

"What the hell--?"

As Pam lunged for him, he hastily turned and nearly collided with zombie Dennis, who had the same dead look in his eyes and dried blood down his chin. Brian cried out with horror and shoved Dennis backward and away from him. Pam grabbed Brian from behind and bit him on the neck. He cried out in pain and surprise, shoved her away, and turned to run while clutching his bleeding neck. Zombie Dennis grabbed him and tackled him to the floor. He fought against Dennis, who was now on top of him, and attempted to keep his bloodstained teeth away from his face. Pam dove to the floor, grabbed Brian's thrashing leg, and bit into his calf through his pants. Brian screamed. Dennis overpowered him and sank his teeth into his throat.

✝

$\mathcal{T}$he Winter Harbor Hotel was an impressive ten-story, elegant three-hundred-room beachfront hotel with acres of sprawling gardens, a large, in-door pool, several hot tubs, and many other resort amenities. Despite the hotel's grandeur, it was void of life. Tourist season had ended and the resort had the appearance of a ghost town. The beach was empty and there weren't any boats in the harbor.

The hotel's massive kitchen was nearly empty. A heavyset man in his late thirties, wearing a white chef's outfit, loaded dishes into the massive dishwasher. Rafael was head chef for the resort and possibly the only remaining kitchen staff employed during the off-season. Supposedly, a renowned chef from some exotic beach resort overseas, Rafael was transplanted to Winter Harbor a little over a year ago. It was rumored he'd taken the job at Winter Harbor Hotel because he suffered from work related stress, but he was the most laid-back guy on the entire island. His true reasons for leaving his high paid gig to work on the island remained one of those little mysteries. Jetta and Hunter entered through the employee's entrance. Rafael appeared delighted to see them. He was delighted to see anyone these days. As a people person, he had a tough time dealing with the solitude that off-season unfortunately brought.

"Hey! Company! What brings you to my dungeon?"

"Morning, Raphael. Carter wants me to fly him to the mainland for his meeting," Jetta announced cheerfully. "And Hunter needed to get out--"

"Hunter had a psychotic episode last night," Hunter bluntly interrupted. "She's afraid to leave me home alone."

"Dude, you're always welcome in my kitchen. You can help peel potatoes," he teased then smiled and winked at Jetta.

"I owe you, Rafael."

"Yeah, yeah. Just go." Rafael waved her off and joined Hunter at the island counter. "So, Hunter, tell me about some of your more exciting military coups."

"I would, but then I'd have to kill you," Hunter casually replied.

Rafael chuckled softly, leaned on the counter, and grinned boyishly while deviously raising his brows. "How many men have you actually killed?"

"Shot or blown up?"

Rafael appeared to consider the question then grinned. "Let's start with the ones you'd shot and work our way up to, you know, the whole blowing up thing."

Jetta groaned and rolled her eyes. "I'm going to the hanger for the helicopter," she announced. "You two behave."

She knew Rafael was a good man, but he had a morbid sense of humor when it came to Hunter. Perhaps that was because of Hunter's candor and grisly storytelling. It didn't really matter. She preferred not to stick around for story hour.

t

*T*he elegant, empty lobby had one set of large, heavy doors leading to the beach and a second set on the opposite side leading to the circular driveway. The lobby was decked out with hand-carved woodwork, exposed ceiling beams, and handcrafted furniture. Stacy worked behind the front desk, which encompassed most of the back wall and was a work of art in itself. It was locally handcrafted with an elegant marble top. A serious looking woman in her late thirties, Elise Raymond, approached the desk with a scowl on her face. Visually, she was a cross between a librarian and a schoolmarm, but her attitude screamed prison matron.

"Stacy, have you seen Desmond?" Elise demanded.

Stacy immediately appeared on her best behavior and stared at the woman with possible fear. "No, Ma'am."

"Typical," Elise scoffed. "There's not a single reliable man on this entire island. He said he'd have the Internet working this morning." She looked at her watch and frowned. "You'd better take your break. I'll keep an eye on the desk."

"Yes, Ma'am." Stacy made a hasty exit to avoid further contact with Elise.

Elise was a miserable woman and therefore made it her mission to ensure no one else was happy. She was a self-proclaimed man-hater and had little use for the entire male population. The stronger their will, the more she despised them. Sheriff Palmer was on the top of her 'loathe' list. However, it wasn't just men she despised. A strong-willed woman earned high ranking on the same list. Jetta secured that title years ago and still held it today.

An Asian woman in a housekeeper's uniform lurked around the corner not far from the elevators and watched Elise at the front desk. Stacy approached the corridor and saw the housekeeper, Ming, in an apparent state of hiding.

"Are you just getting in?" Stacy asked softly then appeared concerned.

"Yes," Ming said softly and nodded toward the front desk. "What sort of mood is she in this morning?"

"Her usual sort of mood," Stacy replied. "I'd avoid her if I were you."

Most of the staff tried avoiding Elise as a general rule. It didn't need to be stated. Stacy continued along the corridor to avoid being a party to Elise's wrath on poor Ming. Ming was an undeniably attractive, petite woman in her mid-thirties with her long, silky hair worn up in a ponytail. Even her bland, gray housekeeping uniform couldn't diminish her natural beauty. Avoiding Elise in the morning, particularly on days she was late, was becoming a challenge. Ming watched Elise busily working on the computer, saw her opportunity, and then quietly hurried for the elevators when it appeared as if she wasn't looking.

"Ming--"

Ming hesitated before the elevator and nearly had her finger to the button. Of course, nothing got past Elise. She appeared chilled by the familiar female voice and uncertainly turned. Elise beckoned for her like a mother scolding a child. Ming uncertainly approached the desk.

"Did you just get in?"

"My daughter woke up sick this morning," Ming said timidly. "I had to find a sitter."

"You're a good worker, Ming, but you're always late."

"I'm sorry, Ms. Raymond. I'm trying."

In addition to men and strong-willed women, attractive women also reached the top of Elise's least tolerated list. It was a very long, complex list. The elevator doors opened to reveal Bishop in a tasteful suit that still cried mob hit man. Elise cast a look across the lobby at Bishop with apparent loathe and gave Ming a dismissing wave.

"We'll discuss this later. You'd better get to work," Elise gruffly announced.

"Yes, Ma'am," Ming said softly and hurried for the elevator.

Bishop held the elevator door open for Ming's hasty departure. Ming quickly darted inside the elevator and hid around the corner, waiting for the doors to close. As Bishop approached the front desk, Elise placed a clipboard on top. He picked up the clipboard and studied it without looking at her. In second place, beneath Sheriff Palmer, was Bishop. Elise didn't like him at all, and she made that apparent.

"The tub in 413 is clogged, and the sink in 320 is leaking," Elise informed him with little emotion and a refusal to look at him.

"Try maintenance," Bishop remarked. "I'm not a plumber."

Her patience with Bishop appeared to reach its boiling point. "What exactly is it you do around here, Mr. Kane? Because I never see you doing much of anything," she hissed.

"I'm Mr. Braxton's assistant. I assist Mr. Braxton. What I do is none of your business."

"We work on a skeleton crew in the off-season and fill in where we're needed," she scoffed. "We should discuss your duties."

"I know my duties, Ms. Raymond. There's nothing to discuss, and if there was, it wouldn't be with you," he announced simply.

The elevator doors opened to reveal Desmond, Lee, and Lee's father, Carter Braxton, the resort owner. Carter was a distinguished looking man in his late forties. He wore an expensively tailored suite with several, equally expensive pieces of jewelry. He flaunted his wealth, which didn't impress the locals. Carter and Desmond paused near the elevators to talk. Lee kissed her father on the cheek and approached the front desk. Lee was once again bell of the ball in a slinky, pale dress with strappy pink heels. She approached Bishop with disinterest. Much like Brian, he wasn't her type either, so she had little use for him.

"The penthouse lock isn't working properly," Lee informed him.

"I'll call maintenance about it," he replied.

Elise was obviously offended with Bishop's game playing. "You'll call for a door but not a tub?" she demanded.

Bishop picked up the desk phone and eyed Elise with little emotion. "That's different. This is assisting Mr. Braxton--via Miss Braxton."

Elise rolled her eyes, hurried from behind the desk, and approached Carter and Desmond by the elevators. Both men tensed to her approach but there was no escaping her.

Lee shook her head and chuckled softly. "You certainly like pushing 'Frau Hitler's' buttons," she remarked.

"She's a man-hater," he stated simply. "I find that extremely irritating." Bishop then shifted his attention to the person on the other end of the phone. "Steve? Hey, it's Bishop. Can you check the penthouse lock? I've got daddy's little girl breathing down my neck and it's only a little after nine." There was a moment of silence. Bishop grinned, cast a look at Lee, and continued with his conversation. "Thanks, Steve." He hung up the phone.

Lee glared at him with annoyance. "You're easy to hate, Bishop."

"Ah, but that's different," he announced. "You hate me for me; not for my gender. I can respect that."

Lee rolled her eyes even though it was obvious she wanted to laugh. Elise, Desmond, and Carter walked down the nearby corridor. Bishop watched them disappear down the hall then threw his arms in the air with disgust.

"Great! Now I'm stuck at the desk."

Jetta walked off the elevator, crossed the lobby, and approached the front desk. She eyed both and appeared curious. Neither was exactly front desk material.

"Who's at the desk?"

Bishop and Lee casually pointed to the other.

Jetta picked the lesser of two evils and turned to Lee. "Does your father still need transportation to the mainland?"

"Yes, he'll be back in a few minutes," she replied then slyly grinned. "I'm going along to do some shopping."

"The helicopter's on the roof when you're ready," Jetta informed her then turned toward the elevators.

Jetta preferred the solitude of the roof to making small talk with Lee or Bishop. It would turn into either a debate or an argument, and she just didn't have the strength for either today. Hunter's episode last night kept her awake until the early hours. Jetta saw Elise returning with Desmond and suddenly felt the need to hang around. Unlike everyone else, Jetta didn't back away from the challenge of Elise. She had no fear of her and even less respect for the woman who made Desmond's life so miserable. Elise appeared to be giving Desmond a verbal lashing, and he appeared to be taking it as usual. Her treatment of Desmond was extremely irritating and borderline abusive. Elise seemed to enjoy belittling him probably because he didn't fight back. Desmond wasn't a fighter, despite the admiral's attempts to toughen him.

"I'm sorry," Desmond said timidly to Elise. "Mr. Braxton had me working on his computer this morning."

"Had you explained the situation--" Elise began, saw Jetta watching them, and then immediately silenced. She abruptly switched gears and chose not to verbally attack him in front of Jetta. "Just get it done, Desmond."

"Yes, Ms. Raymond."

Jetta and Desmond exchanged looks. Desmond quickly looked away to avoid the familiar lecturing in her eyes. He followed Elise behind the front desk. Jetta wished he'd learn to stand up for himself, especially to Elise. She wasn't his boss. Technically, they were equals, but Elise certainly didn't see it that way, and Desmond wasn't about to challenge her authority either. Elise looked at Jetta with those piercing eyes and pinched her lips for an added, authoritative look. It was necessary for her to order everyone about and Jetta was no exception. Actually, Jetta thought it gave Elise some perverse pleasure.

"Shouldn't you be manning your aircraft, Miss Cross?"

Jetta stared at Elise with little emotion. It was almost amazing how predictable she was. Usually Jetta went with the silent stare approach. It was her father's favorite move. She'd heard the story from several of his men of the time the admiral got vital information from a prisoner by just staring at him. The 'stare' tactic worked wonderfully on Elise. She'd squirm then become flustered before excusing herself. For some odd reason, Jetta felt particularly confrontational after watching Elise belittle Desmond.

"What is it about me that threatens you?" Jetta asked calmly and without emotion.

Elise appeared surprised that Jetta actually spoke to her. "I'm not threatened by you," she snapped. "I just can't respect a woman who doesn't act like a lady. But it's not really your fault that you were raised by some hard core Navy Seal and his section eight counterpart."

Desmond looked up from his computer with his mouth hanging open. It was never wise to insult Hunter to Jetta's face. An insult to Hunter and his sanity was one of her many 'hot' buttons no sane person ever wanted to push.

"Don't bring Hunter into this," Jetta retorted with a hiss in her voice. "He's a decorated hero. He nearly died saving my father and his entire team."

Bishop and Lee were now silently watching the exchange. Both knew things could turn ugly fast. It was possibly for their own amusement, but there was a greater chance they just enjoyed watching Jetta stick it to the miserable woman.

"The guy's a psychopath and should be committed," Elise scoffed through pinched lips.

The lobby fell eerily silent as all eyes were on Jetta. Jetta suddenly grabbed for Elise behind the desk. Bishop swiftly caught Jetta around the waist and pulled her away from the desk. If he hadn't intervened, she would have gotten Elise. Elise jumped with surprise, saw Bishop had her contained, and then shook her head with distaste at the display. Desmond covered his face and avoided watching. Despite the fact that she wanted to hit the woman, Jetta composed herself. Bishop relaxed and released her.

"Your aggression isn't particularly surprising, considering you live with a couple of natural born killers," Elise announced callously, now appearing overly confident.

Jetta showed no emotion to the comment. Without warning, she again lunged for Elise behind the desk. Bishop again caught her around the waist and now held her against him from behind. Jetta wasn't even concerned about being held against Bishop. She used his body as leverage to brace herself while she kicked at Elise with both feet. Lee attempted to keep from laughing at the spectacle but failed. She enjoyed watching Jetta embarrass herself by acting like one of the boys. It was satisfying on many levels.

"Barbaric. You're just like them!" Elise scoffed.

"Keep it up, Elise, and I'll let her have a piece of you," Bishop remarked lowly while struggling to keep the thrashing woman from escaping his arms.

Elise knew Bishop would follow through with his threat. She walked out from behind the desk and passed them while scoffing, "Military brat--"

Jetta karate kicked at Elise as she passed and nearly clipped her hip. Elise gasped with surprise then hurried for the nearby corridor. Bishop struggled to hold Jetta. She nearly got away from him that time.

Lee maintained her humor with the entire display and watched Bishop struggling to subdue the agile woman in his arms. "Wow, you've got your hands full there, Bishop," Lee teased. "Good luck with that."

Lee walked away while laughing. Jetta relaxed despite Bishop's arms around her waist while he held her firmly against him from behind. She didn't appreciate being subdued by him. She didn't want him to think he could control her. She knew she could get away from him, but that would require physically harming him. Since she wasn't angry with him, she didn't want to go that direction if she could avoid it. He still didn't release her, making her more irritated with him and bringing her closer to using excessive force.

"You can let go of me now."

"If it's all the same, I think I'll give Elise a head start."

"I'm not going to chase after her. And I'm not exactly thrilled with your gun poking me in the hip," Jetta growled.

Jetta considered both statements. Ironically, they were both lies. She did intend to chase Elise, but that was just to watch her run, and she was rather appreciative of firearms, so his pressing against her wasn't an issue. Bishop appeared to give her comment some thought then reluctantly released her. She turned toward him and was about to speak when she briefly saw the gun in his shoulder holster. Shoulder holster? Jetta eyed the shoulder holster with some surprise. Then what was poking her--? She allowed her eyes to stray below his belt. She stared only briefly, groaned by what she saw, and rolled her eyes.

"Oh, for God's sake--"

Bishop appeared amused by her reaction. "It's not my fault," he announced while grinning. "It's hot watching you turn bad-ass commando on Elise."

Desmond stared at them from behind the desk and appeared more stunned than anything.

"Tell Carter I'm on the roof," Jetta scoffed.

She hurried for the elevators while avoiding looking at Bishop. She'd seen enough of him--literally.

Chapter Four

The mailman's truck pulled up to Dennis Albright's house. Ted, a mail carrier in his mid-fifties, got out of the truck with a package, eyed Brian's car in the driveway alongside Dennis' sedan, and approached the front door. He knocked on the door. There was no response. He knocked again. The door opened to reveal zombie Pam with fresh blood down the front of her white, satin nightgown. Ted appeared horrified as she reached out and grabbed his arm. As he dropped the package and pushed her back, she savagely bit into his arm. He screamed and pulled his arm free, losing a mouthful of flesh to Pam's teeth. He clutched his bleeding arm, bolted down the porch steps, and ran for his truck. He jumped into the truck while panting heavily, threw it into gear, and stepped on the gas. As the tires squealed, the truck lurched forward instead of in reverse and crashed into the porch. Ted appeared slightly dazed then looked out the side window and saw the barefooted Pam approaching. He reached into the glove compartment, fumbled through several papers, and removed a .357 Magnum. As Pam approached his truck, he aimed the gun at her and squeezed the trigger while screaming.

The gun fired, striking Pam in the chest. She was thrown backward onto the ground and appeared motionless. Ted jumped out of his truck with the gun in his hand and clutching his bleeding arm. He slowly approached the motionless woman on the ground. He uncertainly knelt alongside her and felt for a pulse. He set his gun down and fumbled with his cell phone. As he pressed buttons in mild alarm, Pam's eyes opened. She suddenly grabbed his arm, pulled

27

him on top of her, and bit him in the throat. Ted cried out to her teeth sinking into his flesh while he pushed against her and reached for his gun on the ground alongside him. He grasped the gun as blood flowed from his mouth then drew his last breath. Zombies Dennis and Brian appeared on the porch and approached Pam while she devoured the fallen man.

✝

*J*etta's helicopter was waiting on the landing pad on the hotel roof an impressive ten stories above the town and ocean. Winter Harbor was visible beyond the hotel tower. The opposite side provided a beautiful view of the ocean. Jetta leaned casually against the helicopter and flipped through her clipboard. Jetta's father had started the helicopter transportation and tour business for the summer tourist season when he thought he would retire the first time around. His distaste for tourists and civilian life nearly destroyed the business within the first month. Although it wasn't her first career choice, Jetta reluctantly took over the business at a young age and dealt with the tourists each summer. She loved flying and couldn't imagine leaving Winter Harbor, which pretty much sealed her fate as island tour guide.

The business's simultaneous beginning and near failure was also around the time Hunter was recovering from his final brush with death. Her father had already started the business and was prepared to launch it on his return home later that month. When a mission they were on went south and his entire team nearly died, it should have been her father's wake-up call to enjoy retirement. However, that month he spent in and out of the hospital worrying about Hunter and attempting to fly tourists to and from the island had the opposite effect on him. At seventeen, Jetta accepted both the responsibility of the business and caring for Hunter's recovery, naturally with help from her good friend Desmond. Running a business and making her own schedule was the only way she was able to keep Hunter from being placed in an undesirable facility in the crucial first year of his recovery. Jetta often felt like a glorified taxi driver to the rich and pampered. As she gazed across the roof to Lee talking on her pink cell phone and wearing her matching pink high heels, she knew today was no different.

Lee paced the roof with her cell phone to her ear. "I hope to find some pink heels," she said into the phone. "Well, yeah, I have pink heels, but I need a different shade to match that new dress I bought. I want to look hot for that party. There are going to be some excellent prospects. Quality men around this island are scarce. Honestly, I don't know why Daddy wanted to move here in the first place."

Carter and Bishop appeared on the roof. Lee looked at the rooftop door and saw them approach.

"Oh, Daddy's here. Gotta fly," she said with a giggle to her own witticism.

Lee disconnected her call and approached the helicopter. She eyed Jetta then the door. Jetta glared back in response. Lee groaned, opened the door herself, and climbed inside. Carter cheerfully smiled at Jetta as they approached. He was obviously overly pleased to see her.

"I call shotgun," Carter announced.

Lee glared at her father from inside the back of the helicopter and indicated Bishop with a sharply raised brow. "You're not seriously going to make me ride with him, are you?"

Carter looked at Lee, fidgeted, and uncertainly smiled. "Of course I'll ride with you, sweetheart." He slyly grinned at Jetta. "Next time--"

Jetta smiled but didn't comment. Carter had the delusion that they were going to get together despite her obvious lack of interest in him. If she had a type, it certainly wasn't someone like Carter. Among other reasons, it was well-known of Jetta's dislike for wealthy men, an obvious trait picked up from her father. Men of wealth and power gave the orders. Men who gave the orders got other men killed; good men like Hunter.

✝

*T*he helicopter flew over the calm ocean on course for the mainland. It was a beautiful, sunny day, and the ocean was peaceful and vacant. Jetta skillfully flew the helicopter with all seriousness, while Lee discussed pink high heels with her father in the back. Jetta allowed her mind to stray only a moment once and listened to Lee talking about pink high heels. Who the hell cared about pink high heels? She couldn't imagine even Carter really caring about Lee's quest for yet another pair of pink high heels. Bishop sat in the co-pilot's seat alongside Jetta and examined several buttons. He reached for one.

Jetta snapped out of her pink high heel daze and smacked his hand with amazing reflexes. "Don't touch my toys."

Bishop gave her a dirty look. "Didn't your father ever teach you it's not ladylike to be a bully?"

"My father didn't teach me anything about being a lady," she retorted. "Did yours?"

Bishop glared at her and didn't appear humored. "He told me to never hit one," he replied. "Of course, I'm assuming you don't qualify."

"I haven't been accused of being a lady yet," she bluntly remarked.

Bishop looked at her and appeared surprised by the comment. A strange smile suddenly crossed his face. He chuckled softly. Jetta felt compelled to smile in response. She knew Bishop's reputation with women. They genuinely disliked him. Perhaps that was why she found him particularly interesting. She was having a tough time dismissing his rugged good looks. There was just something about him that she found strangely attractive. What she found most disturbing was the sexual thoughts she sometimes entertained while around him. Not to say he was her type, but if she would ever consider having a fling, he was possibly first on her list. She was sometimes appalled at herself for the many times she thought about him that way. Despite her distaste for wealthy men, she liked the look of a man in a suit, and he certainly wore his suit well. Apparently, she was attracted to the Italian mobster type. The thought actually made her laugh.

Her mind strayed back to the earlier incident within the lobby when she caught a healthy glimpse of what *wasn't* his gun poking her in the hip. She wasn't sure she wanted to think of Bishop in a sexual manner. It undoubtedly wouldn't end well for either of them. As she fiddled with a few switches, she cast a glance at his crotch and immediately shamed herself from doing so. She didn't know what was wrong with her today. Despite the quick glance, he caught her looking. She concentrated on flying and pretended nothing happened. If she acted casual, maybe he wouldn't think much of it. She glanced at him out of the corner of her eye. The grin on his face was almost unbearable. He enjoyed the fact that he caught her looking! She knew he would never let her live that one down.

†

*T*he helicopter set down on the tarmac of the private airfield on the mainland. Jetta and her three passengers disembarked as a stretch limousine approached. Her timing was nearly perfect once again. Jetta immediately started refueling as the limousine pulled up to her passengers. She attempted to forget about her embarrassing moment with Bishop in the helicopter, but it wasn't easy. Every time she looked at Bishop, he was grinning at her. The bastard enjoyed her sneaking a peek. She was feeling particularly self-conscious now. If it hadn't been for that eyeful she got in the lobby, she wouldn't be in this predicament. The image of him in the lobby again entered her mind. She cursed herself for allowing her thoughts to stray to that again. Obviously, there was something wrong with her. Was her biological clock ticking? It had to be hormonal. Why couldn't she have more female friends? She needed someone to explain women to her. It was very frustrating being without her mother all these years. There were times it was tough being one of the boys when she actually wasn't.

A large, African-American man, roughly 6'4" and with muscles to spare, approached Jetta from behind. He had a determined walk and a stern look on his tough face.

"Cross!" Ziggy, the tough man, shouted gruffly as he was just about on her.

Jetta spun with a startled gasp. Bishop, Carter, and Lee were equally alarmed and turned as well. They saw the large, impressive man directly in front of Jetta. Ziggy suddenly picked up Jetta while laughing and swung her around like a rag doll. He kissed her quickly on the lips and grinned. Jetta hid her smile and smacked the big man's broad shoulders.

"Damn it, Ziggy! Don't do that!"

Ziggy continued to laugh and set her down but didn't release her. "Tell you father; then I'll stop. How the hell is Hunter?"

"Still fighting the war."

Ziggy shook his head while snorting a laugh and finally released her. "That guy's got more demons than hell. Poker game--main hanger. We'll catch up then," he informed her cheerfully, saluted, and then walked away.

Lee shook her head and appeared disgusted. "I just don't get it."

Carter approached Jetta and watched as Ziggy disappeared. "Old friend?"

"One of my father's military buddies," she replied with a grin on her face. "The biggest teddy bear you'll ever meet."

"Yeah, he's big all right," Carter remarked softly. "Are you sure you don't want to join us for lunch?"

"Thanks, but there's a poker game with some of my dad's old military buddies in the main hanger. It's my idea of a good time. They're easy marks."

"Easy marks? I thought military men were good at cards?" he asked with surprise.

"Yeah, they are--against other men, but when they get distracted, they tend to lose," she informed him then grinned. "I know how to distract them."

Carter allowed his eyes to stray to her low-cut tank top. He met her gaze, grinned, and laughed.

"Oh, you are devious."

"Hunter calls it playing the odds."

✝

*T*he main hanger was filled with cigar smoke. Jetta sat with Ziggy and five other brawny men playing poker on top of an old crate. Jetta removed her jacket to reveal her tank top, which seemed to distract a couple of the men. She increased her bet while sucking on an ice cube. She casually removed the ice cube, played with it a moment as the game progressed, and then casually ran it along her cleavage. Ziggy watched her a moment then chuckled and folded. He knew her game and he wasn't playing.

"What was the bet?" Perry asked while attempting to keep his eyes off her cleavage.

"Ten dollars--sucker," Ziggy replied.

"I fold."

Jetta popped the ice cube back into her mouth and exposed a pair of sevens. There were several groans. Jetta smiled, seductively leaned forward, and collected her winnings.

"Girl, you get more mileage out of a pair than anyone I've ever seen," Ziggy said with a grin. "And I don't mean your cards."

Jetta laughed.

"Ah, it's cheaper than porn," Perry said.

"It's a matter of strategy," she informed them. "Don't put down my system."

Bishop was leaning against the open hanger door with his hands in his pockets and casually watched the game from a distance. Ziggy noticed him then glanced at Jetta and indicated Bishop across the hanger.

"Your boyfriend is back," Ziggy muttered.

There was a round of laughter. Jetta eyed the guys while rolling her wade of cash and tucked it down her shirt. All five strained to watch.

"Don't let the suit fool you. He's paid too well for an assistant, and he's carrying," she informed them.

"Bodyguard or hired goon?" Perry asked.

"Carter's a little too straight to need a hired goon. He has some serious attitude," Jetta said. "He's been working for Carter for nine months, and no one still knows what he does. It's a mystery. I can't figure him out."

"Ex-military?" Ziggy asked.

"No, I would have spotted that a mile away," she replied. "I've been waiting for him to get into it with someone, so I can see his fighting style, but he's intimidating enough without getting physical. No one's challenged him yet."

"Want me to engage him?" Ziggy asked with a cheap grin on his face.

"He's liable to shoot you."

Ziggy appeared offended and glared at her. "Remember who you're talking too. I fought alongside your father and Hunter. I think I can handle myself."

"Still, I'd rather not unnecessarily provoke him. I like our relationship the way it is," she informed him.

"And what way is that?" Perry questioned.

"I tolerate him; he ignores me. It works on every level." Jetta stood. "Sorry, boys. We'll have to continue this conversation next time. Duty calls."

"Hey, bring Hunter next time. I want to see if he still has that sharp mind for details," Perry announced.

"Just don't piss him off, it makes him cranky," she replied. "He's not fun to deal with when he's in one of his moods."

"One of his moods?" Perry suddenly laughed. "You think you know him, Jetta?" he asked. "Hell, there are dark corners of his mind I don't even want to know about."

"Stop that, Perry. None of us are saints," Ziggy firmly reminded him. "We've all done things we'd rather not discuss."

"I've lived with Hunter every day for the last seven years," Jetta informed them. "I bathed him when he came home from the hospital; I held him when he learned Caroline left him; and I talk him down when he's off fighting the war in his mind. I think I know him. I know him better than all of you combined. After seven years of mostly just he and I, I'm willing to venture I know him better than even the admiral. The only thing that ever frightens me about Hunter is when he gets it in his head that I'm in some sort of danger."

"Why?" Ziggy asked. "What happens then?"

"He forced me into a closet once and made me hide in there for nearly three hours before I managed to convince him there wasn't a very large terrorist in the house."

"Oh, that guy," Ziggy announced with his eyes wide.

"You know him?"

"Not exactly, but we did see what he did to the guy after the fact," he informed her. "It was one of those highly classified, bullshit missions that we're not supposed to talk about. This big guy, bigger than me, butchered two of our men and had your father in his clutches. Hunter went in to rescue him. By the time we got there, Hunter was sitting on the hood of a jeep smoking a cigar. He was covered in blood with what was left of the dead terrorist at his feet. No one ever got the whole story from him, but judging by the carnage and destruction, it was one hell of a battle."

Jetta flashed a smile. "I know what happened to 'Tank'."

"Tank?"

"That's what he called him," she explained.

"He told you the whole story?" Ziggy asked with surprise. "Even your father couldn't get it out of him. We never knew why he wouldn't tell us what happened."

"He's relived that battle a dozen times over the years," she replied casually. "I know it by heart."

They all seemed interested and nearly jumped out of their folding chairs.

"Tell us! What happened?" Perry asked as his eyes lit up with delight.

"Sorry, I was sworn to secrecy--all twelve times." Jetta smiled teasingly. "Catch you boys later."

There was a round of groans. All five men hugged her before she was allowed to leave. Ziggy grabbed her and kissed her quickly on the lips when she least expected it. She hid her smile and pointed a warning finger at him. He smiled and chuckled. Jetta left her father's former military buddies and approached Bishop by the hanger doors.

"How long were you waiting?" she asked.

"Long enough to watch you fleece five brawny men with little more than crappy cards, an ice cube, and some strategically placed cleavage."

"I made a lot of money off that ice cube. Don't knock it."

"I wasn't knocking it," Bishop casually replied. "I'm actually thinking I'd like to play poker with you."

Jetta sharply eyed him as they left the hanger.

Chapter Five

$\mathcal{T}$he sheriff's cruiser pulled up to Dennis Albright's house. Sheriff Palmer and Deputy Styles got out of the car and stared at the mail truck crashed into the porch.

"Now we know why Ted never reported in," Deputy Styles remarked.

Deputy Styles was newly imported to Winter Harbor fresh from the police academy. He barely made the minimum drinking age, although he looked even younger then he actually was. Styles was enthusiastic for his work and a bit overzealous about fighting crime, which was putting it mildly. There were rumors he kept his cape in the closet alongside his utility belt. His boy next-door good looks were only magnified by his over starched, freshly pressed uniform and his painstakingly polished badge. Sheriff Palmer seemed the outcast wearing yesterday's uniform fresh from the floor and yet to be identified leftovers from breakfast still attached to his old, worn cowboy boot.

Palmer and Styles approached the mail truck and looked around.

Styles nodded at one of the cars as they passed. "That's Brian's car, isn't it?"

Palmer nodded. "If old Ted was hurt, why didn't Dennis or Pam call for Doc?" he asked mostly to himself.

They paused near the truck and stared at the dried blood on the ground next to Ted's cell phone. They saw the open front door and exchanged looks. Both removed their guns and slowly approached the house.

"I'll cover the back," Styles announced and hurried around the house before Sheriff Palmer could protest.

Sheriff Palmer shook his head at his deputy's enthusiasm then walked onto the front porch and toward the open door. He slowly entered the foyer and immediately noticed the dried blood at the bottom of the stairs. He clutched his gun with anticipation as his mind raced. *'Whose wife are you banging?'* his earlier question echoed through his mind. It seemed that Sheriff Palmer might have found that answer. Ted may have walked in on a domestic dispute in progress. Palmer walked along the hall while remaining cautious and alert. There was a loud crash followed by a gasp from the kitchen. Palmer ran for the kitchen and jumped into the doorway with his gun aimed. Styles held his shoulder while half bent over in agony. The back door had been crudely busted open. Palmer lowered his gun and shook his head.

"Did you even check to see if the door was unlocked before you went all *Dirty Harry* on it?"

"I was going for the element of surprise," Styles sulked while rubbing his shoulder.

"Kid, you *are* an element of surprise."

Both suddenly noticed the large pool of dried blood on the kitchen floor past the island counter. It had obviously been there several hours or longer.

"What the hell happened here?" Styles asked. "Looks like a massacre."

"With that much blood, someone's in trouble," Palmer informed him. "There's more at the bottom of the staircase. I want the entire house searched. We have three vehicles. Someone has to be here. They certainly didn't walk to Doc's office."

Styles nodded while staring at the blood. He appeared sickened by the sight. A faint scratching sound was heard from the closed basement door. Both turned toward the door with their weapons aimed. Palmer nodded Styles to the door. Styles looked at him with obvious horror. Palmer more firmly nodded him to the door. Styles uncertainly approached the door, placed his hand to the knob, and looked back at Palmer. Palmer clutched his gun and nodded. Styles pulled open the door. A cat hissed, ran past them, and out the open kitchen door. Both men groaned softly and lowered their guns.

†

*D*uring tourist season, the hotel lounge was the most happening place on the entire island in the evening. Unlike the tavern, it was elegant with plenty of rich, cherry woodwork. The bar was almost as eye-catching as the front desk and nearly twice as long. Only top-shelf liquor was displayed behind the bar. Locals rarely visited the hotel lounge during the tourist season. The prices reflected the ritzy glamour of the hotel and most wanted nothing to do with the wealthy class of tourists. However, once tourist season ended, they lowered their prices in an attempt to attract more locals. It usually only worked on nights they had live bands playing on their small stage. Given the early hour, the lounge was nearly empty. Hunter sat at the bar with a glass of brandy before him while Tyler leaned on the bar from the other side. At the moment, Hunter was his only customer. Tyler glared at Hunter and showed no mercy in his eyes.

"Well, let's have it," Tyler said lowly with a hint of annoyance in his tone. "This is your last chance, smartass."

Hunter stared back at him and showed little emotion. There was no way Hunter was about to let Tyler win. Their standoff was chilling.

"Damnation," Hunter finally replied.

Tyler stared at him in silence and with surprise. He turned toward the nearby laptop on the bar and typed in the word 'damnation'. The screen revealed, 'password accepted'. Tyler suddenly laughed and looked back at Hunter.

"You did it, we're in!" He shook his head with disbelief.

Hunter smirked and indicated his empty brandy glass. Tyler continued to laugh while filling the glass.

"How did you figure it out?"

"Once we eliminated her cat's name and birth date, it wasn't that difficult," Hunter replied with a shrug of his shoulders. "She's not exactly a complex person."

Tyler worked frantically on the laptop while grinning like a schoolboy. "I can't believe we hacked Elise's computer password in three tries."

"I don't understand why you'd want to," Hunter casually replied. "What's so interesting in there?"

"What's not? Everything she does is computerized," he said. "That bad performance review she gave me included. I just need to change a few words, and--" Tyler suddenly grinned. "--my evaluation warrants a pay raise."

"Jetta will be so disappointed in me," Hunter muttered while sipping his brandy. He wasn't exactly suffering with guilt. The free glass of brandy he'd won was worth it.

"Ah, don't sweat it, Hunter," Tyler informed him. "Women are always disappointed in us men. It's the way of the world, my friend."

Elise entered the lounge. Tyler shut his laptop and returned it beneath the bar.

"Speaking of the devil," Tyler scoffed. "I wonder what she intends to scold me about this time."

"Being born with testicles, perhaps?" Hunter teased.

Tyler couldn't help but chuckle. Elise paused by the bar and glared at both men. Tyler immediately fidgeted, but Hunter didn't bother looking at her.

"You're not supposed to serve him, Tyler," Elise remarked lowly.

"I've passed the legal drinking age twice," Hunter casually informed her without bothering to look away from his glass. "Would you like to see my ID?"

"I wasn't speaking to you," Elise retorted to Hunter.

"Oh?" he remarked and finally looked at her with a wildly unpredictable look in his eyes.

The manner in which he looked at her obviously disturbed her, causing her to subconsciously step back from him.

"I'm not a child, Ms. Raymond. Please don't speak to me like one," he informed her with little emotion. "I'm a paying customer, and at these prices, you should be grateful someone's willing to pay. As a paying customer, I think I have a right to know why you believe I should be refused service."

"Fine," Elise remarked while folding her arms across her chest. "You're a mental case. It's a well-known fact that alcohol and psychotropic meds don't mix. In the best interest of this hotel, you won't be served alcohol."

"Nice to know you've accepted the position as my shrink, but, unfortunately, I don't require those services," Hunter remarked and maintained his emotionless expression. "I am not currently on any medication, psychotropic or otherwise, although I do take vitamins for severe joint pain. That being said, if you would like to refuse to serve me based on an unfounded medical condition, you can speak to my attorney."

Elise stared at Hunter while obviously searching for some response. Despite her quarrel with Jetta earlier in the lobby, she wasn't about to push Hunter in the same manner. It wasn't just that she didn't like Hunter, she was almost certainly afraid of him. It wasn't surprising. Many people in town were afraid of Hunter. He had one or two episodes in public, which quickly got around town. Elise frowned and left the lounge.

Hunter casually sipped his drink and grinned. "I think she likes me."

"If you believe that, you really do need a shrink."

A young couple entered the lounge, looked around, and appeared humored by the emptiness. They approached Hunter and Tyler at the bar.

"Are we the only people staying at the hotel?" Allen asked Tyler.

Colleen sat on the stool next to Hunter and offered a polite smile. Hunter returned the smile then minded his brandy.

"No, there are maybe two dozen guests this week," Tyler informed them. "It's going to be pretty dead next week. We'll be lucky if we have two guests."

Colleen immediately frowned. "Yeah, us."

"Winter Harbor Island isn't exactly your fall/winter destination," Hunter remarked then eyed the couple. "The water is far too cold. Even the beach gets cold toward evening this time of year. What brings you here so late in the season?"

"Forgive my blunt friend," Tyler teased. "He's the inquisitive type."

"I am?"

"No, you're actually the rude/sarcastic type, but I was being polite," Tyler remarked.

Hunter considered the comment then chuckled and reluctantly agreed with him. "Yes, I believe you're right."

Colleen laughed and didn't appear offended in the least by Hunter's bluntness. "Allen and I just got married. This is technically our honeymoon."

"And people say I'm crazy," Hunter scoffed then chuckled. "Why would you choose Winter Harbor in the fall for your honeymoon?"

"Long story short," Allen remarked. "We were supposed to go on a cruise and missed our departure."

"That's a really long story," Colleen said with an uneasy chuckle.

"We saw a brochure for Winter Harbor Hotel, heard there were vacancies, and said 'what the hell'."

"The pool's heated, and we had the hot tub all to ourselves last night," Colleen announced. "Besides, we're on our honeymoon. We have each other. What more do we need?"

Hunter was about to speak when Tyler poured him another drink. He grinned at Tyler and held back his comment. Tyler maintained his pleasant smile at the young couple.

"Well, congratulations on your wedding," Tyler announced cheerfully. "I think a bottle of champagne is customary. On the house."

"Thank you," Colleen replied happily.

Tyler removed a chilled bottle of champagne from beneath the bar, popped the cork, and poured the champagne into two, long-stemmed glasses for them.

"If you really want to enhance your honeymoon--" Hunter began.

"Hunter," Tyler scolded.

Hunter glared at Tyler then looked back at the couple and smiled charmingly. "Winter Harbor offers helicopter tours of the island. I know the pilot personally."

"Helicopter tours? I think I saw a brochure in the lobby," Colleen remarked then appeared giddy while looking at Allen. "What do you think, dear?"

"We'll check into it tomorrow," he replied.

They clinked their glasses together and sipped their champagne.

Tyler looked at Hunter, grinned, and shook his head. "That was smooth."

"What did you think I was going to suggest? Combat training?"

"With you, it's hard to tell," Tyler remarked.

"What's with you people? A guy runs naked through town one time--"

Tyler appeared surprised and interrupted him. "You ran through town naked?"

He glared at Tyler and was immediately offended. "No, not me. I was referring to you. You ran through town naked, yet I'm the one you think is demented. I don't know what this world is coming to."

Chapter Six

*J*etta's helicopter shut down on the hotel roof. As the rotors slowed, Bishop, Carter, and Lee got out while Jetta finished her landing protocol. Lee had several department store bags dangling from her arms. Carter held a couple of her bags as well. He waited nearby for Jetta to disembark the helicopter. Hunter was seen across the roof casually waiting by the roof door. Despite his perceived harmless appearance, he looked like a soldier on patrol. Carter approached Jetta as she climbed out of the helicopter.

"How about joining us for a quick drink in the lounge?" Carter asked with a cheerful grin that conveyed he had something more in mind.

"I'd like to Carter, but I have Hunter."

"I'm sure he wouldn't mind a drink."

Jetta held back her laugh. It wasn't as if she didn't know what Hunter was doing while she was gone--and it wasn't peeling potatoes with Rafael. "I'm sure he's had a few already, even though he's not supposed to drink." She then muttered, "I have Tyler to thank for that."

Carter remained close to her and appeared unwilling to back off this time, which made Jetta unusually tense. Bishop standing nearby while taking in the entire conversation wasn't exactly helping matters either.

"Besides, I never drink and fly," she informed him. "I should get the helicopter back to the hanger."

"Come on, Jetta. One drink," he pleaded while adding his version of a charming smile. "You can leave the helicopter here tonight."

Carter was too used to getting his way because of his wealth. He really had no clue how to be charming. Lee approached the roof door and eyed Hunter with distrust. Hunter opened the door for her and smiled politely. She hurried past and glared at him as if he were a bug beneath her pink shoes. Jetta observed the exchange and felt the hostility boiling up inside her. She looked at Carter and suddenly smiled while entertaining a devious thought.

"Okay, one drink," she replied.

Jetta looked across the roof at Hunter by the door and signaled something to him. He motioned something back then disappeared through the door. Both Carter and Bishop appeared curious by their signals.

"Did you just tell him to steal second?" Carter asked with a chuckle.

"No, I told him we were having a drink in the lounge, and he said he'd meet me there. As long as I don't do this--" Jetta made another motion. "--we're okay."

"What does that mean?" Carter asked.

"Rear assault. Take no prisoners," she replied with a devious grin.

Carter laughed. Bishop gave her a curious look and appeared to wonder if she was kidding. Jetta caught Bishop's look and grinned at him. He didn't look confused too often, so she had to enjoy it when she could.

†

*T*he elevator door opened to reveal Lee. She stepped out and looked across the lobby to the front desk. Desmond remained behind the desk while busily working on the computer. Stacy was conspicuously missing. It was undoubtedly her lunch break. Lee studied Desmond a moment, frowned her displeasure, and reluctantly crossed the lobby, approaching him at the desk.

"Have you seen my father?" she asked curtly.

Desmond looked up at Lee, hesitated when he saw her approaching, and then smiled timidly. "I, uh, think he went to the lounge with Jetta and Hunter."

Lee stared at him as if the world suddenly came to an end. Her look hardened, and she was obviously bothered by what he told her. "He's having drinks with Jetta?"

Desmond noted her mood change and attempted to soothe it. "And Hunter. Bishop too, I think."

She glared at him with the anger evident in her eyes. "She's young enough to be his daughter."

"Well, I--"

"You're friends with her," Lee snapped hotly. "Tell her to stay away from my father. She's obviously only after his money."

"I don't think--"

"The bitch!"

Lee turned and stormed across the lobby for the awaiting elevator. Desmond watched with surprise as she disappeared into the elevator.

"Bye," he said softly then sighed, shook his head, and returned to working on the computer. "Jetta's right. She's definitely not the woman for me."

✝

*T*yler remained behind the lounge bar but appeared mostly bored. Jetta, Carter, Bishop, and Hunter sat in a corner booth with their drinks before them.

"Not much of a bar scene," Hunter remarked.

"Welcome to off-season. We have maybe twenty guests," Carter informed him.

"Do you import the call girls?"

All eyes were suddenly on Hunter. Carter appeared surprised if not speechless by the question. Jetta hid her smile and tried to keep from laughing. After a few drinks, Hunter's candor often kicked into overdrive. She hated to encourage him, but she appreciated that side of his personality.

"Excuse me?" Carter questioned.

"Sheriff Palmer said there were high-priced call girls prowling around the hotel lounge," Hunter announced with all seriousness. "I was just wondering if you imported them. I've never seen a high-priced one before. I bet they smell good."

Bishop turned his head and tried not to laugh. Sheriff Palmer had mentioned something to that effect, although it was quite possibly in jest. There was no telling with Sheriff Palmer's crude sense of humor.

Carter appeared offended. "We don't offer hookers in my hotel," he said firmly.

"Oh, they're freelance then?"

"No," Carter retorted. "We don't allow prostitution of any kind here."

Hunter appeared baffled and considered his comment a moment. "Huh, then you should probably talk to the girls in the spa," he remarked. "With what they charge for a massage, you know it's ending happy."

Jetta looked away while smiling. Now Hunter was just playing with Carter. He was well aware that the massage therapists were professionals. Sadly, on more than one occasion, her father's men had scheduled massages and complained about their lack of *services*. Bishop chuckled softly despite the glare he received from Carter. Carter wasn't nearly as amused by Hunter's candor. As much as Jetta was enjoying watching Carter squirm, she knew Hunter would torment him for hours if she allowed it. She was convinced Hunter was a cat in a former life. He enjoyed playing with his prey before killing it.

"Maybe you should find a new subject, Hunter," Jetta gently suggested.

"Oh, I'm sorry, Jetta," Hunter replied and shifted in his seat. "I keep forgetting you're mixed company and not one of the boys." Hunter looked at Bishop across the table from him and indicated Jetta with a slight nod. "You should hear her at home. She has a mouth like a sailor on shore leave."

Bishop appeared humored by the comment. "Don't listen to anything she says," he casually informed Hunter. "No one's mistaking her for mixed company."

"Excuse me?" Jetta snapped.

Bishop grinned at Jetta. She didn't know what was going through his head, but he never grinned at her like that before. She was almost positive he was entertaining thoughts about her minor indiscretions. Jetta squirmed for the first time. It wasn't often she was made uncomfortable. Hunter noted the exchange, appeared curious, but easily dismissed it. He then looked at Bishop's jacket several times and found a new interest. Bishop noted his look and stared back.

"Something on your mind?" Bishop questioned.

"Is your weapon military?" Hunter asked.

Bishop glanced at his open jacket and the barely visible pistol concealed in the shoulder holster. He looked back at Hunter. "Yes, it is."

"May I see it?"

Bishop reached into his jacket for his weapon. Carter appeared alarmed and stopped him from removing the gun. Jetta caught

Hunter's extended hand then glared at Bishop. That was the last thing she needed.

"Hunter is on a firearm free diet."

"What she means is--I'm not allowed to handle weapons in fear I may accidentally shoot someone," Hunter remarked then glared his disapproval at Jetta. "Despite that I've never shot anyone *accidentally* in my life."

"Not my rules, Hunter. Speak to the admiral," she said sternly.

Carter appeared equally annoyed with Bishop. "And we don't pass guns around inside the hotel."

Bishop frowned, pulled his jacket open, and allowed Hunter to see the holstered gun. Hunter eyed it from across the table.

"Impressive," Hunter remarked with an approving nod. "Browning Hi Power 9MM pistol. MI5 British Intelligence." He looked at Jetta and grinned. "James Bond."

"How do you know that?" Bishop asked.

"I know my weapons, Mr. Kane," Hunter replied. "That's the real thing too. Is it registered?" Hunter suddenly cringed and looked at Jetta with surprise and possible annoyance. "Why did you kick me?"

"Getting a little personal there, Hunter?" Bishop remarked.

"That's why," Jetta muttered to Hunter.

Hunter wasn't impressed and appeared matter-of-fact with her. "He's hardly a professional hit man, Jetta," he retorted. "The gun hasn't been fired or even cleaned in months. No professional would disrespect his firearm that way."

All three stared at Hunter with surprised looks.

"Meaning what?" Carter asked.

"He carries it for protection with little intent to use it," Hunter informed them. "Much like the condom in his wallet."

Bishop stared at him with surprise or possible embarrassment. "Excuse me?"

"When you had your wallet out earlier, I'd noticed your condom had expired over nine months ago," Hunter replied. "They do have a shelf life. That means you haven't had intercourse since--" Hunter suddenly yelped and looked at Jetta. "Why did you kick me again?"

Jetta glared her response.

Hunter studied her expression and appeared to understand. "Oh--" He looked back at Bishop. "I'm sorry. That was rude of me."

"You're very observant, Hunter," Carter announced with an uneasy laugh.

"Yes, it gets me kicked a lot."

"Saying things out loud is what gets you kicked," Jetta muttered.

"Discretion, I forgot," he replied then looked at Carter with a slightly humored expression. "My mind betrays me. Last week I called Jetta mommy."

Carter smiled and chuckled.

"We need to get going. Thanks for the drinks," Jetta said to Carter.

"I wouldn't mind another brandy," Hunter casually informed her while raising his glass and casting a look at Tyler behind the bar. "They serve the good stuff here."

"I think you've had enough."

As Tyler was about to approach with the bottle of brandy, Jetta firmly motioned him away. He was a little too quick with the bottle of brandy, she thought. Tyler frowned and returned to the bar.

Hunter looked at Jetta with concern. "Am I slipping?"

"Just a little."

He immediately looked at Carter and smiled politely. "Thank you for the drink, Mr. Braxton."

All four stood.

Hunter extended his hand to Bishop in an attempt to be polite. "It was a pleasure, Mr. Kane."

Bishop eyed him suspiciously then shook his hand. Jetta turned to Hunter, took the gun from him, and returned it to Bishop. Bishop appeared stunned and uncertainly accepted his gun. Hunter was really good at lifting things, especially things he coveted. She knew his flaws, and it annoyed him to no end.

"We really need to go," Jetta announced firmly.

"How about dinner tonight?" Carter asked her.

"I should probably stay home tonight."

"Then how about tomorrow night?"

"That's not a good idea right now," Jetta informed him. "I'll talk to you tomorrow."

"Yes, of course."

She hurried Hunter from the lounge. Tyler grinned slyly at Hunter, almost as if indicating he knew he was in trouble. Hunter smirked in return and secretly gave him the middle finger. Tyler laughed and shook his head as they left. As Jetta and Hunter entered the lobby, she linked onto his arm and slowed her pace. There was a long silence. Hunter was contemplating if he was in trouble or not. With Jetta, it was sometimes hard to tell. It wasn't her fault. Since she was technically a woman, there would be times he didn't understand her. She should have been a boy; then he wouldn't have to be so polite around her all the time.

"It's my fault, isn't it?" he finally asked.

"What's that?"

"You turning down a date with Carter."

"I turned down a date with Carter, because I don't want to go out with him," she stated flatly.

"Why not? He's rich and handsome."

"He's old enough to be my father, and his daughter is my age. And that's just the tip of the iceberg."

"Yes, and she hates both of us," Hunter muttered.

"As much as I'd like to date him just to spite her, I'm not the least bit attracted to him. He gives me most of my off-season work too. When it doesn't work out, he may realize it's just as easy to charter a boat."

She knew Hunter wanted to see her happily dating. He was routinely on a mission to get her into the dating scene. Sometimes, she wondered if he wasn't just trying to get her out of the house for *whatever* his reason. Her mere presence hindered his devious nature, of this, she was certain.

"I suppose that is best," he replied then swiftly changed the subject to something more amusing for him. "Was it just me or did you find the sexual tension back there staggering?" Hunter asked with a quizzical look.

"Actually, I thought Carter was behaving for a change."

"No, not Carter. I was talking about Bishop. With the lustful way he kept looking at you, I feared for your virginity."

"I think you're losing your instincts, Hunter," Jetta informed him. "Bishop has little interest in me."

She certainly would notice if someone like Bishop was interested in her. Truth was Bishop wasn't interested in dating anyone. It was a well-known fact. To her knowledge, he'd never even hit on any women. Perhaps it was because he was too busy insulting them. She was convinced he was only really in love with himself anyway. It was the only explanation.

"Ah, so you're attracted to him too?" he teased and suggestively raised his brows. Hunter enjoyed watching Jetta squirm. It was a difficult task getting her flustered, but he was convinced someone had to do it.

"I'm not attracted to Bishop," she scoffed and tried not to entertain the thought in front of Hunter. She didn't want that image from the lobby infecting her mind again. It already got her into enough trouble. "He's like a rash that won't go away."

"He's definitely going to need some fresh condoms before you two start dating," he announced with a deep sigh and completely ignored her entire statement. "I'm not ready to start changing diapers."

Jetta glared at Hunter then smirked. "Now you're just messing with me for your own amusement."

Hunter chuckled softly and patted her hand on his arm. "I'm easily amused these days."

"After six glasses of brandy, I'd say you're half lit."

"Who said anything about six glasses? I had two while you were gone. Ask Tyler."

"I did," she replied. "He said you had two, which means you had twice that much, and then another two with us. That makes six."

Hunter looked at her and frowned his disapproval. "I don't like when you act like me," he remarked. "It's very unattractive."

Chapter Seven

*B*arb and Stan Zion's renovated farmhouse was nestled alongside their landscaping shop, which resembled a large hanger with an office. The pristine property had a large greenhouse, lavish flowerbeds, a gazebo, fishpond, and amazing landscaping. A massive rose trellis cascaded down the side of the house from the second story and was the envy of every gardener in Winter Harbor. The sheriff's cruiser pulled up to the house. As Palmer and Styles got out of the car, an attractive sixteen-year-old girl, Teresa Zion, appeared from the house and stepped onto the porch. Teresa stood and impressive 5'9" and was the heartthrob of every boy in town. She had long, blonde hair and big blue eyes. In a few years, she would almost certainly be Lee's rival.

"Evening, Sheriff," Teresa said cheerfully then looked at Styles with a lustful grin. "Deputy Styles--"

"Hey, Teresa," Palmer replied casually. "Are your folks home?"

"No, they went to work on Doc's landscaping."

Palmer approached the house while Styles remained near the car. The sheriff looked back at him and appeared curious.

"You coming?"

Styles appeared tense while attempting to act casual. "No, I'm good. I'll, uh, just wait here."

Palmer shook his head then approached Teresa on the porch.

"Can I get you some iced tea, Sheriff?" Teresa asked and again looked at Styles and smiled sweetly. "Deputy?"

Styles managed a smile and gave a wave of no thanks.

"No, we're kind of in the middle of something," Palmer informed her. "There was an accident over at Albright's place. Did you happen to hear anything?"

"No. What sort of accident?"

"Ted's mail truck hit their porch."

"Is Ted okay?"

"That's what we're trying to figure out," Palmer remarked. "We've got a bunch of cars, but no one's home. No one came by for help?"

"No. I've been home all day."

"Shouldn't you have been at school?" he asked sternly.

Teresa fidgeted then smiled timidly. "Headache."

"Yeah, from the smell of booze, I can understand that," Palmer casually remarked. "I'll discuss that with your parents later."

Teresa immediately tensed and subconsciously played with her small, gold hoop earring. Her seductive attitude quickly drained away, transforming her back into a little girl. "I may have some information for you, if you promise not to say anything to my parents about the drinking," she quickly offered.

"I'm listening."

"Brian Fitch's car is at their house a lot when Dennis leaves," Teresa timidly informed him. "Last night, it was parked in the woods when I went for a walk, but I thought it was odd that Dennis' car was still at the house."

"What about when you came home from the tail gaiting party in the woods?" Palmer questioned.

Teresa's expression dropped with surprise that he somehow knew what they were doing last night. She fidgeted and attempted to compose herself. "Brian's car was gone."

"Consider this a warning, Teresa," Palmer firmly scolded. "Next time I find out you and your friends are drinking, I'll do more than talk to your parents. You're smarter than this." Palmer turned to leave then suddenly paused and turned back to her. "And stop hitting on my deputy. You can do better." Palmer approached the cruiser and eyed Styles with disapproval. "I know these country girls can be a bit of a culture shock to you city boys, but the next time she hits on you, speak up."

"It's not just her, it's all of them," Styles protested. "There must be something in the water."

Palmer grinned deviously and chuckled softly. "I'm guessing it's what's in the uniform."

t

Cross' beach house appeared isolated on the beach and far from anyone. Even during tourist season, there was little activity on that particular stretch of beach. The beach was broken up by a large rock formation detaching it from the tourist spots located around the hotel. Wealthy locals, who valued their privacy, owned the few homes that resided along that stretch of beach. Jetta and Hunter sat on the porch with cups of tea before them. Jetta watched the ocean as the sun set while Hunter read a book.

"You don't have to baby-sit me, Jetta," Hunter casually informed her while seemingly engrossed in his book. "You can go out with your friends."

"I'm not baby-sitting. I'm keeping you company."

"Ergo--baby-sitting."

"Desmond has to work late, so I have nowhere to go anyway. Why are you trying to get rid of me? Building a bomb in the basement?"

Hunter didn't bother looking up from his book. "Don't be silly," he announced simply. "We don't have a basement."

Jetta glared her disapproval. She didn't understand his perverse pleasure in tormenting her. There were times she had difficulty telling his lucid moments from his fits of insanity. She sometimes wondered if he was playing her.

"Besides, I haven't blown up anything since, well, me."

She couldn't even look at him after that comment. Jetta hated being reminded of his near death experience. There were several weeks while he was in the coma that they didn't even know if he would survive. His wife abandoned ship at 'possible brain damage', and her father drank himself into depression. Ironically, when her life fell apart, Desmond stepped in and brought order to the chaos that surrounded her. He proved he was capable of taking charge even if he rarely applied it to his own life.

Hunter looked at her over his small reading glasses. "I hate to think I'm the reason you don't have more fun."

Jetta snapped out of her trance and looked at him. She hated to tell him that her lack of dating didn't have anything to do him. Perhaps, in part, it did. She grew up in Navy Seal central. Her father's men were the end-all-be-all of mankind. She idolized her father, Hunter, and their entire team from a young age. How could any man possibly compare to them?

Hunter casually returned to his book. "Lord knows I had my share of fun. Of course, had I known Caroline would leave me while

I was in a coma, I may have reconsidered that Bangkok massage parlor invite." Hunter looked up and reflected thoughtfully. "Imagine; I could have been out there contracting venereal diseases with the rest of the boys. Such a shame." Hunter sighed, shut his book, and removed his glasses. "I'm suddenly in the mood for Chinese."

Jetta eyed him then grinned. "Food or women?"

"I suppose we could start with the food and hope the latter follows," he replied then chuckled softly.

"We'll take a ride out to the mainland tomorrow and see if we can find a little of each for you." Jetta considered her comment then stared off a moment. Just because she didn't date, that didn't mean he shouldn't enjoy himself. Her expression turned serious as she looked back at him. "You know, if you're *lonely*, I'm sure Ziggy could find you some temporary company."

Hunter tried not to laugh. Temporary company, paid for or free, wasn't really his style, but he enjoyed letting her think he had stud potential. "Not that lonely, Jetta. But I appreciate the offer." He replaced his glasses and returned to his book, although he was too distracted by inappropriate thoughts to concentrate. "Who's that cute Asian housekeeper?"

"Ming? She's widowed and has a six-year-old daughter. I think she has enough on her plate at the moment."

"So she doesn't need a mildly insane, fifty-two-year-old commando in her life?" he asked quizzically. "Must be something wrong with her. I'm both domesticated and housebroken."

Jetta stood and hugged Hunter around the neck from behind. "Her loss. I'll happily keep you all to myself." She kissed him on the cheek.

Hunter set his book down and clung to her arms around his neck. "I can't imagine why you want me, but I'm glad you do."

Jetta moved around his chair and collapsed onto his lap. He teasingly let out a painful groan.

"I don't remember a time when you weren't in my life, Hunter," she said with a sigh and rested against him while staring out at the ocean.

"Probably because you were still a twinkle in your father's eyes when we first met," he teased while holding her.

"I'd sit on your lap and you'd tell me stories."

"Then your father would yell at me because you had nightmares afterwards."

"You bought me my first semiautomatic."

Hunter nodded with a reflective smile. "Yes, I remember. You shot me in the foot."

"Scars build character."

"You say that every time I'm shot," he informed her. "I have a little too much character as it is."

"Then it works. See, I was right," she teased. Her look turned serious. "One day other people will appreciate you as I do. I just wish I didn't have to constantly defend you to you."

"Maybe you don't know me as well as you think you do. You don't know who I was--what I did."

"I know all I need to know, which is more than you think I know. Besides, I know who you are to me. Nothing else matters."

"I guess I've had quite a bit of influence on your life growing up," Hunter said as he held her against him. "If your mother was alive today," he remarked with a reflective sigh, "she'd undoubtedly smack the hell out of me."

Chapter Eight

*T*he vast countryside was peaceful at night as it usually was outside Zion's farmhouse. Several interior lights were on, indicating the occupants were still up despite the late hour. The tastefully decorated living room was moderately outdated and not nearly as impressive as the exterior. Stan sat on his lounge chair reading the paper, while Barb relaxed on the sofa with her needlepoint. Teresa entered the living room and hugged her father from behind.

"I'm going to bed," she announced then smiled deviously. "You kids behave."

"Night, dear," Stan replied.

"Good night, Teresa."

Teresa headed for the stairs and hurried up them.

"I wonder what happened next door," Barb remarked.

"Well, knowing Pam, she probably poisoned Dennis to be with that pig, Brian," Stan bluntly informed her without looking up from his paper. "Poor, old Ted probably saw something he shouldn't have and needed to be taken out."

Barb appeared alarmed and stared at her husband behind his paper. "Do you really think so?"

Stan suddenly laughed, lowered his paper, and looked at her. "How should I know? Maybe Dennis caught them in bed together and shot them both."

"You're terrible."

"Why? I didn't shoot anyone."

Barb groaned and hid her smile so not to encourage him further.

✝

Zion's farmhouse appeared peaceful alone in the field. Teresa's second floor bedroom light went out. Only a moment passed before Teresa quietly climbed out of her darkened bedroom window, walked along the porch roof, and climbed down the massive rose trellis. As she jumped to the ground, she was suddenly grabbed from behind. Teresa let out a startled scream and turned to face a teenage boy, Jeremy. Jeremy was a jock, as indicated by his varsity jacket. He wasn't particularly attractive in appearance, but he had a muscular build, which created popularity among Winter Harbor High School girls. He chuckled at Teresa's nervousness. She playfully smacked his arm.

"Not funny, Jeremy. What if my parents heard?"

"You're jumpy tonight."

Teresa shifted and appeared uncomfortable. "Sheriff Palmer stopped by this afternoon and smelled booze on me from the party last night."

"You did drink a lot," he teased with a laugh. "Don't worry about Sheriff Palmer; his bark is worse than his bite."

"I don't know; he barks pretty loud," she muttered. "He somehow knew we were tail gaiting in the woods last night."

"Of course he knows we were tail gaiting in the woods. That's what he did when he was our age," Jeremy informed her. "All our parents did." He then appeared to consider something. "How did you get inside last night without waking your parents?"

"I didn't," she replied. "I slept in the office."

Jeremy pulled her into his arms and grinned lustfully. "We should check it out. Sounds quiet."

"I don't know," she replied and pulled out of his arms. "What if my father needs something from his office? Maybe we should just drive to our usual spot."

"Can't," he said. "My father took away my car keys when he caught me sneaking in late last night. I had to walk all the way here."

"It's a half mile through the woods from your house," she scoffed then appeared humored. "Considering you're on the track team; that should be nothing."

Jeremy again pulled her into his arms and against him. He grinned boyishly. "Come on; let's break into your father's office."

She grinned while caressing his chest and moved her lips close to his. "We don't have to. He doesn't keep it locked." She pulled out of his arms, took his hand, and led him toward the landscaping building.

The office was dimly lit from the building's exterior vapor light shining through the solitary, dirty window. Teresa and Jeremy entered the office through the outer door. Jeremy immediately pulled her against him and kissed her passionately as he pushed the door shut with his foot. She pulled away and guided him toward the barely visible sofa. They fell onto the old, worn sofa and kissed aggressively while groping each other. Despite the dim lighting, it was obvious the office was poorly maintained. Something clattered outside. Jeremy pulled away from his position on top of Teresa and looked around the dimly lit room.

"What was that?" he asked with a note of concern.

"Probably a cat."

She pulled him back down on top of her, and they resumed kissing. There was another clatter. This time, it was closer to the office. Jeremy pulled away and looked around. Something moved past the dirty window. He groaned with annoyance and climbed off Teresa.

"I think I saw someone outside the window," he told her, as he hurried across the room for the window. He strained to look out through the layer of thick dust on the glass. "It might be one of the guys screwing around." He looked back at Teresa on the sofa. "I should check it out."

He hurried from the office, leaving the outer door open. Teresa groaned, rolled her eyes, and flopped on the creaky, old sofa.

"I hate boys with short attention spans," she muttered.

†

*J*eremy crept around outside the landscaping building with a devious grin on his face. It obviously wasn't the first time his friends had played tricks on him, and, this time, he was determined to give them a good scare first. As he rounded the corner to the office window, he noticed several rakes and shovels were lying scattered on the ground. He looked around but didn't see anyone. He appeared disappointed that it hadn't been his friends; and any chance he had of scaring them would have to wait until another time. He frowned and shook his head with disgust.

"Damned cats," he scoffed.

As he turned, he saw a shadow moving behind the far side of the building. Jeremy appeared curious then grinned. Maybe his friends hadn't disappointed him after all. He hurried along the side of the building and kept his back to the wall near the corner. He grinned and lunged around the corner. There was a loud crash followed by Jeremy's startled cry.

✝

*T*eresa lie casually on the sofa in the dimly lit office and attempted to examine her fingernails. Jeremy had been gone nearly fifteen minutes, and it was unlikely he was going to return. It wouldn't be the first time he cast her aside for an opportunity to goof around with his friends. She'd outgrown him. Truth was; she'd outgrown all boys her own age. A shadow was cast upon her from something blocking the open doorway. She looked up and saw the outline of a man standing in the office doorway. Teresa groaned with annoyance and sat up.

"Well, it's about time. I was going to start without--"

Teresa stared at the man in the dim lighting. With the house light behind him, she barely recognized Brian in the doorway. Teresa uncertainly stood while staring at him.

"Brian?" she asked with surprise then appeared relieved. "Jesus, Sheriff Palmer was looking for you. He thought something happened to you."

Zombie Brian moaned softly and took a step toward her.

She stared at him a moment then smiled seductively. "What?" she playfully teased. "See something you like?"

He moaned again and took another step closer. Teresa raised her brows suggestively and appeared pleased.

"Ah, screw Jeremy," she announced then grinned. "I can't tell you how many times I've thought about you in *that* way." Teresa quickly approached Brian, slammed the door shut behind him, and grabbed his hands. He attempted to lunge for her neck, but she had already turned and was pulling him behind her. "Your hands are so cold," she said while giggling as she pulled him to the sofa. "I'll warm them up for you."

Teresa cast herself onto the sofa and aggressively pulled him on top of her. Zombie Brian grabbed her shoulders and lunged for her neck. Teresa met him halfway and passionately kissed him. She suddenly muffled a scream and thrashed against him as he bit her lips. In the dim lighting, it almost appeared as if he was kissing her. The office door opened to reveal Jeremy.

"You're right. It was just a cat," he announced. "And who the hell puts a wheelbarrow--?"

Jeremy hesitated and stared at the outline of what appeared to be a man kissing Teresa. Her screams were muffled as she firmly grasped his shoulders while attempting to push him away; but that's not how it looked to Jeremy.

"Teresa! What the hell?"

Jeremy turned on the light. Zombie Brian lifted his head and snarled at Jeremy, revealing blood stained teeth, and blood dripping down his chin. Teresa's mouth appeared torn away as she gasped and spit up blood. Her eyes rolled back, and she started to convulse. Jeremy stared, horrified at the sight, cried out, and ran from the office. Brian returned to devouring Teresa's face. He ripped off her ear, chewed on it, and then spit her earring onto the floor.

✝

*J*eremy ran from the garden center toward the house. Zombie Ted appeared alongside the house with the .357 Magnum still clutched in his hand. His eyes were glossed over, and his left arm was missing. He had dried blood along the large, devoured part of his neck and down his clothing. Jeremy saw Ted's condition and tripped up the steps. He scrambled to his feet as Ted got closer and bolted into the house. Jeremy entered the well-lit kitchen, slammed the door behind him, and locked it. There was a thump against the door. He backed away from the door and quickly looked around. The back of Stan's head was visible in his lounge chair within the living room. Jeremy hurried toward the living room and stopped just in the archway. A woman in a satin nightgown knelt before Stan in the chair. She moaned while moving her head against him. Jeremy appeared surprised by what appeared to be a sexual situation.

"Mr. Zion, this is an emergency!" Jeremy cried out. "Please, they're out there! They got Teresa!" There was no response. Jeremy, who was now beyond hysteria, stepped into the living room. "Mr. Zion--"

Jeremy stopped alongside the chair to see zombie Pam kneeling over a clearly dead Stan while eating his innards. She stopped and looked up at Jeremy with intestines hanging from her mouth. Jeremy appeared horrified but held back his scream. He quickly turned and collided with Barb. She screamed and punched him in the face. He stumbled back a step while clutching his mouth. Barb gasped with surprise. Zombie Pam looked at them and started moving to her feet.

"We have to get out of here!" Jeremy cried out.

Jeremy and Barb ran for the living room door. Zombie Dennis appeared in the doorway before them. Both screamed at the bloodstained, decaying man. Jeremy pulled Barb behind him and up the stairs. She stumbled up the steps in an attempt to keep up with his long strides. He pulled her into Teresa's darkened bedroom. Jeremy slammed the door behind them and locked it. Barb gasped and sat on the bed while sobbing and panting. Jeremy hurried for the window and looked out while Barb clutched her bleeding wrist.

"We can climb across the roof and down the trellis," Jeremy informed her.

"Are you sure?"

He turned toward her and nodded. "Trust me, I've done it before."

"I'm so weak, I don't think I can," Barb said softly while gasping for air. "I'm having trouble breathing, and my chest hurts. I think I'm having another anxiety attack."

"I'd run for help, Mrs. Zion, but I don't know that the bedroom door will hold," he informed her. "It's not safe leaving you here. I know you can do it."

She uncertainly nodded. "I just need a minute to catch my breath."

"Okay, you rest a minute," Jeremy announced and attempted to relax despite his anxiety and adrenaline rush. "I'm going to take a look outside."

Jeremy hurried toward the window and climbed onto the porch roof. From his vantage point, he could see the entire yard and the nearby fields. Everything appeared clear. They just needed to scale down the trellis and run for the fields. If they made it to the woods, they'd have some cover. The woods would also be the quicker path to Millers Road. He returned to Teresa's bedroom window and climbed through it. Jeremy quickly approached Barb, who sat on the bed with her head resting against the bedpost.

"Okay, it's clear. We need to go," he informed her.

She didn't respond. He appeared concerned and touched her shoulder. Barb lifted her head, snarled, and attempted to bite him. Jeremy cried out and pulled away with horror as she leaped to her feet. He ran for the window with Barb in pursuit. He quickly climbed out. Zombie Barb grabbed his ankle and tried to bite his leg. Jeremy cried out while attempting to kick his foot free. On the third try, he pulled his foot away from Barb and slammed the window shut on her fingers. She screamed and thrashed while attempting to pull free. She fell backwards, leaving her crushed fingers within the closed window. Jeremy hurried along the porch roof. The yard and field were still clear.

Zombie Ted stood on the porch below and looked at the roof to the sounds above. Jeremy climbed onto the trellis, quickly scaled down it, and jumped off at the bottom. Ted snarled and ran for him, dropping his gun near the edge of the porch. Jeremy saw him and quickly turned to run. He suddenly came face-to-face with zombie Teresa, who was missing all flesh from her nose to her chin, exposing her teeth and jawbone. He cried out with horror at her gruesome appearance. Teresa knocked him to the ground with a snarl and landed on top of him. He fought against her while attempting to keep her teeth away from his face. She sank her teeth into his forearm, easily tearing through his skin. Jeremy punched zombie Teresa in the face, striking her fleshless jaw, as he screamed and attempted to pull his arm free from her teeth. He managed to pull his arm free, despite the large amount of missing flesh, and tossed Teresa off him. He scrambled to his hands and knees and almost made it to his feet when Teresa jumped on top of him and knocked him face first to the grass. As he attempted to buck her off his back, she sank her teeth into his neck. Jeremy screamed and thrashed against her.

Chapter Nine

$\mathcal{D}$t was a beautiful, sunny fall morning. Hunter cheerfully poured pancake batter onto the skillet while lively swing music played. He danced by the stove while busily making breakfast. Jetta entered the kitchen, stopped when she saw him, and leaned in the doorway to watch. She enjoyed catching his exceptionally good moods. It helped balance the heartbreaking moments when he was fighting the war in his head. He sang into the spatula and spun around to the music. He saw Jetta and suddenly stopped with surprise or possible embarrassment.

"In a good mood?" she teased.

Hunter smiled cheerfully, grabbed Jetta's hand, and swing danced with her. She laughed as he spun her around. He was actually a very good dancer, and it wasn't the first time they swing danced together. He released her, grabbed his spatula, flipped the pancake into the air without missing a beat, and caught it with the skillet on the way down. He returned the skillet to the stove, pulled Jetta into his arms, and kissed her quickly but passionately on the mouth. He broke off the kiss leaving Jetta stunned.

"Morning, Caroline," he announced cheerfully.

Jetta stared at him with horror in her eyes. "Oh, God--"

Hunter returned to his pancakes and appeared oblivious to what he had inadvertently done. Jetta quickly removed her cell phone and pressed a button while moving to the far end of the kitchen. She got her father's voicemail, which wasn't unusual. Taking personal calls while on covert missions was generally frowned upon.

"Hey, Dad, it's me," she said into the phone. "I think we have a real problem. Call me as soon as you can. Love you." Jetta disconnected the call, sank into thought, and then made another. She watched Hunter dance around the stove without a care. Someone picked up on the other end. "Hey, Doc. It's Jetta." There was a moment of silence as she listened to Doc through the phone. "Hunter thinks I'm Caroline. He's in a great mood, but I'm really worried. He's never mistaken me for her or anyone else before." There was another pause as Doc responded on the other end. "Yes, we'll be there around nine." The line went dead. "Hello? Doc?" Jetta disconnected the call and attempted to call him back. Her cell phone hummed.

"How many pancakes, my dear?" Hunter asked.

Jetta stared at him with a dumbfounded expression. She wasn't sure if she should play along or not. There was a knock at the front door. She almost welcomed the interruption. She smiled weakly and indicated the door.

"Hold that thought," Jetta announced then hurried from the kitchen.

Jetta crossed the living room to the front door and opened it to reveal Sheriff Palmer. He managed a smile but appeared tense. Given the early hour and his questionable mood, he probably hadn't had his coffee yet.

"Morning, Jetta."

"Whatever you think he did, Sheriff, he didn't do it. He was here all night," she said defensively.

"No, I'm not here about Hunter," Palmer remarked then fidgeted. "We sort of have a problem that now sort of involves you."

Jetta groaned softly. She didn't have time for this. "I'd love to play guessing games with you, Sheriff, but I have a pancake situation in the kitchen."

"And I have three bigwigs from CDC breathing down my neck over my missing person's case."

"CDC?" Jetta asked. "What does CDC have to do with a missing person?"

"Beats the hell out of me, but they want you to pick them up at the federal building on the mainland and take them on a tour of the island."

"Don't these high profile types have their own transportation?" she asked.

"I don't know, but you don't question these boys, or they'll go up your ass with a microscope," Palmer stated firmly then appeared embarrassed. "Excuse my language. I didn't have my coffee yet," he muttered.

"I really can't, Sheriff. Hunter just lost his reality button, and I need to get him to Doc by nine."

He suddenly appeared enthusiastic. "Is that all?" Palmer asked then grinned. "Hell, I can do that. I'll drop you off at the hanger and run Hunter to Doc just down the road."

"My helicopter is still on the hotel roof from yesterday."

"Better yet. I'll have Doc see him at the hotel."

Jetta was suddenly suspicious of Sheriff Palmer. He was up to something, which was actually pretty normal for him. "Someone has to keep an eye on him," she informed him sternly.

"We'll look after him. Trust me, it's under control." Sheriff Palmer's look suddenly turned serious. "Do you have any coffee?"

†

*H*unter sat alongside Jetta in the back of Sheriff Palmer's police cruiser and stared out the side window with a look of disgust on his face. He was in a foul mood now, which was never good, but being lost in his own mind *and* in a foul mood was borderline frightening.

"Who doesn't have time for pancakes?" he muttered. "I made those special. Now they're ruined. They'll be like little Frisbees by the time we get back."

"Rafael will make you some special pancakes at the hotel," Palmer grumbled from the driver's seat.

And then there was Sheriff Palmer with his own, special kind of foul mood to add to the explosive situation. Caffeine withdrawal. Jetta was regretting that there hadn't been any coffee on hand, but she wasn't expecting Sheriff Palmer knocking at her door so early. He usually didn't bug her until closer to lunchtime, so he could score a free lunch.

"What good will that do? I made those special for my darling wife," Hunter said then took Jetta's hand, smiled suavely, and kissed it.

Palmer gave Jetta a bewildered look through the mirror. "His wife? Did my invite get lost in the mail?"

"It's a long story, Sheriff."

"I don't do long stories before I've had my morning coffee," he growled then shook his head with disgust. "Who doesn't make coffee in the morning?"

"You mean besides you?" Jetta asked then immediately regretted saying it aloud.

Sheriff Palmer glared his annoyance at her through the rearview mirror. There was no joking with the sheriff during his morning coffee crisis.

✝

*H*unter sat at the island counter in the hotel kitchen with a massive pile of extra-large pancakes half-eaten in front of him. Rafael leaned on the counter while grinning as he watched Hunter enjoy every bite.

"These are fantastic," Hunter remarked.

"Glad you like them, dude."

Palmer leaned against the main counter and watched Hunter. Desmond entered with Doc Trenton, a short, graying man in his early sixties. Doc was a third generation, Winter Harbor doctor. His father and grandfather all practiced in town before him. His son was also a doctor, but he opted to work for a practice on the mainland. Although Doc insisted his son would take over when he retired, most in town doubted it. There just wasn't enough money in being a small town doctor. Freshly baked apple pie was an acceptable form of medical payment, which would explain the doc's girthy midsection. Doc approached Hunter and joined him at the counter.

"Morning, Hunter," Doc announced pleasantly. "That's certainly a lot of pancakes you've got there."

"I'm sure Rafael will make you some, Doc."

"Maybe later. How are you feeling?"

"Getting a little full," Hunter replied and pushed the half-eaten plate of pancakes away then wiped his mouth.

"Do you remember when you were talking to Jetta this morning?" Doc asked.

"No."

"This morning," Doc informed him in a casual tone. "You were making pancakes, and you spoke to Jetta."

Hunter tensed and stared at Doc. He realized something was wrong. Jetta wasn't at the house this morning. He was positive it had just been him and-- "I, uh, I don't remember talking to her," he said with uncertainty.

"You called her Caroline."

Doc's words shattered him. Hunter suddenly groaned and held his head in trembling hands. How could he have made that sort of mistake? How could he have kissed Jetta as he would a lover? There was no way to recover from this blunder.

"Oh, this is not good," Hunter gasped while staring at the counter. His mind was racing. He couldn't make any sense of what he had done.

Bishop and Carter entered the kitchen and headed behind the counter to join Palmer, Desmond, and Rafael, who still leaned on the island counter across from where Hunter sat. Doc studied Hunter closely and watched him tremble. When Hunter trembled, it usually meant he was confused and searching for answers. If he was unable to jolt himself back into reality, it just caused more confusion. The situation needed to be immediately defused.

"It's okay, Hunter," Doc gently informed him. "These are just side effects from the injuries you'd sustained during the blast."

"She must hate me," he said softly.

"No, Jetta doesn't hate you," Doc reassured him. "You know how she feels about you."

"It seemed so real." Hunter no longer trembled but didn't look up.

"I heard you had several drinks yesterday in the lounge," Doc announced. "This may have caused swelling in your brain. You should drink a lot of water today--"

Hunter suddenly glared at Doc with hostility. Did he hear him correctly? "That's your solution? Drink water?" he demanded in a tone that startled everyone. "I mistake Jetta for my ex-wife, and you recommend I drink water?" His eyes turned dark and frightening. "What kind of horse doctor are you?"

Doc stared at Hunter's dilated pupils and immediately tensed. Hunter was on the verge of 'flight or fight', and that usually only went one way for him. Desmond tensed with concern as well.

"You need to relax, Hunter," Doc said firmly.

Hunter bolted upright, and his chair crashed to the floor. Doc jumped from his own chair and took a step back. Rafael quickly backed away from the counter.

"Relax?" Hunter demanded in a chilling tone. "I fucked up with the only person in the world who matters to me, and you want me to relax? And drink water!"

"Oh, boy," Rafael murmured softly.

Doc calmly reached into his bag and removed a sedative syringe. Palmer moved around the counter and positioned himself a safe distance behind Hunter. Desmond saw what was about to unfold and approached Hunter in an attempt to keep him calm.

"Hunter, listen to me," Desmond said calmly.

"I want to talk to Jetta," Hunter lashed out.

Hunter couldn't figure out what was wrong with these people. Had they done something with Jetta? Why wouldn't they let him see her? He needed to find her before something bad happened to her. His body twitched.

"Jetta will be back," Desmond informed him gently. "She had to pick up some people from the mainland." He eyed the syringe then Doc. "Is that necessary, Doc?"

"That depends on him."

Desmond looked back at Hunter and tried to lighten the mood. "Why don't I take you home?" he said then grinned playfully. "Hey, we'll play that video game you like. The commando one. I've been practicing. I think I can beat you this time."

Hunter glared at Desmond through piercing, dark eyes. "You need to grow a pair before that will happen," Hunter growled. "I want to talk to Jetta."

They weren't going to keep him from her. Hunter knew he had to do something and fast. He didn't know what these men were capable of and in what sort of danger Jetta was. How long had they been pretending to be his friends to infiltrate his home? He was pretty sure he'd be able to get the lanky one to talk. Palmer grabbed Hunter from behind.

Desmond held his hands up in alarm. "No, don't--"

Hunter immediately rammed his elbow into Palmer's midsection, knocking him backward. He then kicked Desmond in the abdomen, knocked the syringe from Doc's hand, and swept Doc's feet out from under him. As Doc crashed to the floor, Hunter spun back for Palmer, who was in the process of reaching for him. Hunter grabbed his arm and flipped him over his hip, dropping him to the floor alongside Doc. Hunter leaped over the island counter, startling everyone. Bishop stepped into his path. Hunter swung at Bishop. Bishop blocked the punch and two others that immediately followed. Hunter spun into a roundhouse kick for Bishop's head. Bishop ducked and kicked Hunter in the side just hard enough to jolt him. As Hunter straightened, he had Bishop's gun in his hand and aimed it at him.

There were several gasps. Bishop stared with alarm at his own gun aimed at him. The silence was deafening. As Hunter stared at Bishop, he heard Jetta's voice echoing through his mind. '*I think you're losing your instincts, Hunter. Bishop has little interest in me.*' He then heard his own voice in response. '*Ah, so you're attracted to him too?*' Was this man Jetta's boyfriend? Something clicked in his mind. With one hand, Hunter disassembled the gun into several parts and casually dropped it to the floor. Bishop exhaled loudly with relief. Rafael hurried to Doc's side and helped him to his feet. Doc grabbed the discarded syringe. Hunter again jumped over the island counter to avoid further confrontation with Bishop and nearly collided with Rafael, who stared at him with fear in his eyes.

"Dude--" he gasped.

Rafael wasn't a fighter and didn't relish the thought of being pummeled by his friend. Hunter suddenly stood rigid while staring past Rafael. Ming stood across the kitchen with her six-year-old daughter, Fei Yen, clinging to her leg. She stared with surprise at the unfolding events. Hunter leaned closer to Rafael, causing him to jump anxiously.

"Pretty lady at ten o'clock," he whispered with enthusiasm. "Introduce me."

She was the most beautiful woman Hunter had ever seen! He thought, perhaps, he had seen her somewhere before, but his mind was playing tricks on him. Perhaps there was something in the pancakes. Rafael stared at Hunter with his mouth hanging open then uncertainly looked back at Ming. He forced a grin and leaned closer to Hunter.

"Let Doc give you the shot, and I'll introduce you, dude," Rafael remarked softly.

Hunter rolled up his sleeve while staring at Ming and extended his arm to Doc. Doc injected Hunter with the syringe. Everyone breathed a sigh of relief. As Hunter rolled down his sleeve, Rafael cautiously guided him closer to Ming. She appeared apprehensive as they approached but didn't back away.

"Ming, this is Hunter," Rafael announced politely. "Hunter, this is Ming and her daughter, Fei Yen."

Hunter smiled charmingly and extended his hand to her. "It's a pleasure to meet you, Ming."

Ming uncertainly eyed Rafael. He gave her a reassuring nod. She accepted Hunter's hand and returned the smile.

"It's nice to meet you, Hunter."

"We were having pancakes," Hunter announced cheerfully. It was the only line he could come up with on short notice. "Would you like join us?"

Rafael appeared enthusiastic, hurried behind the counter, and looked around the room. "Yes, let's all have pancakes."

Ming uncertainly smiled and nodded. Desmond and Palmer appeared sore but unharmed while watching the instantaneous transformation. Hunter picked up the stool and dusted it off for Ming. She smiled and joined him at the counter while Rafael allowed

Fei Yen to climb over him like a jungle gym. The other men collected near the main counter.

Bishop watched Hunter with astonishment and uncertainly shook his head. "He's rather--"

"Skilled?" Desmond replied.

"That too."

"He should be committed," Palmer scoffed.

"You shouldn't have grabbed him," Desmond softly interjected. "I had it under control. You're the one who set him off."

"How the hell was I supposed to know he was some sort of ninja?" Palmer demanded. "Quinn made him out to be a retired crossing guard. I'm going to have words with that bastard next time I see him."

"I told Jetta and Quinn that medications won't resolve the underlying issue," Doc informed them firmly. "He has a fragment of shrapnel pressing against his brain. The only way to fix it is with very delicate and expensive surgery that his insurance simply won't cover."

"How dangerous is he?" Palmer demanded to know. "He easily could have killed someone just now."

"But he didn't," Desmond announced.

"That's beside the point," Palmer scoffed.

"99.9% of the time, he's not dangerous at all," Doc replied. "What you saw just now is rare--and avoidable." Doc glared at Palmer. "Desmond knows how to deal with him. He did have it under control."

Palmer fidgeted then frowned. "Yeah, sorry about that," he muttered.

"He's going to be very tired for a few hours," Doc announced. "Desmond should take him home and let him sleep it off."

"Stay with him as long as you need," Carter informed Desmond then looked at Doc. "How much would that surgery cost?"

"Nearly a million dollars."

Everyone appeared stunned and groaned softly.

"How much does that little shot cost?" Palmer asked.

Doc smiled and laughed softly.

✝

*M*ing waited impatiently for the elevator in the lobby. Elise stood before the front desk, noticed her, and immediately crossed the lobby toward her and the elevator. Elise wore her usual grumpy expression, which meant she once again intended to unleash her wrath on poor Ming. Ming saw her, recognized the look, and fidgeted.

"Ming--"

"I was on time, Ms. Raymond," Ming quickly protested. "Mr. Braxton needed my assistance in the kitchen. He said he'd talk to you."

"Yes, he talked to me. This isn't a day care, Ming," Elise announced and impatiently folded her arms across her chest. "Why is Rafael baby-sitting your daughter?"

"He's not, Ms. Raymond," Ming replied then hesitated. "I mean, he's just keeping an eye on her for a few minutes until my mother gets here."

"This is a business, not a day care center," Elise scoffed. "This is the last time I'm going to tell you about this. If it happens again, you'll receive a written warning, and it'll go on your record. Now get to work."

Elise turned and walked back to the front desk. Stacy immediately looked down and pretended to be working. Ming frowned as the elevator doors opened. She said something in Chinese, most likely a curse word, entered the elevator, and cast her back against the wall.

Chapter Ten

*J*etta stood by her helicopter on the federal building roof and watched as the three aging government men in cheap suits, Daniels, Anderson, and Milton, loaded several duffel bags into the back of the helicopter. Something about the way they talked quietly among themselves made Jetta immediately suspicious of them--or *more* suspicious of them. She had her father's distrusting instincts. It was going to be a long, trying day.

"That's a lot of equipment for a missing person investigation," Jetta casually remarked. "Why exactly is the CDC interested in a missing person anyway?"

"Now you, of all people, know we can't divulge our interest in this case," Daniels informed her.

"I'm sorry, have we met before?" she asked.

She knew they hadn't. She would have remembered someone like Daniels. Although not unattractive, he reeked of a superior attitude, which made him unappealing. He was the sort of man who'd make her father's skin crawl. He made her skin crawl, and she wasn't entirely sure why. If she had Hunter's instincts, she'd know why.

"No, we haven't met, but we know your father, Admiral Cross," Daniels replied. "That's why we agreed to having your sheriff send you. You know better than to ask too many questions."

If Daniels had an ounce of intelligence, he'd realize hiring her was a mistake. She smiled despite her distrust for the man and his position.

"I'm assuming that's my cue to shut up and do as I'm told," she remarked with a grin.

"And you're smart too. I like that," Daniels announced cheerfully. "That means I shouldn't have to repeat myself more than once."

"My father taught me well," she replied then muttered under her breath, "which is very unfortunate for you."

They weren't going to get along, she was already certain of that. Jetta removed her cell phone and pressed a button. There was the same interference. She shut her cell phone and glanced at the three men, who were just about ready for take-off.

"My cell phone isn't working for some reason," she informed them. "Anyone have a phone I can borrow? I have a sick friend I need to check on."

Anderson removed his phone, pressed in a code, and handed the cell phone to her. She was immediately suspicious that he needed to enter a code to activate the phone. Jetta made her call, waited a moment with the cell phone to her ear, and then cringed at the voice on the other end.

"Hi, Elise," Jetta said into the phone then paused while listening and frowned. "Yeah, good morning to you too. Is Desmond there?" Silence. "Oh, I see." Silence. Jetta rolled her eyes. "I'm sorry your Internet still isn't working. Can you transfer me to the kitchen?"

Jetta made a face and held the phone away from her ear. Elise was heard shouting from the other end.

✝

Elise stood behind the front desk with the phone to her ear and the irritation evident on her face while talking to Jetta. Stacy sheepishly looked up from her position behind the desk not far from Elise. It was a common occurrence for Elise to go off on some poor, unfortunate soul several times a day. It was usually Desmond or Ming who suffered her wrath. Elise had already made her quota for the day, but she must have been feeling particularly confrontational, especially when Jetta wasn't standing in front of her.

"This is a hotel, as everyone seems to forget," Elise announced with hostility. "Our business is the guests, not socializing with the staff. And another thing--"

Bishop approached the front desk and picked up the clipboard. He appeared mildly interested in her rage-induced conversation then

71

glanced at Stacy. Stacy grimaced slightly as if answering his silent question.

"That crazy bastard struck the sheriff and poor Doc," she shouted into the phone. "We aren't running a mental ward for your charity case--"

Bishop realized with whom she was talking, grabbed the phone from Elise, and placed it to his ear. Jetta was heard cursing through the phone. Even Stacy heard the cursing from her position several feet away.

"Wow, that was some colorful language," Bishop announced into the phone. "Even better than phone sex. I'm actually blushing." Jetta's murmuring shouts were heard even with the phone against his ear. Bishop frowned. "Okay, now that's just plain rude. Do you want an update or not?" Silence. He suddenly grinned. "See, you can be nice. Desmond took Hunter back to your house to sleep off his sedation cocktail. Doc says you'll just have to ride it out like you always have." Bishop listened to her on the other end and nodded in response. "I believe Desmond intends to stay with him. Carter was very understanding." A sly grin crossed Bishop's face. "You're lucky he wants to get in your pants." Jetta's cursing could once again be heard through the phone, surprising Bishop. He grinned playfully almost as if enjoying it. "I don't think I've ever been called that before." The phone clicked and went dead. Bishop eyed the phone, shrugged, and hung up. "Must have been a bad connection."

Elise folded her arms across her chest while glaring at him. "You're disgusting," she scoffed.

He gave her an innocent look. "Me? I was being a complete gentleman," he announced proudly. "Can I help it if she has a mouth like a sailor?" Bishop attempted to hide his grin and looked back at the clipboard in his hand. "Talk about a turn on," he muttered softly.

Elise rolled her eyes with disgust then realized Stacy was watching them, apparently listening to their conversation. Since she was obviously no match for Bishop, Elise turned her wrath on Stacy instead. "Shouldn't you be working?"

Stacy immediately looked back to her computer screen and frantically typed nothing in particular. Bishop frowned with disapproval.

"How do you expect the poor girl to work with her boss throwing a tantrum?" Bishop remarked.

Elise glared at Bishop and appeared stunned by his disrespectful comment. She immediately turned angry. "I'm talking to Carter about you. I find you offensive, and I don't have to take your sexual harassment."

Elise hurried out from behind the desk and stormed across the lobby. Bishop and Stacy watched her until she vanished around the corner into the hallway. Bishop shook his head then looked at Stacy and grinned.

"You're welcome."

Stacy hid her smile and laughed softly.

Chapter Eleven

*J*etta flew the helicopter over the woodlands and fields several miles from town. Daniels occupied the co-pilot's seat while Milton and Anderson sat in the back and fiddled with high-tech gismos. Jetta remained suspicious of the government men claiming to be CDC. Since minding her own business was simply out of the question, she opted to eavesdrop on the conversation being had in the back while acting disinterested. It was a learned skill.

"Our first stop is the Albright house," Daniels informed her while barely looking up from his high-tech tablet. "Do you know where that is?"

"Yes, I know where that is," Jetta replied. If she didn't know the area, she'd make a very poor tour guide. She was amazed Daniels was smart enough to tie his own shoes. "I've lived in Winter Harbor my whole life. I've flown over this island so many times; I know every back road, fishing pond, and pothole."

"Knowing the area that intimately might be helpful. Take us to the Albright house," he announced. "And be sure to circle once before landing."

That was an interesting request. She wondered what he knew about Dennis and Pam that she didn't. To her knowledge, Dennis was predictable and completely boring, and Pam was flighty and over-sexed.

"Expecting enemy fire, Daniels?" she teased.

Daniels glared at her. Jetta caught his look and laughed softly. He was obviously wound too tight and needed a little teasing to loosen him up. Milton looked out the window and indicated Zion's farmhouse as they passed.

"Who lives in that farmhouse?" Milton asked.

"That would be Stan and Barb Zion. They own a landscaping business," Jetta casually informed them. "But I suspect they're secretly criminal masterminds. No sane person can be that into plants and flowers."

Daniels now ignored her. She could almost feel him rolling his eyes at her. Maybe extracting emotion from him wouldn't be as difficult as she first anticipated.

"We should check out that farmhouse as well," Milton informed her with little emotion. He obviously didn't care for her jovial personality either.

Milton was almost as stiff as Daniels was, she thought. She was two for two. She held out little hope that Anderson would be less pompous and even remotely interesting. She was also sure he'd hate her too. Jetta didn't know which one of *The Three Stooges* turned her on most. They were equally stiff, boring as hell, and void of personality. She was beginning to think those qualities were a job requirement--along with the cheap suits and bad haircuts.

"You know, I can get into all this cloak-and-dagger superspy stuff, but what exactly is it you're looking for?" she finally asked. "You're certainly not looking for any missing person."

Daniels glared his irritated response. She caught his look and concentrated on her flying.

"Minding my own business," Jetta muttered.

†

*T*he sheriff's cruiser drove along Millers Road with the lights flashing. It pulled up to a wrecked car that had apparently swerved from the road and struck a tree head on. Palmer and Styles got out of the cruise and approached the mangled car. The driver's side door was open and there appeared to be no one inside. Palmer paused before the open door. There was blood on the steering wheel and more on the seat. As Styles investigated the skid marks on the road, Palmer walked to the front of the car and looked over it. He lowered himself to the driver's side headlight. There was dried blood on the broken headlight. A shadow loomed over him. He straightened and turned, nearly colliding with Styles. Palmer jumped with surprise then shook his head.

"I wish you wouldn't sneak up on me," Palmer retorted. The sheriff was a little on edge after the frustrating morning he'd had. He also had too many unanswered questions over the last twenty-four hours, and his disgust was starting to show.

"I wasn't sneaking," Styles protested, although his tiny smirk suggested he may have been. "Judging by the skid marks on the road, I'd say the car swerved to avoid something. Never even had a chance to hit the brakes."

"I'm guessing he was avoiding a deer," Palmer replied and indicated the bloodstain on the headlight. "Didn't exactly miss though."

"What happened to the driver?"

Palmer returned to the open door with Styles directly behind him. "Looks like Roger was hurt in the crash. I'm guessing someone came upon the accident and picked him up. Probably took him to Doc."

Styles stared inside the car over Palmer's shoulder. "Kind of strange."

"What's that?"

"There's no damage done to the inside of the car, yet there's so much blood."

Palmer looked at the door window then the steering wheel and appeared bewildered. "You're right, that is strange. We'll radio Rosemary and have her call Doc. See if someone took Roger to his office."

"You'd think if someone did take him to Doc, he would have informed us about the accident by now," Styles said. "I mean, the crash must have happened at least an hour ago by the looks of the blood."

"This day is starting to give me a rash," Palmer muttered while frowning.

†

*J*etta stood alongside the helicopter just outside Dennis Albright's house and again attempted to make a call on her cell phone. The same static-filled humming sound was heard. She shut her phone with disgust and wondered if her cell phone issues were directly related to whatever it was those government types were looking for. She watched the three men poke around outside the house before entering. They were suspicious to say the least. What they were looking for or expecting to find was a mystery to her. She suspected they didn't even know what they were looking for. Sheriff Palmer should have been the one baby-sitting them, and she resented him just a little for pawning them off on her. There was no denying he was a devious man. She sometimes felt he did these things to her on purpose. It possibly had something to do with the admiral fleecing the good sheriff in poker nearly every time he returned home. Palmer was a sore loser when it came to cards. Sadly, the admiral was a gloating winner; and Hunter enjoyed egging both on. She was suddenly nostalgic for poker night. Jetta looked at her watch, groaned softly, and rolled her eyes. It was going to be a long day. She reached into the helicopter and removed her radio.

"This is Eagle One to the sheriff's office," Jetta said into the radio. "Do you copy?"

There was a lot of static on the radio, which she rarely experienced. "Yeah, Jetta," Rosemary in dispatch responded. "What can I do for you, honey?"

"Hey, Rosemary, where's Sheriff Palmer? This high-profile baby-sitting job is trying my last nerve."

"He's investigating a crash on Millers Road," came Rosemary's reply.

"Millers Road? I'm near Millers Road at the Albright house," Jetta informed her. "I didn't see any crash."

"It's a few miles from the tavern. Near the shoreline."

"Near my house?" Jetta suddenly asked and appeared curious. "Roger that. Tell Sheriff Palmer I'm about two seconds from tossing these three into Millers Pond. If he wants them alive, he'd better contact me ASAP."

"Roger that, honey, and good luck," Rosemary teased. Her giggle was an added insult.

"Over and out," Jetta said with a groan.

Anderson hurried from the house with the meteor in his gloved hands. Milton and Daniels hurried after him onto the porch and removed a biohazard box from one of the duffel bags. Jetta watched them gently place the rock into the biohazard box and then stash it in the duffle bag in an unsuccessful attempt to conceal the box from her prying eyes. Biohazard box? Jetta wondered what was so important about that rock that it required a biohazard box. Did a rock have something to do with Sheriff Palmer's missing persons? There couldn't be any connection. That wouldn't make sense. They quickly approached the helicopter with their bags and seemed excited with their find. Jetta tried to make sense of what she had just witnessed.

"We need you to take us to the sheriff's office," Daniels informed her.

That was an excellent idea, Jetta thought. Let Sheriff Palmer deal with them.

†

*T*he helicopter landed on the upper level of the empty parking garage in town not far from the sheriff's office. All three men got out. Daniels removed the duffle bag containing the biohazard box. Jetta watched them while turned sideways on her seat half out of the helicopter. She was happy to be rid of them, although she was wondering why they didn't remove the other three duffle bags in the back.

"Wait here for us," Daniels ordered.

Wait here? She thought her baby-sitting job was finished. Jetta was quickly losing patience with them. "I'd love to spend the day flying you boys around on your covert mission, but I need to check on my friend," Jetta firmly insisted.

"So--call him," Daniels informed her.

"My cell phone doesn't work," she snapped.

How quickly men with Ph.Ds. seemed to forget the little things. Anderson removed his cell phone, pressed in a code, and handed it to her. Jetta studied the cell phone then looked at the men hurrying away from her.

"I have to refuel back at the hanger," she called after them.

"Be back in half an hour," Daniels said firmly as they hurried inside the parking garage elevator.

Jetta shook her head as she climbed back into the helicopter and studied Anderson's cell phone. "Yeah, I'll be back," she muttered to herself. "After I make a quick stop."

†

*H*unter and Desmond sat on the deck at Admiral Cross' beach house while drinking hot tea. They sat a long time in silence and watched the ocean while a warm, salty breeze blew past them. Although Hunter appeared sedated, he was alert and painfully aware of the earlier events in the hotel kitchen. He was troubled by his actions and still attempted to make sense of them. He remembered hitting Desmond, which was troubling enough, but he was more alarmed that he pulled Bishop's gun on him. He remembered feeling justified at the time, which scared him. He questioned whether he would have felt equally justified if he had pulled the trigger. He couldn't bring himself to look at Desmond. He was Jetta's best

78

friend, and he struck him without regard, and at the time, without remorse. The things he said to him were cruel and disrespectful to someone he considered a friend. Hunter knew Desmond's ego was fragile enough without him destroying it altogether. He wasn't sure how he would correct the situation or if Desmond would even consider forgiving him. He knew he'd have to say something soon. The silence was becoming unbearable.

"I'm sorry I hit you this morning," Hunter said softly.

"Barely even felt it," Desmond teased.

Hunter eyed him while raising his brow in question then smiled and chuckled softly. Maybe Desmond was tougher than he thought. Desmond grinned in response. Apparently, their friendship was still intact, allowing Hunter to relax.

"Sheriff Palmer is pissed, huh?"

"Yeah, but that's his natural state," Desmond informed him. "I wouldn't worry too much about it."

"I wasn't, actually. For as often as he cheats at poker, he's lucky this is the first time he's been hit."

Desmond grinned and chuckled. Jetta's helicopter was heard approaching. Both looked at the sky with anticipation. The helicopter gracefully skimmed the coast then landed on the beach. Hunter and Desmond shielded their eyes from the blowing sand. As the helicopter shut down, they hurried toward it. Jetta jumped out as Desmond and Hunter approached. She was relieved that Hunter wasn't too heavily sedated.

"Are you okay?" Jetta asked him.

Hunter pulled her into his arms and held her against him. "I'm so sorry about this morning. Can you forgive me?"

"Why?" Jetta asked with a humored laugh while pulling back to meet his gaze. "You certainly kiss a hell of a lot better than Ziggy."

Hunter smiled and released her. Two for two. He had good friends. Of course, he'd need to check into this Ziggy kissing her business. He was familiar with Ziggy's reputation. He was extremely popular with the ladies, and that wasn't the sort of man he'd approve for Jetta.

"You should have called," Desmond announced. "I would have picked you up at the hanger."

"I'm still on the clock," she replied with disgust. "It was hard enough getting away from our government friends." Jetta tossed Anderson's cell phone to Desmond. "Can you hack this?"

"No problem."

"I'd love to know why their cell phones work and none of ours do," she said.

"Isn't cutting off communication one of the first rules of engagement?" Desmond asked.

"That's take no prisoners," Hunter casually informed him.

Desmond cast a glare at Hunter. "I sometimes think that's the only rule you know," he scoffed.

Hunter grinned and raised his brows suggestively. Jetta motioned for Hunter to follow her. He walked with her to the back of the helicopter. She opened the door and unzipped one of the duffel bags to expose automatic weapons. Hunter appeared surprised then smiled with boyish glee.

"But I didn't get you anything."

"Okay, genius, tell me what these government types are up to," she announced.

Hunter rummaged through the bags and examined several items with fascination. "Best guess?" he remarked. "They're preparing for a shock and awe. Night vision goggles; bad boy assault toys--" Hunter grinned and removed a rocket launcher. He caressed it lovingly. "Hmm, I think I'm in love."

"Yeah, put it back."

Hunter frowned and returned it to the bag, since it obviously wouldn't fit in his pocket. He played with several gismos he found within the bag and appeared fascinated with each one.

"The phone is encrypted," Desmond informed her while approaching and shaking his head. "Your friends are not exactly the trusting type. I'll need to get my laptop back at the hotel in order to hack it. Can I keep this?"

"Yeah, sure." Jetta looked back at Hunter as he dug around inside the bags. She motioned him out of the duffel bags and cursed herself for not knowing better. It was a bad idea letting him into them in the first place. "I have to go. They're probably waiting," she announced then indicated Desmond to Hunter. "Keep Desmond out of trouble."

Hunter offered a humored smile as she climbed back inside the helicopter. As the helicopter started, Hunter and Desmond hurried away to avoid the flying sand. Both men returned to the deck and watched her fly back toward town. Hunter hid his boyish grin while concealing something in his pocket. He figured it was Jetta's fault. She knew him well enough to know she should have checked his pockets. He was ashamed to admit he actually enjoyed when she frisked him. It was one of those moral dilemmas with which he often struggled. How mad would she really get? He needed a new toy anyway. Desmond slipped the cell phone into his jacket pocket and looked at Hunter, who was preoccupied with his coveted new toy.

"Are you coming with me?" Desmond asked.

Hunter looked at Desmond and maintained his casual appearance. When he was up to something, it was often hard to tell. It came from years of practice. Desmond was always easily fooled. He was far too trusting.

"Am I allowed to stay here by myself?" Hunter asked casually. If he wanted to play with his new toy, he needed to get rid of Desmond.

"I'm comfortable leaving you here."

"Then I'll stay. I'm a little tired."

"I'm trusting you," Desmond warned him while wagging his finger for added effect. Obviously his first mistake. "Jetta will have my ass if you burn the house down."

"God, she has you whipped," Hunter scoffed while rolling his eyes.

Desmond glared at him and appeared offended by the remark. "Look who's talking."

Hunter considered the comment and grinned. "Touche."

✝

*T*he helicopter lowered to the upper level of the parking garage in town square. Jetta saw her tour group waiting impatiently near the elevator minus their precious, cleverly hidden biohazard box. She was only ten minutes late. Considering how devious she had been in the last forty minutes, she made good time. Jetta jumped out and offered her best fake, apologetic smile. Smiling at her enemy while deceiving them came a little too easy for her.

"Sorry, I had to visit the little girl's room."

That actually wasn't a lie. She had stopped there too. Judging by their disapproving looks; they either didn't believe her or simply didn't care. It was evident they were irritated that she put them behind schedule, although their schedule seemed sketchy at best. Anderson seemed to realize his phone was missing and gave her a bewildered look.

"Where's my phone?" he asked.

"Oh, uh?" Jetta patted her pockets then put on a false look of alarm. "The sink in the ladies room," she said with a soft groan.

Anderson frowned his disapproval.

"I could run back to the hanger and get it," Jetta offered. There was no telling what sort of trouble she could get herself into if they gave her another thirty minutes.

"Forget it. Let's go!" Daniels snapped.

Daniels had already lost precious minutes as it was, and his attitude was showing his displeasure with her.

"I charge extra for surly," Jetta retorted.

Chapter Twelve

Later that afternoon, Lee stood before the front desk and talked to Stacy while showing off the new pink high heels she wore. Although they were obviously uncomfortable, Lee was proud of them all the same. Jetta entered the lobby through the driveway entrance with a look of exhaustion and approached the desk. She hated being without her car. She also had Sheriff Palmer to blame for that too. Even though it was less than a mile away, the walk from the hanger seemed to take forever some days. Lee and Stacy looked at Jetta as she wearily leaned on the desk near them.

"Someone's certainly putting in the overtime today," Lee teased while taking a little too much pleasure in Jetta's predicament. "I hear Sheriff Palmer passed off his baby-sitting job onto you."

"Is that the story he's telling?" Jetta asked.

"He bragged a little, yes," Lee replied with a look of humor on her face.

Jetta shook her head with disgust and straightened. She would deal with Palmer when she had more energy. "Is Desmond around? My cell phone isn't working."

"Maybe you should try paying your bills," Lee scoffed.

"None of the cell phones have been working since this morning," Stacy offered. "It must be the mainland tower. The landline phones are still working. Desmond is in his office."

"Thanks."

Jetta headed across the lobby toward the corridor beyond the elevators.

Lee watched her leave then shook her head. "Is it just me or is Jetta turning into her father?"

"She's certainly as popular as he is."

Lee suddenly glared at Stacy. "You're kidding, right?"

"I don't understand why you're so bugged by her," Stacy remarked. "So what if she's popular? She's never stolen a man from you or even said one bad thing about you. And your father adores her--"

"Yes, he adores her, and it makes me sick," Lee scoffed and removed her uncomfortable, pink high heels with disgust. "How would you feel if your father wanted to get into my pants?"

"I wouldn't doubt he does," Stacy replied simply.

"And how would you feel if I became your new step-mom?" she demanded.

Stacy considered the comment for a long moment then appeared curious and glanced at the pink high heels in Lee's hands. "Would I be allowed to borrow your shoes?"

Lee rolled her eyes, groaned, and walked away. Stacy stared after her with a look of surprise.

"I guess not."

†

*T*he hotel lounge was empty and quiet. Tyler stood behind the bar and peeled labels off empty beer bottles. Jetta and Desmond sat at a table near the back. Desmond had his laptop set up in front of him and worked on Anderson's cell phone. Jetta was still irritated with the government guys and Sheriff Palmer. Once again, poor Desmond had to suffer through her rants.

"Those idiots are driving me insane," Jetta scoffed. "Fly here-- fly there. Mind your own business. I'm telling you, Desmond, they're up to something. What's with all the assault rifles? And I saw them putting a rock or something into a biohazard box. What the hell was that about? Have we all been exposed to radiation poisoning or something? I'm lucky they even allowed me to take a break."

He finally looked up and appeared surprised by her comment. Apparently, he hadn't been paying attention to most of her rant. "You're going back out?"

"And I'm charging them accordingly," she informed him while allowing her head to fall into her hand.

Desmond returned to fiddling with the cell phone. "None of the cell phones seem to be working, but for some reason, this one still does."

"I hope you can crack it."

"Must have something good on it," he remarked.

Anderson's cell phone chirped and came to life.

Desmond grinned proudly. "Damn, I'm good."

The cell phone suddenly went blank. Desmond appeared stunned and stared helplessly at it.

"What happened?" Jetta asked.

"I don't know. They must have done something to it. Some sort of security precaution to prevent hacking," he informed her then appeared disgusted. "I guess they don't want anyone seeing what's on it."

"Can you get it back?" she asked.

"No, it's fried. These guys are good."

"Yeah, but so are you."

Desmond frowned. "They're better."

Chapter Thirteen

*I*t was around four-thirty that afternoon. Hunter sat on the deck with his reading glasses on and studied the electronic device the size of a cell phone in his hand. He played with one of the buttons, aimed it at a female jogger passing by, and watched the heat-seeking blip on the screen. He grinned and appeared pleased with his new toy.

"Well, aren't you the sophisticated little guy," he said. "Let's take you apart and see what makes you tick."

Hunter entered the house, shut the door behind him, and walked through the kitchen. He paused only a moment to glance at the floor in front of the refrigerator, just to be sure, and then continued into the hallway beyond the kitchen. Hunter entered the study and rummaged through several drawers. The study obviously belonged to the admiral indicated by the military gear hanging on the walls and the gun cabinet reinforced with bars behind the glass. Hunter removed a set of tiny screwdrivers from the desk drawer, left the study, and returned to the kitchen.

Hunter sat at the island counter with the heat-seeking device in front of him, put on his glasses, and removed one of the tiny screwdrivers from the case. There was a soft tapping on the glass deck doors. Hunter groaned softly, set his toy down, and removed his glasses with disgust. He was always being disturbed while he was up to something devious. As he approached the nearby doors, he saw zombie Teresa standing before the glass doors staring at him. All flesh was missing on her lower face and the entire front of her body was covered in dried and fresh blood. Hunter suddenly stopped and stared at her a moment from several feet away.

This was a first. Usually when he saw dead people, they were lying motionless on the floor. His mind was obviously playing tricks on him again. He was convinced he'd seen this girl before, although he didn't remember her being nearly as unattractive as she was now. He figured he should ask her what she wanted; since it seemed obvious she wanted something. He uncertainly approached the door, reached for the handle, and was about to open it when he suddenly hesitated. He flipped the lock on the door and approached the kitchen phone on the nearby counter. Hunter decided he should probably discuss this with Jetta first. He dialed Jetta's cell phone number and received a strange humming sound. He hung up and instead dialed the hotel's phone number. As it rang, he casually leaned on the counter.

"Winter Harbor Hotel. This is Stacy," came the familiar voice on the other end.

"Is Jetta Cross available?" Hunter asked.

"Hunter?" Stacy asked.

"Yes," he replied. "Who's this?"

"Hunter, it's Stacy."

"Uh, Stacy who?"

"Oh, okay," she replied with the sound of concern in her voice. "One moment."

There was a moment's pause.

"Hunter?" came Jetta's voice.

"Jetta, uh, hey, I'm, uh, seeing dead people," he said timidly while shifting uncomfortable at the counter.

"Hunter, there are no dead people. I assure you, you're alone," Jetta informed him over the phone.

Hunter casually looked at the glass doors. Zombie Teresa ran her bloodstained hands along the glass, leaving bloody smears, while watching him. He stared at her exposed teeth and jawbone. She was rather repulsive, he thought.

"Are you sure?" he asked and now felt tense.

"No one's there, Hunter," she gently assured him. "No one died."

Hunter stared at the glass doors and maintained his doubt. Zombie Jeremy now stood alongside zombie Teresa and tried to open the door. The lever handle jiggled slightly. Jeremy was missing the flesh from the back of his neck and part of his shoulder. His spine near the base of his skull was visible. Hunter wondered what kind of bomb caused that sort of damage.

"Yeah, they look pretty dead to me. Sort of like zombies," he replied casually. "Am I having another episode?"

"I'm sure that's all it is," she said from the other end.

✝

*J*etta stood before the front desk in the lobby with the phone to her ear while talking to Hunter. Desmond stood alongside her and listened to the conversation while appearing curious. She looked at Desmond, frowned, and shook her head.

"Dead people again," she said softly.

"I got this. Tell him I'm on my way," Desmond said and hurried across the lobby for the parking lot doors.

Elise and Stacy were behind the desk and stared at Jetta with strange, bewildered looks. Elise shook her head with disgust but refrained from commenting.

"Hunter, Desmond is on his way," Jetta said into the phone. "I have to baby-sit our government friends another few hours."

"What should I do about the dead people? They want to come inside," Hunter asked from the other end.

"Tell them you're not allowed to talk to strange dead people. House rule," Jetta informed him.

"What if they don't care?"

"Try hitting your reset button," she said simply. "I promise they'll go away."

Daniels entered the lobby with his usual look of impatience. He spotted her and quickly approached. Jetta saw him approaching, groaned, and rolled her eyes.

"I'll be home as soon as I can. I'm not doing any night flying for these bozos. Will you be okay until Desmond gets there?" she asked.

✝

*H*unter studied zombies Teresa and Jeremy as they attempted to enter the house and pawed at the glass. The dead jogger now joined them at the door. He watched them while holding the phone to his ear and appeared distracted.

"Uh, yeah. I'll be fine," he said into the phone.

"Okay. Behave until I get back," Jetta announced from the other end.

88

"Yeah, bye," Hunter replied. He hung up the phone and approached the glass doors. He stared with disbelief at the collection of dead people on the other side of the glass and uncertainly shook his head. "What the hell was in that injection Doc gave me?" He firmly waved off the zombies. "Go away. You're not real!"

They continued to paw at the door. Hunter shut his eyes and inhaled deeply. When he opened his eyes, the three zombies remained outside the door and continued to stare at him with dead eyes. A fourth zombie, Ted, was now approaching. Hunter stared at Ted's missing arm and shook his head.

"Damned reset button," Hunter muttered. "Wish they made little screwdrivers for that too."

He heard the front door opening in the living room. That couldn't be Desmond already. Desmond had a bit of a lead foot, but even he couldn't get here that fast from the hotel. Hunter turned and casually headed into the living room. A female zombie entered through the open front door. He stared at her as she made her way toward him. Now who the hell was she? The first time he was surrounded by women, and they were all repulsive! He shamed himself for being so shallow. He was sure they had lovely personalities. Hunter uncertainly took a step toward her then hesitated. Something seemed wrong.

"I'm just having an episode. You're not real," he sternly informed her. She didn't seem impressed. Hunter turned and walked away from the female zombie. She followed after him. Hunter looked back at her and was becoming annoyed. "Why are you following me?"

Another male zombie entered through the open front door as well and joined the female zombie in her pursuit of Hunter. Hunter groaned, waved them off with disgust, and walked away.

†

*O*t was around the same time that afternoon when Sheriff Palmer's cruiser pulled up to Zion's farmhouse with the lights flashing. Palmer and Styles got out of the car and looked around. Everything seemed unusually quiet. Styles remained tense.

"So Jeremy didn't come home last night," Styles bluntly remarked as he looked around. "Is that any reason to storm the Zion homestead?"

"I thought you enjoyed storming places," Palmer teased. "Or are you afraid of a certain blonde teenager?"

"Of course I'm not afraid of Teresa," he scoffed then uncertainly looked around. "I just don't want anyone getting the wrong idea, that's all."

Palmer chuckled while obviously taking pleasure in his deputy's discomfort. "Don't worry; it's my job to watch your back, Styles. I'll make sure Teresa doesn't molest you."

Styles frowned to the sheriff's twisted sense of humor and followed him onto the porch. Sheriff Palmer knocked on the door then glanced around. Nothing seemed out of the ordinary at the farmhouse.

"Jeremy's father said he was probably visiting Teresa last night," Palmer remarked. "I had Rosemary call here, but no one answered. It's probably nothing, but after that strange business at Albright's house, I'd rather not take any chances."

"Rosemary said Jetta's pissed at you," Styles remarked. "Maybe you should avoid her for a while."

"Are you kidding? She loves me. I let her father win at poker all the time. Jetta and I get along great," Palmer announced with a bold grin.

"Uh, I don't think so," Styles replied.

Palmer stared at the door, appeared curious, and knocked again. They waited another couple of minutes, but there was still no response.

"Want me to go around back?" Styles asked and was already taking two steps away.

Palmer grabbed Styles arm and pulled him back alongside him. "No, you can stay right here," he said firmly.

Palmer attempted to open the door, but it was locked.

"Should I break it down?"

"That won't be necessary," Palmer remarked, removed the spare key from under the welcome mat, and showed it to his deputy while grinning. "I know where just about everyone in town keeps their spare key."

Palmer unlocked the door and opened it. Styles attempted to enter ahead of him. Palmer casually pulled him back and entered first. The deputy frowned and followed behind. Both looked around the kitchen. Everything seemed in place and nothing was out of the ordinary.

"Stan? Barb?" Palmer called out.

There was no response. Styles followed Palmer into the living room. They briefly looked around then stared at Stan's easy chair. The chair was covered in dried blood.

"Son-of-a-bitch," Palmer scoffed.

Both drew their guns and quickly looked around.

"Just like at Albright's place," Styles said while nervously looking around. "This is getting really weird. What's going on around here?"

"I don't know, but I don't want you touching anything," Palmer firmly announced. "You have a look around inside the house. Check every room and closet. I'm going to look around the landscaping building and office."

Styles nodded and walked through the house. Palmer glanced at the floor. A small trail of blood led to the partially open living room door. He followed the blood and looked out onto the rear porch. The blood stopped halfway across the porch. Palmer remained suspicious and walked toward the front of the house. He stepped off the porch and suddenly hesitated. The .357 Magnum revolver lay on the ground alongside the porch. Palmer removed his handkerchief and picked the revolver up by the barrel to examine it. There was dried blood on the handle. He sniffed the barrel and appeared surprised. It had been recently fired. He carefully wrapped the revolver in his handkerchief and placed it in his jacket pocket. He uncertainly headed around the side of the house. Palmer stopped by the massive rose trellis and stared at the large amount of dried blood on the grass. He uncertainly looked up the rose trellis and observed the crushed flowers and leaves. Someone had recently climbed the trellis. Actually, it appeared to have seen a lot of recent activity. He attempted to put all his clues together, frowned with discuss, and headed for the landscaping building.

Sheriff Palmer entered the office and turned on the light. The dingy room barely brightened to reveal old, dusty furniture and a cluttered, metal desk. He looked at the sofa, appeared concerned, and approached it. The entire first cushion was soaked with dried blood. A bloody handprint was visibly noticeable on the side of the cushion. Palmer crouched alongside the sofa and studied the bloody handprint. He placed his hand up to it. The bloody print was definitely that of a woman. He looked at the floor. A blood-covered, gold hoop earring lay on the floor alongside the sofa. The clasp was still connected and it contained some flesh. He removed his pen and pushed the earring away from the blood.

"Teresa," Palmer gasped softly. He uncertainly straightened, appeared concerned, and looked around the room. "What the hell is going on around here?"

†

*J*etta's helicopter landed at Zion's farmhouse only moments later near the landscaping building. The sheriff's cruiser remained out front with the lights flashing. Jetta shut down the helicopter and watched her three passengers disembark. Jetta uncertainly got out of the helicopter and looked around. The entire farm was eerily silent. Sheriff Palmer typically did a lot of talking no matter what the occasion. That she didn't hear him was concerning. None of the three men seemed to notice, or perhaps they didn't care. Jetta slowly reached inside the helicopter and removed a small revolver from beneath the pilot's seat.

"I've just about had it with this messed up day," Sheriff Palmer was heard shouting from the landscaping building.

Somehow, that gruff, shouting voice relieved Jetta. Palmer appeared from the landscaping building with a look of disgust on his face while replacing his gun to its holster. All three men hurried toward him. Jetta replaced her small revolver to its rightful place beneath her seat.

"Did you find anything?" Daniels demanded.

"Yeah, more blood but no bodies," Palmer scoffed. "What the hell is going on around here? It's like some crappy PG-13 horror movie."

A gunshot was heard from inside the house. Jetta jumped with surprise and looked at the house. She was very familiar with the sound of gunshots but rarely heard them away from the shooting range. All four men ran for the house. Styles suddenly emerged from the house and onto the porch with his gun still in his hand. He looked shaken and out of breath.

Palmer stopped before him and appeared alarmed. "What happened?"

"I--I don't know," Styles stammered. "I had to break into the upstairs bedroom and Barb attacked me. We struggled on the floor. Next thing I know, the gun went off and she went down. I think she's dead."

Daniels returned to the helicopter, grabbed one of the bags, and ran inside with Anderson and Milton in tow. Palmer watched them run into the house and groaned loudly with a look of disgust and irritation on his face.

"Damned yahoos are going to compromise my evidence," Palmer cried out. He was about to run in after them when he noticed blood on Styles' pants leg and immediately became concerned. "Is that her blood or yours?"

Styles pulled up his pants leg to reveal a freely bleeding gash. "Oh, Jesus, that's mine! I must have cut it when she tackled me to the floor. I never even felt it."

"Oh, that's it. That is it," Palmer shouted then turned and pointed at Jetta. "You--take him to the hotel. Have Doc fix his leg. You're finished with these damned yahoos. I want them off my island!"

"I can go?" Jetta asked with enthusiasm.

"Go. Take Foo Wong Chung with you," he shouted back then scoffed lowly, "Probably cut his damned leg kicking down the damned door." Palmer headed for the open front door. "This day can't possibly get any worse!" As he headed inside, he was still heard ranting as his voice trailed off. "Damned yahoos!"

Jetta looked at Styles and the gun he still held. He noted her look, eyed his gun, and sheepishly holstered it. She helped Styles toward her helicopter and offered a sympathetic smile.

"I have an emergency kit under the seat. We'll patch you up and get you to Doc."

Chapter Fourteen

*I*t was a little before five o'clock. Desmond's car pulled up to Cross' beach house from Millers Road. Desmond got out of his car and looked at the front door now standing open. He uncertainly approached and slowly entered the living room. Desmond looked around with some concern. Several lamps and photos were lying shattered on the floor. The state of the room suggested a struggle had taken place. Even while taking on multiple, imaginary terrorists, Hunter never made a mess. At least not the sort of mess others could see. The amount of damage seemed impossible. It had only been twenty minutes since Jetta talked to Hunter.

"Hunter?"

There was no response. Desmond now appeared alarmed as he approached the kitchen and slowly entered. The French doors were broken with dried blood smeared on them. He appeared horrified and looked at the island counter. Chairs were toppled and there was dried blood on the counter and on the floor. A man's shoes stuck out on the floor from behind the island counter. Desmond gasped and hurried for the counter. The male zombie lie motionless, face down, with his head turned unnaturally to the side. Desmond stared at the zombie with a look of shock. He uncertainly looked behind the counter. The female zombie lie behind the counter with a butcher knife through her forehead. Someone appeared behind Desmond. Desmond turned with a startled cry. Hunter casually stood alongside the counter with his empty teacup.

"Did you want some tea while we wait for Jetta?"

Desmond stared at the casual look on Hunter's face. He uncertainly looked at the motionless zombies then back at Hunter. "What--what--what the fuck!"

"Coffee then?" Hunter asked with a curious tilt of his head.

Hunter never knew anyone could be so upset by the offer of tea. Desmond was wound too tight for someone so young. Maybe Ziggy needed to find Desmond some temporary company. It seemed like he needed it more. Hunter stepped over the dead female zombie and poured more hot water into his cup.

"I'm hungry for pizza. Maybe we could have some delivered, although the phone doesn't seem to be working," he informed Desmond while casually dunking his teabag. "What time will Jetta be home?"

Hunter again stepped over the body and headed back through the broken doors for the deck. Desmond uncertainly followed Hunter onto the deck and suddenly stopped. He watched Hunter step over zombie Ted's body and stared at the man with his arm missing. Ted's head was methodically bashed in. Hunter casually relaxed in his chair. Zombie Teresa was across the deck on her hands and knees with her head wedged between the vertical rungs on the railing and struggled to free herself. Zombie Jeremy was seen at the bottom of the steps and pawed at them while attempting to pull himself up without use of his severely broken legs. He snarled at Desmond. Desmond stared at Jeremy's bloodstained teeth, missing flesh, and blood-soaked clothing. The female jogger lay awkwardly on the steps having been impaled through the eye by a broken railing onto which she'd obviously fallen.

"Oh, my God! They're--they're zombies!" Desmond suddenly cried out.

Hunter appeared surprised and looked at Desmond. "You mean they're actually real?"

Desmond stared at Hunter with his mouth hanging open and appeared unable to respond. He suddenly exploded, "Of course they're real!"

Hunter looked at all four zombies with little emotion. "Huh? How about that?" he remarked then casually sipped his tea.

Desmond stared at Hunter with possible shock at his calm demeanor. "What's wrong with you? We need to call Sheriff Palmer!"

"The phone isn't working," Hunter reminded him then set his teacup down and finally stood. "Do you think there are more of these zombies?"

"I don't know, but we need to get to the hotel and find Jetta," Desmond announced in a state nearing hysteria.

Hunter stared at Desmond a long moment. Something clicked in his mind, and his expression suddenly hardened. Jetta was in trouble? Did he let that happen? He certainly wasn't going to allow a bunch of zombies get their decaying hands on her. Those sons-of-bitches were going to regret even thinking about touching her! Anger and rage swept over him.

"Keep an eye on them," he gruffly ordered then hurried inside the house.

Desmond remained horrified while staring at zombies Jeremy and Teresa, who tried in vain to reach him while snarling. Hunter returned from the house with one of the military swords from the living room wall. Desmond gasped and jumped out of his path. Hunter casually walked down the steps to zombie Jeremy, who reached for him, and lobed off his head with the sword. Desmond watched with surprise and appeared almost sickened. Zombie Teresa pulled free from the rung and staggered to her feet. She snarled and lunged for Desmond. Hunter suddenly appeared with the sword, swung for her neck, and decapitated her in front of Desmond. As her body collapsed to the deck, her head flew over the railing and landed in the sand below. Desmond uncertainly looked over the railing to see Teresa's face staring back at him. He appeared unable to move or speak.

"First rule of engagement," Hunter firmly announced, startling Desmond back to reality. "Take no prisoners."

Desmond just stared at Hunter and the coagulated blood covering the sword he held. The look in Hunter's eyes was serious; and it was frightening.

Chapter Fifteen

*J*etta sat in the pilot's seat of the helicopter as the countryside whizzed past. Styles moaned softly from the co-pilot's seat. She looked at him then the blood soaking through the bandage wrapped around his calf. His head rested against the co-pilot's door, and he barely moved now. Her concern for his condition was evident by the speed she was traveling. She looked at him several times while attempting to concentrate on her flying. For a brief moment, she debated taking him straight to the mainland hospital. His injury didn't appear that severe, but if something happened while they were in the air, she wouldn't be able to do anything about it, especially while flying over the ocean. She needed to get him to Doc. Doc could make the call and fly with her, if necessary.

"Are you still with me, Deputy?"

There was a chilling moment of silence. Jetta felt her hand twitch on the controls. He groaned softly and lifted his head. She glanced at him several times. Styles painfully straightened in his seat and looked at her.

"Yeah, I'm still here," he replied then laughed weakly. "My first injury in the line of duty. I was sort of hoping it'd be something more heroic; not wrestling a suburban housewife to the ground."

"I can't believe Barb attacked you like that," Jetta remarked. "Do you think drugs were involved? The Zion's just don't seem the type."

"It had to be drugs. The woman was possessed. She tried to bite my face off," he announced then cringed in pain. "I guess that's when I injured my leg." He sank into thought and suddenly appeared alarmed. "Oh, God, I hope I didn't accidentally shoot myself. I'll never hear the end of it from Sheriff Palmer."

"No, that wasn't from a bullet," Jetta informed him. "I've seen bullet wounds of almost every kind."

"You have?"

"The guys in my father's team take pictures of their wounds and send them to me," she announced then made a face. "I think they actually do it just to gross me out."

Styles was oddly silent a moment then he suddenly appeared pale and trembled. "I killed her," he gasped with realization. "Oh, my God! I killed Barb Zion!" He sobbed softly. "I've never even drew my weapon on anyone before. I don't even remember pulling the trigger."

Jetta uncertainly looked at the sobbing deputy. Oddly enough, she had been in this same situation many times with Hunter since his near death experience. She had gotten good at soothing tortured souls.

"Sheriff Palmer said there was blood all over the sofa in the landscaping office," Jetta announced gently.

Styles sniffed and stared at the fields flying past them. "There was blood all over the living room too," he said softly. "And at Albright's house. We didn't find any bodies. All that blood and not a single body."

"It's possible Barb went insane, Deputy," Jetta said gently, although she couldn't imagine Barb being capable of killing a fly. "I don't think you had much of a choice when you pulled the trigger. If you'd hesitated, you may have been the one killed."

He slowly nodded, wiped his eyes, and leaned his head against the seat. "How does your father do it?" he said softly. "All those missions in all those scary places."

"I don't know, he doesn't talk about it," she replied. Jetta indicated the town of Winter Harbor rapidly approaching. "There's the hotel. Think you can walk?"

Styles forced a smile and nodded.

✝

*T*he elevator doors opened within the empty hotel lobby. Jetta helped Styles out of the elevator. He avoided weight on his injured leg and leaned heavily on her shoulder. Stacy saw them from her position at the front desk, appeared alarmed, and hurried for them.

"What happened?"

"Styles was injured out at Zion's place," Jetta informed her. "Can you call for Doc? He's in a lot of pain."

"The phones stopped working half an hour ago," she replied with concern.

Jetta considered her options. "I'll fly back to the hanger and run to Doc's office," she said. "It's only a block away. I'll return here with him."

Jetta handed Styles off to Stacy. She helped the deputy to a sofa as Jetta hurried back to the elevator. Styles painfully collapsed on the sofa and appeared pale and exhausted. Stacy looked at the blood-soaked bandages wrapped around his injured leg. She appeared mildly panic-stricken and uncertain of what to do.

"Is there anything I can do for you, Deputy?" Stacy asked while fidgeting.

"A shot of alcohol would be great, if you've got it," he teased while grinning.

She offered a sympathetic smile and hurried from the lobby. Colleen had been standing near the front desk when Styles was brought out of the elevator. She uncertainly approached and stared at him where he lie, exhausted on the sofa.

"What did you do to your leg?" she asked.

Styles looked at her and considered his response. "We were checking out one of the homes," he said with discomfort. "I was injured in the struggle."

Colleen knelt before his leg and met his gaze. "It's okay," she said gently and offered a compassionate smile. "I'm a nurse. Mind if I have a look at it?"

Styles shook his head while cringing in pain. Colleen gently unwrapped the blood-soaked bandages and stared at the gash on his leg. Stacy returned with a glass of whiskey and stopped when she saw Colleen examining the bleeding gash. Stacy gasped and dropped the glass of whiskey. It shattered on the floor. Colleen looked at Stacy with surprise then relaxed.

"Is there a first aid kit?"

Stacy slowly nodded. Her eyes suddenly rolled back, and she collapsed to the floor. Colleen and Styles both looked at the unconscious woman and appeared surprised.

†

$\mathcal{I}$t wasn't even five-thirty that evening and there were several vehicles already parked outside the tavern for Friday night happy hour. Country music blared from the jukebox just inside. Two men got out of their truck and walked across the parking lot toward the tavern door while laughing and joking with each other.

"Okay, stop with the fish stories, Glenn," Herb said while laughing. "I was there, remember? I don't know who you're trying to impress."

"At least I'm not bragging about *other* things like you do," Glenn informed him with a cheap grin. "I've seen you in the locker room. You have nothing to brag about, and, I promise, no one's impressed."

"Oh, you're real funny," Herb sneered then laughed. "Do you think Lee will be here tonight?"

"As if you stand a chance with her," Glenn remarked. "I tried to ask her out once, and she made me feel like an idiot for even talking to her."

Zombie Pam appeared in the shadows alongside the building in her blood-covered nightgown. Both men noticed she was only wearing a nightgown and immediately became concerned for her.

"Pam? What happened?" Glenn suddenly asked. "Did Dennis do something to you?"

They quickly approached her alongside the building. She stepped out of the shadows to reveal her decaying flesh and severe injuries. Both men cried out with alarm. She lunged for Herb and tackled him to the ground. She tore into his neck, ripping his flesh with her teeth. As he screamed, Glenn took a step back with a look of horror on his face. He turned and nearly collided with zombie Stan, whose intestines trailed on the ground several feet behind him. Glenn jumped backward while crying out and narrowly avoided Stan's bloodstained hand. He turned to run and collided with zombie Dennis. Dennis grabbed Glenn and sank his teeth into the screaming man's neck as he tackled him to the ground. He thrashed beneath Dennis as he ripped flesh from his neck. The music blared from within the tavern, drowning the chilling screams as zombie Dennis feverishly fed on Glenn's flesh.

Just inside the tavern, a small gathering of locals were drinking and having a good time. Wes, the bartender, poured drinks to the patrons who mostly gathered around the bar. Shelly, the attractive waitress in a tank top and blue jeans, served a table near the back, where two men, Wayne and Edwin, sat. Wayne was an older man in his late fifties. Edwin was his twenty-something year-old nephew. Shelly hesitated by their table, appeared distracted, and listened while looking around. Both men noted her look, fell silent, and appeared curious.

"Something wrong?" Wayne asked.

"I thought I heard something," Shelly replied then smiled and waved off her concerns. She placed a full pitcher of beer on the table and removed the empty one. "You boys are starting early tonight. What's the occasion?"

"We thought we'd get a jump start on the weekend by blowing off the rest of the day," Edwin teased. "The boss was a little pissed, but he'll get over it."

Shelly grinned and eyed Wayne. "Are you over it?"

Wayne chuckled lowly. "He's buying, so I guess the boss is over it."

Shelly again looked across the tavern, this time toward the door, and appeared bewildered. Both men again stared at her and appeared curious.

"Hearing things again?" Wayne asked.

"I don't know," she replied. "I thought I heard something coming from outside. I'd better have a look."

Wayne stood and stopped her while offering a charming smile. "I'll check it out. You never know what's out there this time of year."

"Bear, raccoon," Edwin teased. "Big foot."

"Give me a break," Wayne scoffed then headed for the door. "No one believes you actually saw big foot."

Shelly remained tense while watching Wayne approach the door. He pushed open the door and looked outside. The parking lot appeared quiet. He turned his back to the open doorway and grinned at Shelly.

"Nothing out there," he announced. He allowed the door to close behind him.

Shelly appeared relieved, smiled at Wayne as he approached, and affectionately patted his chest. "You're the last of the true gentlemen."

"Yeah," Wayne said with a sigh. "Too bad I'm too old for you."

Shelly giggled and returned to the bar. Edwin glared at his uncle and rolled his eyes. Shelly approached Wes at the bar and returned the empty pitcher. Wes gave her a disapproving stare. She wasn't even aware that he was jealous. She looked around the tavern with enthusiasm.

"Good crowd for the early hour, don't you think?" she asked while grinning.

"Yeah, well, don't get too excited," Wes remarked. "There's a home game at the high school tonight. We'll be dead until well after ten."

"Maybe, but we're going to be busy the rest of the night," she replied cheerfully. "If we're lucky, some of the away team visitors will find their way out here as well."

"That'll never happen," Wes remarked. "They drive right past the hotel with that big sign advertising their lounge. That's where the away team visitors will be spending their evening; not with us locals."

Shelly frowned and collapsed onto a nearby stool. "More tips for Tyler, I suppose," she said with disgust. "Do you know they don't even have a waitress working during the off-season? He's going to clean up."

"Thinking about working for team hotel?" Wes teased.

"No, I'd rather work here where I know everyone," she replied. "Besides, I prefer your gruff personality over Tyler's inflated ego any day."

Wes chuckled softly.

Chapter Sixteen

*M*ing drove her car along Millers Road and eyed Fei Yen in her car seat through the rearview mirror. Ming smiled proudly as Fei Yen sang softly. Someone suddenly appeared in the middle of the road. Ming screamed and slammed on her brakes. The car skidded and the man was thrown over the hood and across the windshield with a series of loud thuds. Fei Yen let out a shrill scream from the backseat. Ming threw her car into park, looked at her daughter through the rearview mirror, and hastily removed her seatbelt. There was a loud crash as something struck her car from behind. Her car lurched forward. Ming was thrown forward with tremendous force and struck her head on the steering wheel. She appeared motionless while slumped in the driver's seat as blood ran down her forehead. Fei Yen's shrill scream was heard from the backseat. Ming, with her head resting against the steering wheel, slowly opened her eyes to her daughter's screams. For a moment, she didn't move. She watched the blood from her forehead drip onto her hand. Ming slowly lifted her head and looked around with disorientation. Reality flooded back to her. Despite her pounding head, she quickly looked into the backseat. Fei Yen remained virtually unharmed in her car seat.

"Mommy, mommy!"

"It's okay, baby," Ming said in a failed attempt to sound calm. "I'll get you out."

Ming tried to open her car door. It was stuck! She sharply pushed her shoulder into the door several times, becoming more aggressive with each thrust. The car door suddenly flew open, and she fell out of the car onto the pavement. Ming slowly pulled herself to her feet while clutching her bleeding head and attempted to maintain her balance. Her attention was suddenly drawn to the car's rear panel. The entire front end of the sheriff's cruiser was scrunched into the back of Ming's car. She appeared horrified by the sight. Ming opened the back door and looked at Fei Yen within her car seat.

"Stay put, Fei Yen. I need to check on the sheriff. Be good for mommy."

Ming hurried for the sheriff's cruiser and stopped by his door. Palmer was slumped over the steering wheel with blood streaking his face. The air bag had been deployed and was now deflated. Daniels, Milton, and Anderson were also in the car and appeared motionless. Ming pulled on the door several times before it finally flew open with a grinding metallic creak.

"Sheriff, can you hear me?" she said with concern while gently nudging his shoulder.

Palmer slowly woke with a groan and fell back against the seat. He stared at Ming with some disorientation.

"What the hell--?" Palmer dabbed the blood on his head, looked at it, and then slowly turned toward Daniels in the passenger seat. "Daniels? Hey, Daniels!"

Daniels groaned and slowly came to life. Palmer stumbled out of the car while swaying slightly and opened the back door to Milton and Anderson. Ming was obviously distressed and followed close behind Palmer.

"Sheriff, there was someone in the road," Ming said with mild panic in her voice. "I hit him; I know I hit him."

Ming pointed toward the other side of her car. Palmer stared at her a moment as if unable to comprehend her words while clutching his bleeding head then hurried past her car. She ran after him. There was dried blood on the hood and the windshield, but there wasn't any sign of anyone on the ground around the car. Palmer uncertainly looked around then under the car. Fei Yen suddenly let out a shrill, loud scream. Palmer and Ming turned toward the car. A badly mangled male zombie was reaching for Fei Yen in her car seat through the open door. Fei Yen frantically attempted to open her seatbelt while screaming. Palmer removed his gun and unsteadily ran toward the zombie.

Milton suddenly appeared from the opposite direction and pulled the zombie from the open door and away from Fei Yen, who continued to scream, but was now free from her car seat and against the opposing door. The zombie spun around, grabbed Milton, and sank his teeth into Milton's throat. Ming and Palmer stood motionless with horror while staring helplessly at what they were witnessing. Anderson yanked Milton away from the zombie, causing blood to erupt from his neck, and fell to the macadam with him. The sound of a gunshot rang out. The zombie's head jerked back as the bullet exploded through his skull. The zombie dropped to the pavement. Daniels stood by the car holding an automatic rifle. Palmer appeared horrified then enraged.

"What the hell? You just killed my suspect!" Palmer shouted at Daniels.

"He was already dead!" Daniels lurched back.

Daniels lowered himself to the ground alongside Anderson to assist him with Milton, but Milton had already bled out. His body jerked and thrashed. Daniels quickly pulled Anderson to his feet and away from Milton. Without warning, Daniels shot Milton in the head. Palmer aimed his gun at Daniels and immediately became enraged.

"Drop the weapon, asshole!"

"They're zombies, Sheriff," Daniels cried out. "And there's only one way to deal with zombies. Head shot. Remember that and you'll live longer!"

Palmer kept his gun aimed at Daniels, disinterested in what he had to say. "I said drop the weapon!"

Daniels ignored him and turned to the visibly shaken Anderson, who just stared at Milton's nearly exploded head and the blood spilling onto the pavement.

"Get the bag from the car," Daniels ordered to Anderson then looked back at Palmer.

By the look on the sheriff's face, he was debating whether or not to pull the trigger. In his current state, there was the very real possibility he would.

"They're already dead, Sheriff," Daniels announced in a more calm tone, possibly to avoid being shot by the cowboy sheriff. "You need to listen to me or the consequences could be disastrous for your little town."

Palmer appeared distrustful but uncertainly lowered his weapon regardless. Ming lunged for the backseat, removed her crying daughter from the car, and held her in her arms while shielding her from the gruesome sight on the pavement. Anderson hurried for the police cruiser's open trunk. Another zombie suddenly appeared by the rear of the cruiser and attacked Anderson. Anderson cried out while attempting to pry the male zombie off him as he bit him on the shoulder near his neck. Two more zombies appeared from around the back of the cruiser. Daniels fired at them and struck several in the chest and torso. It was obvious he wasn't a very good shot from more than a few feet away. A stray bullet struck Anderson. He immediately dropped. The two zombies pounced on his nearly motionless body.

"You damned idiot! You shot your own man!" Palmer cried out.

The zombies tore the flesh from Anderson's body and devoured him in a feeding frenzy. Palmer stared at the sight with a look of horror on his face.

"Sheriff!" Ming suddenly screamed while pointing toward the woods near his cruiser.

Palmer and Daniels looked in the direction she pointed. Two more zombies appeared from the woods only a few yards from them. Fei Yen saw them and screamed hysterically while clinging to her mother. Sheriff Palmer suddenly snapped out of his daze, appeared alarmed, and wildly waved his gun down the road in the direction of the distant tavern.

"Get to the tavern!" Palmer cried out.

Ming turned and ran along the road with Fei Yen in her arms. Palmer ran after her and looked back at Daniels.

"Come on, you stupid son-of-a-bitch!" Palmer yelled back at Daniels.

Daniels fired at the approaching zombies and missed with nearly every shot. His weapon suddenly jammed. The zombies were closing in on him. As Anderson rose to his feet with that familiar dead look in his eyes, Daniels stared at him and appeared momentarily frozen with fear. Daniels was suddenly grabbed from behind and spun around to face the enraged Sheriff Palmer.

"I said move it!"

Palmer shoved Daniels in the direction of the tavern after Ming. Ming ran as fast as she could with her daughter in her arms. She was obviously getting too big for Ming to carry let alone run with. Palmer and Daniels ran after Ming. The sheriff was surprisingly fast despite the thumping of his cowboy boots on the pavement. Palmer caught up to them, took Fei Yen from Ming without missing a stride, and carried her as they ran. Daniels attempted to keep up with them, but it was obvious he had spent too much time behind a desk in recent years.

†

*T*he tavern was half-filled with trucks parked out front and every interior and exterior light was on. Country music continued to blare from inside. There was no visible sign of Glenn or Herb's bodies. Ming, Daniels, and Palmer, who carried Fei Yen, approached the tavern now at a brisk pace. Ming uncertainly looked at what appeared almost certainly to be a large puddle of blood on the gravel parking lot. A drunken man stumbled past the door. As they approached, they saw it was zombie Stan with blood down his shirt and his intestines dragging in a lengthy trail behind him. Fei Yen screamed. Palmer quickly passed her off to Ming, crouched down slightly, and aimed his gun at the zombie. Zombie Stan turned toward them and snarled.

"Stop right there!"

"Shoot him, Sheriff!" Daniels shouted.

"Shut up! We don't shoot our own!"

The tavern door opened to reveal one of the patrons. Zombie Stan turned toward the man in the doorway, snarled at him, and bared his teeth. The man cried out in horror and slammed the door. The zombie turned back for Palmer. Palmer stared with his gun aimed and debated what to do.

"Sheriff!" Ming cried out.

More zombies appeared throughout the parking lot and descended upon them. Palmer looked at zombie Stan between them and the door then sneered with disgust.

"Ah, hell--"

Palmer straightened, aimed his gun with determination, and shot zombie Stan in the head. The zombie's head snapped back, and he fell to the ground. Daniels ran for the door and attempted to open it. It was locked! Palmer joined him and pounded on it with the butt of his revolver.

"Open this door, you damned yahoos, or I'll shoot it open!" he cried out with anger.

The door opened. All four hurried inside. The half-filled tavern was alive with men and women dancing and drinking. Country music blared from the nearby jukebox. The four stared at the good time being had by the patrons who appeared unaware of the situation outside.

"Listen up!" Palmer called out.

Either no one heard him or they simply didn't care. Palmer turned toward the jukebox and casually shot it. The music stopped and the jukebox smoldered. There were several startled screams from around the room. The sheriff had succeeded in getting their attention. All eyes were now on Palmer.

"I want every door and window shut and bolted--now!" Palmer yelled. Everyone stared at him with surprise but no one moved. "If you yahoos want to live, you'll do it now!"

His words chilled everyone. Wes and Shelly bolted into action and hurried across the tavern in separate directions. Wes ran into the kitchen area behind the bar. There was a loud crash. Wes could be heard yelling. Palmer ran across the tavern and disappeared into the kitchen. The sounds of gunshots echoed throughout the tavern. The room was eerily silent as everyone stared at the kitchen door with anticipation. Palmer returned with Wes, who held his bleeding arm. Daniels hurried toward them and examined Wes' injury. It was clearly a bite wound.

Daniels appeared alarmed and met Palmer's gaze. "This man's been infected."

"What do you mean infected?" Wes suddenly asked while staring at him with a look of horror.

"In less than an hour you're going to become one of them," Daniels informed Wes.

"One of them?" Wes suddenly asked. "What are you talking about?"

The crowd chattered softly with confusion and still oblivious to what was happening just outside.

"You were bitten by a zombie," Daniels informed him then turned to Palmer. "You need to deal with him now."

"Are you out of your mind?" Palmer demanded with rage showing in his eyes.

"You don't understand, Sheriff. There is no cure," Daniels proclaimed. "Once you're bit, that's it. You saw what happened to Anderson."

"I didn't see nothing," Palmer snapped then turned to Shelly, who jumped at his frightening glare. "I need you to call Rosemary for backup."

"The phones went down a little while ago," Shelly nervously informed him. "There's no cell service either."

Palmer stared at Shelly and appeared oddly calm despite their desperate situation, which was unusual for the sheriff who'd rant endlessly over something as trivial as spilled coffee. This was certainly worse. All things considered, he seemed to be handling the stress rather well. Palmer suddenly turned to Daniels, grabbed him by the shirt collar, and slammed him against the bar. Everyone within the tavern jumped with surprise. Glasses toppled and spilled on top of the bar from the impact. Palmer stared into his eyes with the appearance of a raving lunatic.

"You'd better tell us what the hell is going on around here--and fast, or you're the one I'm going to be shooting, compredes?"

Daniels stared at Palmer with a frightened look. "I can't tell you what I don't know."

"You're lying," Palmer lashed out. "I saw that biohazard box you were trying to hide in that bag in my office! I want to know what was in that damned box, and what the hell is happening to my people!"

There would be no messing around with the good sheriff now. No one within the tavern had ever seen this side of him, and there was no telling what he might do.

"It was supposed to be a harmless meteor," Daniels reluctantly replied with a quiver in his voice while attempting to loosen Palmer's grip on his shirt to no avail. "There was another one just like it found yesterday in a field on the mainland. Our men took it back to the lab to examine it. When they went to take a sample, a toxic gas escaped and sprayed one of the scientists in the face. At first, he seemed okay. An hour later, he attacked and ate his lab partner. Moments after that, his lab partner got back up."

Palmer loosened his grip on Daniels' shirt. Daniels relaxed and was able to straighten slightly despite the sheriff's death grip on his shirt.

"The toxin within the meteor infected him, and he turned into a zombie. He, in turn, infected his partner when he bit him. We were lucky that the biohazard was confined to the lab. It wasn't until this morning that we learned a second meteor had landed on this island. We were in the process of tracking it down when we heard radio chatter from your police scanner," Daniels said gently. "You reported three missing people in the area near where we suspected the meteor had landed. We realized one or more people had already been exposed. We came as quickly as we could to track down the meteor and help find the potentially infected people."

"Why didn't you just say so in the first place?" Palmer demanded and roughly released Daniels.

Daniels attempted to compose himself, but it was obvious Sheriff Palmer's iron fist tactics rattled him. "Things like that tend to alarm even the most rational people and cause mass hysteria. We thought we could handle it quietly ourselves. Besides, would you have believed me?"

"That's beside the point. Consider yourself very lucky I think we need you," Palmer informed him. "So I suggest you make yourself useful, or I'll find my own use for you."

Chapter Seventeen

$\mathcal{D}$oc wrapped Styles' lower leg with Colleen assisting him. Stacy and Elise watched from several feet away. Styles was in a lot of pain, remained pale, and sweated profusely. Jetta sat on the arm of a nearby chair and subconsciously rubbed her chilled arms. Styles didn't look good. She was reconsidering having taken him directly to the mainland hospital. Doc was a good doctor, but she was concerned that there was something more going on with what she'd heard and witnessed throughout the day. It crossed her mind that Styles may have been exposed to whatever it was the government guys were attempting to conceal.

"You're going to be fine, but we should get you to my office," Doc said to Styles with a reassuring smile. "I'd like stitch that up and make you more comfortable."

"If it's all the same, I'd like to rest a few minutes. I'm really weak."

Doc nodded. Elise looked at everyone and started waving her hand around like a magic wand.

"Okay, everyone back to work," Elise commanded.

Everyone scattered as if by magic. Stacy and Elise returned to the front desk. Jetta uncertainly stood and followed Doc across the lobby.

"Maybe I should fly him to the mainland hospital," Jetta suggested softly to Doc. "I can run back to the hanger for my helicopter. I have more than enough fuel."

Doc offered a gentle smile and patted her arm. "He's going to be fine, Jetta. I gave him the good painkillers and started him on antibiotics."

Jetta smiled weakly and nodded. She still wasn't completely convinced. As Doc joined Elise and Stacy at the front desk, Jetta returned to Styles. Carter and Bishop appeared from the elevator and hurried toward the deputy on the sofa.

"I just heard," Carter said to Styles. "Is it true that Barb attacked you?"

"It's true. She came at me like a wild animal. It all happened so fast."

"You just rest. I'll have Tyler bring you a drink," Carter announced with a reassuring smile.

"Thanks, Carter."

Carter glanced at Jetta and grinned while shaking his head. "Looks like you're now our medevac as well, huh?"

"Yeah, looks that way," Jetta said with a sigh then looked around the lobby. "Could someone give me a ride back to my place? I'd like to check on Hunter."

"I'll give you a ride--right after dinner," Carter informed her with a pleased smile.

"I'd like to take a rain check, Carter," she said gently with mild exhaustion in her tone. "It's been a long day, and I just want to get home to Hunter."

"Desmond is with him. He's fine," he informed her. "You have to eat, and I've already given you about six rain checks. Come on--a quick bite."

Jetta reluctantly nodded and walked with him toward the lounge. Bishop approached the front desk and immediately received a glare from Elise.

"Something on your mind, Ms. Raymond?" Bishop asked while raising a brow in question.

"You're in charge of security, right?"

"I'm in charge of the guy who's in charge of security, yes," Bishop remarked.

"Well, no one has seen Phil since he left the tavern an hour before his shift," Elise remarked. "Since you're in charge of him, perhaps you'd like to see if he's sleeping off his bender somewhere on the grounds."

"Yeah," Bishop reluctantly replied with a sigh. "I'll look for Phil."

t

*J*etta sat with Carter in the lounge at the back booth and picked at the food on her plate with little interest. She didn't want to be there. She just wanted to get home and make sure Hunter was okay. It had been a long, exhausting day, and she wanted it over. She wasn't in the mood for Carter or his cheap attempt at charming her.

"I know how worried you are about Hunter, Jetta," Carter said with an almost sympathetic sounding tone.

She doubted he did. If he did, he wouldn't be forcing her to join him for dinner; he'd be giving her a ride home to be with Hunter. She made a conscious effort to remain polite, despite her growing irritation toward him.

"First he thinks I'm his wife, and now he's seeing zombies," she reluctantly replied. "It's hard watching a man you respect and admire losing it like that."

"Doc was telling us about the surgery."

"Did he also mention it's close to a million dollars?" Jetta asked and snorted an uneasy laugh. "Even war heroes aren't above insurance limitations. A little respect for him just once from this town would be nice. All they see is some crazy, ex-military whack job. They have no idea who he is and how many lives he's saved over the years."

Carter placed his hand on hers, immediately catching her attention and sparking her distrust. He caressed her hand. Somehow, it seemed he was up to something more than just being understanding and comforting.

"I'm a very wealthy man, Jetta," he said gently and with considerable seriousness. "I could pay for his surgery. I know how much Hunter means to you."

Jetta stared at him then his hand on hers. What should have come off as a kind gesture raised immediate suspicions. "Uh huh. And just what is it you expect in return?"

Her tone caught him off guard. Carter removed his hand from hers and offered a tiny smile. "I just want a chance. I'd like you to get to know me better. A couple of months, that's all. If it doesn't work out, it doesn't work out."

"A man doesn't throw around a million dollars for just a chance, Carter," she remarked firmly, calling him on his so-called generous offer.

"Okay, yes," he replied while shifting in his chair and appeared tense by her curtness. "I'd want it to be a sexual relationship. It's just two months, Jetta. Two months and Hunter can live a normal life again."

"I know you think you're doing a noble thing," she began gently then her look suddenly hardened, "but I don't intend to whore myself out to you. Thanks for dinner."

Jetta stood from the table and left the lounge. Tyler watched Jetta leave then stared at Carter with his mouth hanging open. Apparently, he'd heard enough of the conversation to find disbelief in the indecency of Carter's proposition. Carter caught Tyler's look, sneered at him, and pushed his plate across the table with disgust.

✝

*H*unter entered the study with a casual but determined gait. He had received his next mission, and his orders were clear. It was operation 'clean sweep', although he wasn't sure about going on such an important mission with this new guy. Desmond hurried into the study after him and appeared nearly paranoid while subconsciously running his fingers repeatedly through his hair. He looked behind him every few seconds almost as if the devil was chasing him. No, Hunter was confident that this wasn't the right man for the mission at hand. When he saw the admiral next, he'd have to talk with him about the quality of new recruits.

"We really need to go, Hunter. We don't have time to play around--"

"I'm not playing." Hunter approached the gun cabinet with bars behind the glass and turned to look at Desmond. "First, we need to prepare." As he studied Desmond, he suddenly appeared concerned while mentally questioning his abilities. "You do know how to fire a weapon, right?"

"I must have missed that semester at MIT," Desmond muttered. "Do you have a key for that cabinet? Because I sort of think those bars are there because of you."

"Of course I have a key."

Hunter turned toward the gun cabinet and roughly kicked the back of it several times. The cabinet popped away from the wall to reveal a secret compartment filled with several assault rifles, handguns, stun guns, fancy little grenades, and an assortment of gruesome looking knives. It wasn't that the admiral was paranoid; he just believed in being prepared.

Desmond's mouth fell open as he stared at the weapons with horror. "Oh, this isn't going to end well," he said softly.

He watched Hunter pick up one of the assault rifles and skillfully load and cock it. Desmond jumped to the frightening sound and stared at Hunter. Seeing him with such a large weapon was sobering if not frightening. Hunter tossed him the assault rifle. Desmond jumped with surprise, fumbled with the large weapon, and watched it fall to the floor with a loud clatter. Hunter stared at Desmond with surprise then shook his head, expressing his disapproval.

"You're lucky that didn't fire," Hunter informed him. "That's how men lose toes--sometimes testicles."

Desmond stared at Hunter with a look of alarm and wondered if that had actually ever happened.

Chapter Eighteen

$\mathcal{T}$he Winter Harbor High School football game was nearing the end of halftime with the away team up by ten points. Half the town attended the game and nearly filled the stands. There were more than nine hundred spectators at the game and over one hundred participants. The band played while the cheerleaders performed their rehearsed cheers for the crowd of mostly locals. As the clock ran out, the whistle blew to signal halftime. Both teams hurried from the field and headed toward their respective locker rooms. The home team marching band took the field and played a lively tune to lift the town's spirits.

A three-year-old girl wearing a dress with sunflowers on it walked with her mother while holding her hand. Her mother pointed to the field while smiling.

"We have to go over there--across the field," her mother announced. "Keep an eye out for Daddy."

The little girl appeared excited and bounced around. "Will I get to blow the whistle, Mommy?" she asked.

"We'll have to see, dear."

†

$\mathcal{T}$he away team entered their locker room while shouting and cheering. They were enthusiastic for the game, which they were obviously winning. A man rifled through one of the lockers and caught the attention of one of the players.

"Who the hell is that in my locker?" the player demanded to know then turned angry.

The football player ran for the man inside his locker and roughly pulled him away. The male zombie turned, with blood running down his chin, and snarled at the football player. The partially eaten janitor could be seen stuffed in the blood-strewn locker. The zombie lunged for the football player and knocked him over the bench with a loud crash. The other players saw the attack and immediately tackled the zombie, unaware of the surrounding circumstances. There were several shouts and some screams from the pile-up. The coach ran down the aisle while shouting at his team. He saw the dead janitor in the locker, appeared stunned, and uncertainly approached him. The coach stared at the mutilated janitor with his innards exposed and blood seeping down the locker and onto the floor. The janitor's eyes suddenly opened, startling the coach. He grabbed the coach and bit him on the face. The coach screamed while thrashing against the zombie janitor.

✝

*T*he marching band played on the field while the cheerleaders performed for the crowd. The crowd appeared ready for the second half with renewed hopes for another win. Zombie football players appeared from the away team locker room without their helmets and before the whistle. They ran toward the cheerleaders and the band on the field. When the band turned while playing, the zombie football players tackled half to the ground. Those that didn't fall hit the zombies with their instruments. Several zombie football players chased the screaming cheerleaders while they ran across the field. The crowd witnessed what appeared to be poor sportsmanship and became enraged.

"They're attacking our band!" one of the men from the bleachers shouted.

A group of local men from the bleachers charged the field to break up what they thought was a senseless fight. The zombie football players attacked the home cheerleaders and the approaching spectators on the field. It wasn't until the crowd witnessed blood and torn flesh, that panic spread throughout the bleachers. Men, women, and children thundered down the bleachers in mass panic while screaming. Several people tumbled down the bleachers and the remaining crowd trampled them. The zombie away team coach pounced on one of the fallen woman and tore into her face while she screamed and fought against him.

The three-year-old girl in the sunflower dress stood on the field and cried for her mother as zombie football players charged for her. She was suddenly swooped up by Winter Harbor's star running back, Tanner. Tanner tucked her under his arm and charged for the oncoming team of zombies while being pursued by several others behind him. She screamed as he yelled and plowed through the zombies.

✝

*R*everend Bloom was a heavyset man in his late fifties, who was neatly dressed in a black, clergy shirt and collar. He wore a homemade, silver nail crucifix necklace, which, in spite of its simplicity, was actually somewhat flashy. Rev. Bloom locked the church door while fumbling with his keys and briefcase as he headed for the sidewalk. Faint screams were heard coming from the distant high school football field. He listened a moment, grinned proudly, and shook his head.

"I guess that means we're winning," he said with a pleased chuckle.

He walked down the cobblestone sidewalk and turned toward the rectory. Zombie Pam, in her bloodstained nightgown, stood on the sidewalk several feet in front of him. Bloom stopped when he saw her and immediately appeared concerned.

"Pam? What happened to you?"

Bloom hurried toward Pam then stopped when he saw her gruesome appearance up-close. Zombie Pam lunged for him. He cried out and shoved her away with amazing reflexes. She lost her balance then straightened and pursued him as he turned to run. He swung his briefcase at her and clocked her on the side of the head. She was thrown to the sidewalk and got up more slowly. Bloom ran from her before she could return to her feet. Dennis suddenly appeared from between two parked cars. Bloom cried out and, with great agility, darted past him. More zombies now wandered the streets. A male zombie lunged for Bloom and knocked him to the cobblestone sidewalk. Rev. Bloom screamed while attempting to keep the zombie's teeth away from his face. He clutched his silver crucifix necklace, cried out with horror, and stabbed the zombie in the eye with the pointed end. As the thick, bloody substance oozed from his eye, the zombie collapsed on top of him. Bloom gasped as he pushed the zombie off and sat up while clutching his bloody cross. Rev. Bloom blessed the motionless zombie, saw the others quickly approaching, and scrambled to his feet.

"Lord have mercy!"

✝

*T*he hotel's large maintenance building and security office was located beyond the pool and garden area and appeared almost hidden so as not to distract from the guest's lavish and costly vacation experience. Bishop entered the building and looked around. The main office area was cluttered and filled with tools, parts, and various supplies. Two desks were piled high with clutter. Bishop walked through the disastrous office while visually expressing his distaste. Phil was seen huddled over one of the desks behind the clutter and appeared to be eating his dinner. Bishop eyed the clutter, which mostly constituted garbage, and shook his head with disgust as he approached Phil behind the desk.

"Phil, Elise is on her broomstick again," Bishop informed him as he approached. "You were supposed to walk the property an hour ago. Why do you hate me? You know how I feel about dealing with her."

Bishop stopped near Phil behind the desk. Phil tore the flesh from a man's hairy, severed arm like a turkey leg while blood ran down his chin. He looked at Bishop with dead eyes and bared his bloodstained teeth while snarling. Bishop stared at him with the horror evident in his eyes. Zombie Phil returned to eating the arm. Bishop removed his gun and slowly backed away.

"Yeah, we'll talk later--"

Bishop quickly turned and nearly collided with a male zombie in a green maintenance uniform, who was missing his arm.

"Steve?" Bishop gasped with surprise.

The maintenance zombie snarled at Bishop and closed in. Bishop remained horrified and aimed his gun. The zombie lunged for him and grabbed his arm. The gun fired and fell from his hand. The bullet struck the maintenance zombie in the leg but didn't have any effect on him. Zombie Phil approached Bishop from behind. Bishop looked back at him, appeared alarmed, and kicked Phil in the abdomen, tossing him back several steps. He then spun and kicked the maintenance zombie in the groin, which also had no effect. The maintenance zombie grabbed Bishop's arm and attempted to bite it.

Bishop grabbed the zombie's arm, twisted it behind his back, and shoved him across the room. The maintenance zombie crashed into a mountain of equipment and fell to the floor with the equipment crashing down upon him.

Zombie Phil was almost on top of Bishop now. Bishop was halfway to the floor, reaching for his gun, when another zombie appeared. Bishop stared with horror at the large, burly zombie approaching him.

"Oh, shit!"

Chapter Nineteen

Elise and Stacy stood behind the desk and watched Doc checking on Deputy Styles. Doc sat on the coffee table and patted Styles on the arm. The deputy still remained weak and pale, but he now managed a smile. Doc stood and approached Jetta, who paced the length of the lobby like a caged animal.

"I'm going to get my car," he said to Jetta. "If you'll help me get Styles to my office, I'll give you a ride home."

"I'd appreciate that."

Doc headed for the driveway entrance doors. Rev. Bloom bolted into the lobby and nearly knocked over Doc. Bloom shut and locked the door then turned toward the others as he panted heavily. Everyone stared at him.

"We need to lock the place down!"

Elise walked out from behind the desk and approached Bloom with limited patience. Even a man of the cloth wasn't immune to her detest.

"Have you been drinking, Reverend?"

Rev. Bloom suddenly grabbed Elise by the shoulders, startling her, and shook her firmly. "Lock it down--now!"

A female zombie struck the doors and pawed at them with bloodstained fingers that were missing all fingernails. Everyone appeared alarmed and several screams echoed through the lobby. Jetta ran for the beachside doors and locked them.

"I'll get the kitchen," Stacy called out. "There are doors in the lounge!"

Jetta ran down the corridor after Stacy. Elise just stood immobile and stared at the female zombie outside the door. Within minutes, Jetta and Stacy returned with Carter, Tyler, and Rafael in tow. Three zombies now attempted to get inside.

"What the hell are they?" Carter cried out.

Rafael looked at Carter with all seriousness. "They're zombies, dude."

"Zombies--?" Jetta gasped and suddenly had a chilling realization then appeared horrified. "Hunter!" She ran for the corridor beyond Carter and Rafael.

Carter grabbed her arm to stop her, but she easily pulled free from him. Rafael moved into her path. She ran into him, bounced off his large body, and fell to the floor onto her backside. Jetta immediately scrambled to her feet. Rafael grabbed her by her shoulders and refused to let go.

"I have to get to Hunter. I can make it to my helicopter!"

"And what if you can't?" Rafael demanded.

"I have to try."

"I'm sure Hunter is fine," Rafael said firmly. "You can't go out there."

"You don't understand," she cried out in panic. "He told me he saw zombies. I told him they weren't real. I handed him to them. If he dies, it's my fault!"

"That was almost two hours ago, Jetta," Rafael gently informed her.

"We need to contact the sheriff," Carter announced.

"I'll try the radio," Rafael announced then reluctantly released Jetta. He hurried down the corridor for the kitchen where the radio was located.

"We need to get everyone down here right away," Carter announced and quickly turned toward Stacy. "Stacy, find out which rooms--"

Jetta pulled the fire alarm next to the elevators. The alarm wailed loudly throughout the hotel as lights flashed.

"Or we can do it that way," Carter said flatly. "I'm going to get Lee in the penthouse. Keep everyone calm and together. Hopefully help with arrive soon."

Carter frantically pressed the elevator button. Only a moment or two passed before the elevator arrived. The doors opened to reveal several guests, including Colleen and her husband, Allen. Carter hurried past them and entered the elevator, leaving the guests baffled. Doc assisted Bloom to a nearby sofa not far from where

Styles was located. Bloom suddenly clutched his left arm, gasped for air, and collapsed. The bite wound on his hand was now visible.

"He's having a heart attack," Doc cried out.

Allen and Colleen quickly approached and assisted Bloom to the sofa while Doc ran for his bag near Styles. Bloom collapsed and appeared unresponsive.

"Doc!" Allen called.

Doc hurried for them and took Bloom's pulse. He immediately appeared alarmed and began digging through his medical bag. "Get him on the floor! He needs CPR!"

Allen and another man moved Bloom to the floor while Colleen gave them room. Doc knelt alongside him and tossed Allen a disposable resuscitator.

"Hold this over his mouth and nose and squeeze when I tell you to," Doc announced firmly to Allen.

Allen moved to Bloom's head and placed the device over his nose and mouth. Doc started chest compressions and indicated to Allen when to pump the air. Some of those remaining in the lobby watched Doc while others stared at the zombies collecting outside the glass doors. Bloom opened his eyes and began to move. They stopped CPR and appeared relieved. Rev. Bloom suddenly grabbed Allen, pulled him on top of him, and tore into his neck. Allen screamed and pulled away while leaping to his feet, tearing his flesh, and causing blood to spray everywhere. Doc jumped to his feet while staring with horror. Everyone within the room screamed and panicked. Several guests ran from the lobby. Allen collapsed to the floor while clutching his neck as it gushed blood. Colleen dove to his side and attempted to stop her husband's bleeding.

Zombie Bloom grabbed Doc's ankle and attempted to bite his lower leg. Doc cried out while pulling away, lost his balance, and fell to the floor. His head roughly struck the hard floor. Bloom lunged for Doc alongside him, hovered over his unconscious body, and went for his throat. Jetta was suddenly standing over Doc and kicked zombie Bloom in the face, throwing him across the floor with amazing force. Elise and Stacy grabbed Doc's arms and dragged him out of the way. Bloom moved to his hands and knees, looked at Jetta with dead eyes, and snarled at her. She stared at him with a look of horror as the fear momentarily paralyzed her. For a moment, she was unable to move. Her expression suddenly hardened. She kicked him under the chin, tossing him onto his back. He lie motionless a moment then rolled over and again moved to his hands and knees while snarling viciously. Everyone screamed as he started to get up. Jetta was now filled with panic. She had given him two hard shots, which either should have stopped him. It wasn't possible for him to be moving.

"Jetta!" Styles cried out.

Jetta looked at Styles on the sofa behind her. He tossed her his revolver. Jetta caught the gun, turned to zombie Bloom, and, without hesitation, shot him in the head. Zombie Bloom collapsed to the floor as blood poured from his head. There was more screaming from around the lobby. Allen suddenly sat up, surprising Colleen, and grabbed her arm. As he attempted to bite her, she screamed. Jetta turned with the gun aimed and shot zombie Allen in the head. His head snapped back as he flew backwards. He struck the floor and lay motionless. There was an eerie moment as everyone stood frozen and stared at the large amounts of blood rapidly spreading across the lobby floor from the dead men. Colleen suddenly screamed, jolting everyone back to reality, and then she sobbed uncontrollably. She looked at Jetta, who just stared blankly at the dead man. The gun remained clutched in her hand with her finger tightly on the trigger.

"You killed him! You killed my husband!" Colleen screamed.

Jetta lowered the gun that now trembled in her hand, walked toward the elevators, and slowly sank down the wall while holding her head and the gun. She didn't know what to think. Her mind was suddenly blank. There was a loud thump against the beachside doors, which startled everyone. Stacy jumped with a scream. Bishop stood before the doors with his gun in his hand. His shirt and hands were covered in blood. Bishop pounded on the door with a look of horror on his face.

"Let me in!" Bishop muffled a shout.

Stacy hurried for the doors. Elise suddenly appeared before her and prevented her from reaching the doors.

"We can't let him in! He's been injured! He's going to become one of them just like Rev. Bloom!" Elise cried out.

Stacy stared at Elise with wide, horror-filled eyes. Jetta remained on the floor with her head in her hands while staring at the floor and appeared oblivious to her surroundings. Bishop continued to pound on the glass.

"Unlock the door," Bishop yelled with panic in his voice. "What's wrong with you? Let me the hell in!"

Elise approached the door and folded her arms across her chest. "You've been infected. We can't let you in. Go away!"

"Let me in, you fucking bitch!" Bishop looked behind him and appeared horrified. "Oh, shit!"

Bishop turned as a zombie approached and shot it in the head. The zombie collapsed at his feet. Bishop jumped around to avoid the spilling blood. More zombies approached. He turned back to the door and pounded while Elise stared at him without sympathy. For a moment, it almost appeared as if it pleased her to leave him outside to die.

"We're not letting you in," Elise said bluntly.

Jetta finally looked up and stared at the glass doors as if in another world. Bishop's eyes met hers from across the room. He appeared almost relieved to see her.

"Jetta! Jetta, let me in!" he pleaded with her.

Reality appeared to hit Jetta as she stared at Bishop pleading for his life just outside the doors. She sprang to her feet and ran for the beachside doors while placing the gun down the back of her pants. Elise stepped in front of her and stopped her.

"You saw what happened with Rev. Bloom. Look at him! He's been exposed!" Elise shouted defensively and appeared unwilling to back down. "I won't let you--"

Jetta sneered with disgust and shoved Elise from her path. She grabbed Jetta's arm to stop her. Jetta rammed her knee into Elise's side, spun into a backwards roundhouse kick, and struck her high on the chest. Elise flew backwards and rolled several times from the force of the kick. Jetta ran for the door. Bishop attempted to shoot a zombie nearly on top of him. The gun clicked empty. He kicked the zombie as Jetta unlocked and opened the door.

Bishop bolted into the lobby. Another zombie attempted to push its way inside. Jetta and Bishop pushed the door closed as the zombie pounded against the door. As Bishop held the door closed, Jetta locked it. Bishop appeared emotionally drained while replacing his gun to his shoulder holster. Elise slowly moved to her feet and was dazed from Jetta's forceful kick. Bishop saw Elise and something snapped. He snatched the gun from Jetta's pants, grabbed Elise by the throat with his bloody hand, and slammed her against the wall. Elise gasped with horror while struggling to loosen his grip as he aimed the gun at her face.

"You nearly killed me!"

Bishop's finger was tight on the trigger. Jetta moved alongside him, placed her hand on Bishop's arm, and pleaded with her eyes.

"Don't do this. We're all scared. Please, put down the gun," Jetta said gently.

Bishop maintained his cold stare into Elise's terrified eyes. He lowered the gun and released her. Elise gasped and darted away from him. Bishop headed for the elevators and cast his back against the wall. Jetta slowly approached and stared at him in silence. He stared at the gun in his blood-covered hand while breathing heavily. He was visibly shaken from his ordeal.

"Hey--" Jetta said softly.

Bishop fidgeted, snorted a laugh, and handed her Styles' gun without making eye contact. "Not exactly my finest moment, huh?"

"I'm pretty sure I would have pulled the trigger," Jetta said gently.

He looked at her and appeared surprised. She wasn't kidding either.

"The infection appears to be spread through bites," she remarked while studying the blood covering him. "Were you bitten?"

He looked at the blood covering in him, shook his head, and finally relaxed. "No, I wasn't bitten. Scared half to death though. Is the building secure?"

"I think so. Everyone scattered when Rev. Bloom attacked one of the guests. Will you help bring some order to this chaos?"

"Yeah, sure," Bishop said with an exhausted sigh. "Let me wash this off and get another clip for my gun. You can tell me the plan then."

The elevator doors opened to reveal Carter and Lee. Both looked at Bishop covered in blood and appeared horrified by his appearance.

"My God, are you all right?" Carter asked.

He walked past them without comment and entered the elevator. The doors shut behind him.

Chapter Twenty

*N*early eight hundred men, women, and children screamed while pushing their way into the large high school gymnasium. The commotion among the surviving spectators grew louder. Some people screamed and others cried as the chatter escalated to deafening levels and echoed off the tall ceiling. No one really knew what was happening. Mothers and fathers called for their children while pushing through the crowd attempting to locate them. There were a few joyful reunions but not nearly enough. Faint screams of those being torn apart could be heard coming from the distant football field. Two security guards looked out the open doors, saw a group of blood-strewn zombies approaching in the distance, and appeared horrified.

"The crazy people are coming!" one guard cried out, alerting the others.

The guards began closing the doors. Another man, Hanson, who stood near the doors with them, prevented them from shutting the doors.

"Wait," he cried out. "Look!"

A few others crowded near the doors despite the pleas of others to shut them. Tanner was seen charging across the school grounds toward the gymnasium with the crying girl now in his arms. The away team zombies chased him and were nearly upon him. The people began screaming for him to run faster. Tanner raced through the doors into the gymnasium with the little girl. The guards slammed and bolted the doors behind him. The zombie football players struck the doors with force, causing them to vibrate.

Everyone jumped back with alarm. The crowd started screaming while pushing and shoving their way to the far end of the gym. The pounding outside the doors ceased. The guards listened by the doors. The gymnasium fell eerily silent. One of the guards appeared to relax and turned toward the crowd.

"I think they're gone," he announced.

There was a round of relieved sighs followed by sobbing. Hanson grabbed one of the guards by the arm and forced him to face him.

"We need to check the doors and windows on the entire first floor," Hanson announced. "We have to make sure those crazy people can't get inside."

The guard uncertainly nodded but remained frozen with fear. "I, uh, think the doors were locked already."

"Well, we're going to go out there and find out," Hanson informed him. Hanson looked at the crowd and clapped his hands loudly to get everyone's attention. "Okay, listen up! I need some volunteers to make sure the first floor is secure. Doors and windows locked. Once we go out those doors, I want them sealed behind us until we're sure no crazies got inside."

"Are you insane?" a woman suddenly demanded. "If they're running around the school, you'll be killed!"

Hanson removed a semiautomatic from a concealed shoulder holster and cocked it. Several people gasped. "I'm betting I won't. I'm retired NYPD," he announced. "We're wasting time. I can't cover that much territory on my own."

Another man, Dixon, stood nearby and removed a knife from his boot. "Former Gulf War vet," he announced proudly. "I'll go with you."

"We should find you a better weapon," Hanson remarked. "Maybe someone here has a gun."

"Nah, this is all I need," he replied with little emotion. "I'm pretty good with a knife. But I assure you, there are plenty of folks here packing." Dixon looked around at the large group of men and women. "Most of you are my neighbors," he announced sternly. "That means I know you pretty well. If you're packing, you're coming. If you're not coming, you're surrendering your weapon for our security sweep. I know who you are, so don't make me come and find you."

Several women approached and removed revolvers from their purses. They handed them to Dixon and sheepishly walked away. Two more men approached and reluctantly volunteered to join them rather than surrender their weapons. It seemed as if there should have been more locals with weapons, but there wasn't a lot of time to argue. An attractive but serious looking woman, Remy, brandished her weapon, smirked her intent to join them, and headed toward the interior doors. Dixon and Hanson handed out the guns to the two guards, and one to each of the three other men, two of which would remain posted at both sets of doors. The six men joined Remy by the interior doors.

"I want those locker room doors barricaded until we get back," Hanson announced to the large crowd. "If you've been injured, see this guy." He pulled one of the men from the crowd and pointed at him. He had no idea who the man was.

"Me? Why me?" the man asked with surprise.

Hanson casually shrugged with little concern. "Why not you? Are you local?"

He nodded.

"Good, then you can find someone in here who's either a nurse, doctor, or something close enough."

"I saw the vet, Gina," he announced.

"See, you're doing great already," Hanson informed him then turned toward the door with the other six volunteers and nodded them onward.

They opened the interior door, cautiously looked into the hallway, and left the security of the gymnasium. The two remaining men with guns shut and bolted the door behind them.

✝

*W*ithin the school's main alcove, the six men and one woman regrouped after a brief search of the first floor. More than fifty zombies pushed against the glass doors outside the alcove. One of the guards pulled down the metal gate and locked it.

"The glass should hold," the guard announced, "but it doesn't hurt to have a second line of defense."

"What's wrong with those people?" Dixon asked as he stared at the blood-covered zombies outside the glass. "Some are injured pretty badly. How are they still standing?"

The guard uncertainly shook his head while watching from a safe distance. "Maybe it's mass insanity."

"Rabies maybe," Hanson remarked.

Dixon snapped out of his trance and looked away from the zombies at the doors. "The place seems secure," he informed them. "We locked the stairway doors to be safe, but we should search the upper floors just in case. We may need to use the roof, if things go from bad to worse."

"I was thinking the same things myself," Hanson announced. "This place is like a fort. I think we can hide out in here pretty long. I assume there's a kitchen. A town on an island like this probably doesn't have school lunches catered."

"Yeah, there's a kitchen. Got a delivery this morning," the guard announced. "There's enough food to last a week or longer. Plenty of water too. There's a generator in the basement, so we're covered even if the power goes out."

"You small-town people think of everything," Hanson remarked while shaking his head.

"When you live on an island, you're pretty much isolated as it is," the guard replied.

"Every single one of those pick-up trucks out there has a rifle and a radio in it," Dixon informed him. "If we could get to one of them--"

"There's a radio in the principal's office," Remy casually informed them.

"How do you know that?" Hanson asked.

She grinned. "Because I'm the principal."

"Okay then, let's check on the others in the gym, give them the good news, and have a look at that radio," Hanson announced. "Maybe we can call up someone to help."

Remy led the way back to the gym with the others following her.

Dixon fell behind, walked alongside Hanson, and grinned. "Pretty hot for a principal, don't you think?"

"Let's just worry about staying alive right now. You can ask her out later."

†

*T*he people stranded within the gymnasium were restless but more relaxed then they had been earlier. They at least felt safe for the moment. The loss of lives on the field was devastating and difficult to calculate. It was unknown how many had died. The number of people within the gymnasium was nearly eight hundred, but there had been over one thousand at the game, including those on the field and in the stands. More than two hundred were unaccounted. The thought was sobering. Tanner walked through the crowded gym while holding the little girl's hand. She no longer cried and searched the crowd for her parents.

"See them?" he asked in a soothing voice.

She shook her head. He picked her up and carried her, giving her a better vantage point. She looked around while clinging to his shoulder pads beneath his jersey. They approached a small group of injured people. Gina, the town vet, was tending to their wounds.

Tanner eyed the quiet little girl he held in his arms. "Any of them?"

She shook her head.

"Gina, do you know this little girl?" Tanner asked. "I can't even get her name out of her."

Gina glanced up at him as he held the little girl and shook her head. "She's not from Winter Harbor," she replied. "She must have come with the visiting spectators."

Tanner suddenly grimaced then looked at the little girl and smiled timidly. "You don't have an older brother who plays football, do you?"

Gina uncertainly looked back at them and shared the same look of dread. The little girl shook her head. Both appeared relieved. Tanner nodded toward Gina's small gathering of injured people sitting on the floor and appeared curious.

"Just minor injuries, I hope," Tanner remarked.

"Mostly sprains," she replied. "The crappy, generic first aid kit I found in the gym teacher's office doesn't have nearly enough supplies. I could use more ankle wraps."

"The boy's locker room has all that stuff," Tanner informed her. "I help myself all the time. It's where coach keeps most of his supplies."

"If you could get that, I'd be grateful," she announced and appeared relieved.

"Yeah, sure. Just wraps?"

"I have a few cuts," she informed him. "If you can find anything I can use to close some deep cuts, it would be fantastic. A sewing kit, suture kit, or even some duct tape. I'm sort of desperate here."

The little girl stared at Gina while she cleaned a bleeding wound on a woman's forearm. The little girl appeared squeamish.

"Did a dog bite you?" she timidly asked the woman.

The injured woman, Wendy, offered a weary smile to the little girl in Tanner's arms. "No, a cheerleader bit me," she replied with a humored laugh.

"The world's gone mad, sunflower," Tanner told the little girl. He bounced her in his arms. "How about a piggyback ride to the locker room?"

She appeared excited and nodded. Tanner flipped her over his shoulder and onto his back. She clung to his shoulder pads as he bounced her across the gym toward the locker rooms. Gina smiled, shook her head, and looked at her patient.

"Who would have guessed a jock would be so good with kids?" Gina teased.

"Tanner gets the neighbor's kids ready for school every morning," Wendy replied. "Their mother works early mornings and the father works nights. He stays with them until their father gets home and drives them to school."

"Is that why I see him running to school every morning?" Gina asked.

Wendy nodded. "When their father's late, he's late. Principal Remy cuts him some slack."

The men watching the inside door opened it to reveal the seven returning from patrol. All seven filtered into the crowd and attempted to check on everyone. Principal Remy approached Gina and looked over her patients.

"Everything okay? Is anyone seriously hurt?"

"Nothing serious. We're good here," Gina replied. "Tanner went to get more medical supplies from the boy's locker room. I don't suppose we have access to any painkillers?"

"There might be some in the nurse's office," Remy announced. "But I wouldn't count on anything stronger then over-the-counter pain relievers."

"I suppose anything will do for now," Gina said.

"I'll take anything," Wendy informed them. "The bite on my arm feels like it's burning."

"Bites are nasty," Gina informed her. "I know; I deal with them every day. Sometimes even on myself."

"You were bit?" Remy asked the injured woman with surprise. "What bit you?"

"A cheerleader."

Remy suddenly appeared deep in thought. Few that made it to the gym had witnessed the attacks close-up. "I'm going to check the nurse's office and see what I can find. You just hold on, okay?"

Wendy nodded. Remy hurried across the room and grabbed Hanson by the arm. She pulled him away from everyone and spun to face him.

"What's wrong?" Hanson asked.

"I don't know," Remy replied while looking around with concern. "What happened on that field? Did anyone actually see anything?"

"All I saw was a bunch of football players attacking the band," Hanson replied. "There was a lot of blood, a lot of screaming, and a whole lot of panic."

"Yeah, but what was causing the blood?" Remy asked. "Were they armed with knives or something?"

"I don't know," he replied. "I just assumed, but I didn't see what happened."

"I'm having a very bad feeling right now," Remy announced. "We need to find out what others saw."

"I don't know what--?"

"How do you explain an entire football team going psycho and attacking the marching band? It doesn't make any sense," she informed him. "Maybe it's not insanity. What if it's a virus? Gina's tending to Wendy's injuries. She said a cheerleader bit her. What did a cheerleader from our community have to do with the away team football players going berserk? And why was the cheerleader *biting* Wendy?"

"She was bit by a cheerleader?" Hanson shook his head and looked across the room at Gina and her patients. He looked back at Remy. "Find a window and take a closer look outside. Tell me what you see out there."

"What are you going to do?" she asked.

"I'm going to talk to the bite victim," he informed her. "Maybe she saw something we didn't."

Remy hurried across the room and climbed a ladder to the elevated windows. A small crowd watched her and chattered among themselves. Dixon saw her, appeared curious, and then looked at Hanson crossing the room toward the group of injured people. As Hanson approached, Gina sprang to her feet and hurried toward one of her patients who was having a seizure. She slid onto the floor alongside the man and attempted to stop his spasms. Hanson picked up his pace and hurried toward them. As he passed Wendy sitting on the floor, she fell over. Hanson stood over Gina as she tried to hold the seizing man down.

"What's happening?"

"I don't know," Gina frantically replied. "I think he's having a seizure. I don't usually work with people."

"Was he bit?" Hanson suddenly asked.

The man stopped thrashing. Gina appeared relieved while kneeling alongside him then looked at Hanson.

"Yes, why do you ask?"

The man suddenly sat up with a snarl and lunged for Gina's neck while her back was turned. She saw him and screamed. A bullet struck him in the forehead. As he collapsed to the floor, there was a round of screams from the room followed by total silence. Gina fell onto her backside, stared at the dead man, and then looked at Hanson holding his gun.

"It's spread through bites!" Hanson shouted to the others. "They're not psychotic; they're zombies!"

Gina stared at him and remained horrified. He suddenly looked at her.

"Who else was bitten?"

She stared at him in apparent shock then looked behind him and screamed. Hanson spun around as zombie Wendy tackled him to the floor. His gun flew from his hand and slid across the floor. Gina continued to scream as Hanson attempted to hold the woman's head back to keep her from biting him. A knife was suddenly plunged into the side of her head. She fell limp against Hanson's arms. Hanson tossed the dead woman off him and scrambled onto his backside while breathing heavily. Dixon stared with a look of horror at the dead woman with his knife sticking out of her skull.

"What the hell?" Dixon exploded. "And I really mean--what the hell!"

As Remy stared out the window near the top of the gymnasium, her expression at what she saw outside said it all. Hanson scrambled to his feet and reclaimed his gun. Dixon pulled his knife from the woman's head. Both looked at Gina.

"Who else was bitten?" Hanson demanded to know.

Gina uncertainly looked at the back wall. Another man lie motionless on the floor. A second was already snarling while springing to his feet. Hanson groaned loudly with frustration and aimed his gun at the charging man. His gun fired.

✝

*T*anner bounced the little girl around on his back as he cantered down the rows of lockers toward the office area. She giggled while clinging to his shoulder pads. He stopped with a whinny then helped her dismount.

"Again, again," she cried out with delight.

"On the way back," he replied. "We need to find a big box with a red cross on the front of it."

The little girl looked around then pointed to it near the desk. "Is that it?"

Tanner looked in the direction she pointed, saw the large kit alongside the desk, and grinned at her. "Good eyes, sunflower."

He approached the desk and reached for the large medical kit. A zombie referee suddenly appeared on the floor behind the desk and bit Tanner on the calf. Tanner cried out, kicked the referee off him, and fell to the floor while the little girl screamed. As the referee sprang to his knees and leaped for Tanner on the floor, the little girl pulled on his shoulder pads.

"Get up, get up!" she cried to Tanner then looked at the zombie referee. "Don't bite him, Daddy!"

Tanner appeared horrified by her words and scrambled to his feet as the zombie referee lunged for him. He dodged out of his path. The zombie referee crashed into the lockers and struck the floor. He appeared dazed. Tanner grabbed the little girl's shoulders and forced her to look into his eyes.

"I want you to hide in one of the lockers and don't come out until I get you," he told her firmly.

She sobbed and nodded.

"I need you to be really quiet," he told her. "No piggyback rides if you aren't quiet."

She nodded while holding back her sobs.

"Go!"

She ran across the locker room and disappeared down one of the aisles. A locker was heard opening then closing. Tanner looked around the desk area as the zombie returned to his feet. Tanner leaped across the desk as the zombie referee charged for him. Tanner grabbed a baseball bat alongside the desk and swung for the zombie referee's head. The bat connected with his head, and the zombie was thrown back several feet. Tanner jumped over the desk with the bat clutched in his hands. The zombie referee stumbled slightly then snarled at him. He charged him with less vigor. Tanner cried out and swung the bat for his head. The bat crushed his skull while snapping his neck. The zombie collapsed to the floor and no longer moved. Tanner stared at the dead zombie referee, closed his eyes, and sobbed softly. He sniffed, wiped his eyes, and straightened. He wiped the blood off the bat, grabbed the medical kit, and hurried across the locker room.

"Sunflower," he called as he ran. "It's okay, you can come out now."

The little girl uncertainly crawled out from one of the lockers. Tanner forced a smile and lowered his back to the changing bench. She climbed onto his back, clung to his shoulder pads, and wiped the tears from her eyes.

"Is Daddy okay?"

Tanner held his breath as he carried her on his back through the locker room and fought his tears. "He's resting."

†

*T*anner carried the little girl on his back across the crowded gymnasium. There was no bouncing and little joy to their return piggyback ride. Tanner looked around at the many silent, concerned faces. Something had happened and it couldn't have been good. Tanner approached a clearly emotional Gina with the large medical kit. He suddenly stopped when he saw the four, covered bodies on the floor.

"Tanner, what's that?" the little girl asked of the carefully covered bodies.

"They're resting," he said softly.

Gina uncertainly took the medical kit with trembling hands. Hanson, Dixon, and Remy stood near the bodies with their heads down. Tanner stared at the bodies with the horror evident on his face then looked at Gina.

"What happened?" he asked softly.

"It's a virus that turns the infected into zombies or something," Gina said weakly. "It's spread through bites."

Tanner stared at her and appeared unable to speak.

"Tanner got bit," the little girl announced.

Gina stared at Tanner with horror on her face. Remy suddenly looked at them then quickly approached while staring at Tanner with shock.

"You were bit?" Remy gasped.

Tanner slowly set the little girl down and stared at Remy and Gina. He watched Dixon and Hanson uncertainly approach while softly talking between them. The nature of their conversation was easily assumed.

"Well, yes and no," Tanner replied. He knelt down on one knee and rolled up his uniform pants leg. He tapped his leg pad. "I was protected."

All four groaned and appeared relieved.

Chapter Twenty-one

*M*ostly everyone had gathered within the lounge and had drinks before them to calm their nerves after the earlier events within the lobby. There were twenty-five people including staff and guests still within the hotel. Doc held ice to the back of his head and appeared visibly shaken by his brush with death. Styles sat in one of the chairs with his injured leg propped on another. He was still pale and in some discomfort, but he didn't look nearly as haggard. It appeared the painkillers were doing their job. Jetta sat on a chair near Styles with his gun belt and reloaded the gun. Styles watched her skillfully load his gun with purpose. She looked a little too at home loading the weapon.

"I really hate admitting it, but you're a better shot than I am," Styles said timidly.

Jetta glanced at him and appeared humored by the comment. "While other girls were taking dance and ballet, I was taking karate and weapons training," she remarked then chuckled. "I guess my father was hoping I'd spontaneously combust into the son he'd always wanted."

"I guess he was disappointed when you didn't, huh?" Styles remarked with a soft chuckle.

"I'm pretty sure he thinks I did," Jetta teased.

Styles laughed softly then shifted and appeared uneasy. Something more was obviously bothering him, and he appeared afraid to admit it. "Do you think Barb was, you know, like those outside? Do you think she was a zombie?"

"I'm guessing there's a strong possibility," she replied. "You said Dennis and Pam were missing around the same time you found Ted's truck crashed in their porch. Plenty of blood but no bodies. Well, those government guys put some sort of rock into a biohazard box. I think whatever happened started at Albright's place with whatever they put in that box."

"And it spread to Zion's place?"

Jetta nodded. "Where Barb was then infected, and you were forced to shoot her."

Styles appeared tense and shifted uncomfortably. "What if--what if Barb bit me? It happened so fast, Jetta. It could be a bite on my leg. I could turn into one of those things."

Jetta gave him a sympathetic look and placed her hand on his. He stared at her with fear in his eyes. She stared back into his eyes with all seriousness.

"Deputy, you injured your leg while kicking the door in," she replied gently.

"But how do you know it wasn't--"

"I saw Doc plucking wood splinters from your wound," she said gently. "He was trying to spare your pride by letting you think it happened during the tussle."

Styles stared at her a long moment. He suddenly smiled and laughed softly. Jetta returned the smile and patted his arm. Rafael entered the room with Carter behind him barely keeping up. Despite his size, Rafael had an amazingly fast gait. They approached Jetta and Styles and sat at the table. Neither appeared particularly pleased with what they learned.

"Rafael couldn't reach the sheriff's patrol car or Rosemary at the office on the radio," Carter informed them with a defeated sigh while helping himself to a drink.

Styles appeared concerned and shifted in his chair. "You couldn't get ahold of Sheriff Palmer?"

"Statistically speaking, his cruiser wouldn't exactly be a safe place to hole up," Jetta informed the deputy.

"I did get a hold of the principal at the school," Rafael remarked with some enthusiasm. "There are around eight hundred people from the football game seeking shelter in the gym."

"Did you ask if anyone was bitten?" Jetta asked. "There could be a mass breakout."

"They already found out the hard way," Rafael replied. "Thankfully there was a retired police officer among the visitors. Principal Remy said Dixon is with them. They handled the situation before it escalated."

"Dixon?" Jetta asked then grinned. "I've heard him swapping war stories with my father. He's a good one to have around in a crisis situation."

Styles was nearly ready to jump out of his chair. It was obvious he was feeling the need to be doing something more. "Did you try the coast guard frequency, Rafael?"

"I'm not real savvy on the whole radio thing, dude," Rafael replied. "If you can roll it in flour or sprinkle it with cinnamon, I'm your man."

"Take Tyler," Carter said to Rafael. "He's really good with radios and nautical jargon. I'm sure he can call up someone in the harbor or off the coast."

"Sure--cool."

Rafael stood and headed for Tyler, who was hanging out at the bar and serving free drinks to the weary guests. Bishop entered with a fast, determined gait, approached their table, and collapsed in Rafael's vacant chair. He took Jetta's drink, drank the entire contents of the glass, and then glanced around the table.

"What do we know?" he asked.

"The hotel is secure. None of the infected are getting inside," Carter informed him. "I think we're safe for now. Hopefully help will arrive in a few hours, but we haven't been able to reach the mainland or Sheriff Palmer."

Bishop appeared unusually stressed, which was unlike him. "So what's the plan? Sit and wait?"

"Do you have a better one?" Carter asked.

"No, but Jetta does."

Jetta stared at Bishop and appeared surprised by his comment. She wondered what gave him that idea.

"Yeah, her big plan was a suicide run to get Hunter," Carter scoffed.

"What makes you think I have a plan?" Jetta finally asked out of curiosity.

He looked at her and appeared surprised by the question. "You're the only one here whose father is a bad ass Navy Seal Admiral, and you've spent the last seven years baby-sitting his number two bad ass Navy Seal comrade. You can't tell me you don't have a plan."

She stared at him a moment in silence then turned serious and leaned closer to him. Oddly enough, she did have a plan. "There are two duffel bags in the back of my helicopter with automatic weapons and grenades left by the government guys. There's enough firepower to wipe them all out."

"Your helicopter is at the hanger. How do we get to the helicopter?" Bishop asked.

"We have two guns and enough chemicals from housekeeping to make some really nice Molotov cocktails," Jetta informed him. "We'll have teams of two drop the explosives onto strategically placed cars and clear a path."

Bishop suddenly chuckled. "You do realize you'll wipe out half of the parking lot," he remarked. "I think you've been hanging around Hunter too long."

"Do you have a better idea?" she demanded.

"No," he replied. "I don't need one. I never said I didn't like your plan."

"Whoa! Blow up cars? Take out the parking lot? Help will arrive," Carter insisted while appearing annoyed.

Both ignored him and leaned in closer to discuss their plan of attack.

"We'll need two-way radios from my office, and I know where to find some binoculars," Bishop informed her. "I could go to the roof and scout out the best route to the hanger."

"I'll make a list of chemicals for Rafael," Jetta said. "He'll know where to find everything we need."

"You do realize it's going to be dark before we get all of this together," Bishop announced.

Jetta grinned. "We'll strike at dawn."

"Meet me on the roof in half an hour," Bishop said then quickly left the table.

Carter watched Bishop leave the lounge then looked at Jetta with hostility in his eyes. "You know, this is still my hotel, Jetta. I won't have you destroying it," he informed her.

"We're cut off for a reason, Carter," she snapped. "First the cell phones and then the landlines? Our government friends just popping in because of Sheriff Palmer's missing persons report? You just don't get it, do you?"

"You're being paranoid," Carter remarked as his agitation with her increased.

"What she's saying does make sense," Styles interrupted.

Carter glared at the deputy, silencing him. "She's young and irrational. She's been hanging out with mercenaries for far too long." He then glared back at Jetta. "That's the sort of attitude that gets innocent people killed."

Jetta had nearly had it with Carter. All he cared about was the financial aspect of everything. There were lives a stake, and if she was right, they were all sitting in a kill box just waiting for the government to declare Winter Harbor a total loss. Carter didn't understand. He wasn't from Winter Harbor. He was too used to others doing his fighting for him. The people of Winter Harbor were used to taking care of themselves. They didn't survive by waiting for someone else to take care of them.

"No, Carter," she snapped. "That sort of attitude is what saves lives. We may ding up your precious resort, but the lives we save will be worth it."

"And I'm telling you, we're safe in here!" Carter shouted while pounding his fist to the table.

Styles jumped with surprise then cast a glance at Jetta for her response. Jetta didn't disappoint. She leaped to her feet while glaring at him across the table from her.

"I'm not talking about us!" Jetta launched back. "I'm talking about the eight hundred people stranded at the school!"

"And if they stay inside, they're fine too!"

"They're not fine," Jetta shouted back in anger. "If nearly two hundred people are unaccounted for, that means there are probably two hundred zombies surrounding that school. In great enough numbers, they'll bust through the glass doors in the alcove! And minutes later, they'll bust through the lock on the metal gate! They're not okay!"

Everyone within the lounge was now staring at Jetta while she shouted at Carter across the table.

"You just try and stop me, Carter!"

Jetta stormed from the lounge while everyone watched. Styles suddenly grinned and laughed. Carter glared his disapproval at the young deputy.

"Something funny, Deputy?" Carter demanded.

"I always wanted to meet the infamous Admiral Cross everyone brags about," Styles informed him then grinned. "And I think I just did."

Chapter Twenty-two

*R*afael stood behind the kitchen counter and studied the list of items on the piece of paper he held while Jetta stood across from him. His eyes were wide as he read the ingredients she asked him to gather.

"Whoa, dude!"

"Can you get all that?" Jetta asked.

"Yeah, sure. We have all this stuff. Plenty of it. But if you don't mind my asking," Rafael remarked while glancing at her. "What exactly are we blowing up?"

"Some cars in the lot."

"That bored already, huh?"

"No, I'm making a run for my helicopter at the hanger. The government kindly left a small arsenal of weapons in the back. We need those weapons."

He stared at her a moment in silence while apparently reading her thoughts. "You're going after Hunter, aren't you?"

She suddenly tensed then nodded. "After I drop off the weapons, yes, I'm going after Hunter," she replied. "Did you or Tyler get a hold of the coast guard?"

"No, our frequency is messed up. We can only radio a short distance. A ship would have to be in the harbor to receive the signal," he remarked. "Tyler thinks we've been cut off intentionally. You know how Tyler can be. He has this whole conspiracy theory thing going."

"He may be right," she boldly announced. "I've been running around with those government guys all day, and it all suddenly makes sense."

"So you think they're trying to contain it to the island and we're, like, expendable?" Rafael suddenly asked.

"I don't want to find out. After I get Hunter, I'll fly to the mainland for some real help; the kind that doesn't require government sanctions."

"You know people?"

"Yeah, I know people," she replied. "I know dozens of retired bad asses just dying to relive the glory days."

"Why am I suddenly scared?"

Elise stormed into the kitchen and approached Jetta and Rafael at the counter. Jetta saw the look on her face and noted her determined gait. This obviously wasn't a social call. Of course, with Elise, it never was. Rafael slipped the paper into his pocket and watched with noted concern. Elise stopped at the counter and glared at Jetta with a wildly unpredictable look.

"Who the hell do you think you are?" Elise demanded in her finest prison matron tone.

"Jetta Cross, daughter of Admiral Quinn Cross," Jetta remarked. "It says so right on my birth certificate."

Rafael sheepishly backed away from them and watched from a safe distance. There was no telling where this argument was going to lead.

"Don't get smart with me," Elise snapped. "This is Carter's hotel. You are just the air taxi. You have no right to give orders to employees or willfully destroy hotel property. If you don't back off, I'll have Deputy Styles arrest you for trespassing, vandalism, and anything else he can think up."

Jetta wasn't intimidated by her and didn't even flinch to her threats. Her lack of emotion possibly frightened Elise more than ever. Despite her tone, Elise watched Jetta closely.

"How quickly you forget who kept Bishop from shooting you," Jetta remarked then suddenly raised her brows. "Don't make me regret it."

Elise twitched. "No one's saying we're not grateful for the way you handled that entire incident in the lobby, but I won't allow you to impulsively wreck this hotel."

"Fine," Jetta remarked simply, folded her arms across her chest, and glared at her with a knowing smirk. "Get Deputy Styles and have him arrest me."

"I will!" Elise shouted but didn't move.

"Then do it." Jetta watched her, although she still didn't make an effort to fetch the deputy. She casually tilted her head. "You know he won't do it, don't you?"

Elise fumbled for an answer. "If he doesn't arrest you, I'll have the mainland police do it," she snapped. "And if you cause any damage to this hotel in the meantime, Carter will sue you for everything you and your father have."

"Assuming we survive; be my guest," she remarked with little emotion.

Elise still didn't move. She stared at Jetta with less hostility and appeared more concerned than annoyed.

"I don't know," Rafael said teasingly to Jetta while grinning. "I think you're winning this argument."

Jetta remained casual while staring at Elise and shook her head in response. "No, Rafael, she's weighing her options," she informed him. "See, she's wondering what will happen if those things get in here, and I'm her only line of defense. She's wondering if I'll just let them eat her ass."

"I--I don't have to deal with you," Elise suddenly announced while attempting to maintain her superior attitude. "You're Carter's problem." She quickly turned and left the kitchen almost as fast as she had entered.

"You really know how to handle her," Rafael remarked and held back his humored laugh.

"Don't be too impressed," she announced. "I was actually hoping she'd give me an excuse to hit her."

✝

*J*etta hurried through the lobby toward the elevators then glanced at the lobby doors and hesitated. More zombies collected at both sets of doors. Lee stood before the beachside doors and stared outside with her hand to the glass. Jetta uncertainly approached her and appeared curious. Lee stared at zombie Glenn pawing at the glass while tears streaked her face.

"Lee?"

"It's Glenn," Lee said softly without looking at her.

Jetta eyed the zombie pressed up against the glass. "Did you two go out?" She knew they hadn't but couldn't quite make sense of Lee's turmoil.

"No, I told him he wasn't good enough for me," she replied with a sniff. "He was a good man, and now he's--he's reduced to this. I never even gave him a chance. There were a lot of men I brushed off. How many of them died tonight? I could have treated them better." Lee looked at Jetta with tears streaking her face. "I'm sorry I treated you so badly since I'd arrived. I was just upset that you were more popular than I was. Even my own father wanted to go out with you. And now--now it just seems so petty. Can you ever forgive me?"

"There's nothing to forgive, Lee," she said gently then offered a teasing smile. "But if it makes you feel better, I promise I'll never be your stepmother."

Lee laughed softly and wiped her tears. "That actually does make me feel better." She sniffed and attempted a smile. "I heard from my father that you intend to blow up the parking lot. Something about making a run for your helicopter. Is there anything I can do to help?"

"You can help Rafael make the explosives," she informed her. "Bishop and I are going to the roof to scout out the most direct path to my helicopter at the hanger. It's a long run, and we don't know what to expect once we're beyond the parking lot."

"How about taking one of the cars?" Lee suggested. "I can give you the keys to my car. It's not too far from the building. A three-minute drive and you'll be at the hanger."

"That's an excellent idea," Jetta replied while smiling proudly. Her look then turned more serious. "Why don't you join the others in the lounge? You shouldn't be here alone."

"It's okay," Lee replied timidly. "I want to spend a few more minutes with Glenn."

Jetta nodded, patted her arm, and headed for the elevators.

✝

*J*etta appeared on the hotel roof and walked several feet before hearing Carter's angry voice. She could see Carter standing with Bishop near the half wall overlooking town. Carter's tone was low and threatening. She was certain he was attempting to stop them by threatening Bishop's position at the hotel. She hoped Bishop wouldn't back down to his threats. Without his help, her success rate dropped drastically.

"You have a responsibility to this hotel," Carter lashed out. "When you start demolishing it, the insurance isn't going to pay for the damage you do."

"Are you kidding me? You're worried about repairs? I'm worried about lives, Carter."

"We're safe as long as we stay put! I can't believe she got to you!"

"This isn't about Jetta. This is about saving lives. What about the hundreds of other people? What about our town?"

"Our town?" Carter suddenly asked then laughed. "You're not one of them, Bishop. I've been here a lot longer than you have, and I'm not one of them. Since when did you start caring about others? You never cared about anyone."

"Not showing emotions isn't the same as not having them," Bishop remarked. "If we can get to those weapons, we can save ourselves and everyone else."

"And we're looking at hundreds of thousands of dollars in damages that I don't have," Carter launched back in a state of rage. "If you want to blow up the hotel, you can explain that to your boss, Harlan Rafkin."

"You let me worry about him," Bishop snapped. "You just worry about keeping your remaining guests from being eaten and stay the hell out of my way."

"You're going to regret this, I promise," Carter snapped. "Just because you have a hard on for Jetta--"

Bishop's look turned cold and threatening. "You'll want to carefully consider what comes out of your mouth next."

Carter appeared stunned while staring at him. "Oh, now I see," he remarked. "You're doing this just to get in her pants."

"What the hell is your problem?" Bishop demanded to know as his hostility rose. "People are dying, and you think I'm doing this just to score with Jetta?"

"It's a stretch, but it makes more sense than actually believing you care about what happens to the people in this town," Carter remarked. "Give it up, Bishop. You don't stand a chance with Jetta. She's not letting you between her legs."

Bishop suddenly punched Carter in the groin. Carter gasped and doubled over while clutching himself. Bishop collected himself and casually glared at him.

"Shake it off, Carter," Bishop remarked lowly. "That was only a warning shot. If I'd actually wanted to hurt you, you wouldn't walk right for a week."

Carter slowly straightened with discomfort and finally looked at Bishop. He was obviously surprised Bishop had hit him. Bishop's glare was stern and threatening.

"Now, I'm asking you nicely to refrain from using vulgarities where Jetta is concerned."

"Yeah, sure," Carter said softly while glaring at Bishop. "It won't happen again."

Carter muttered something under his breath and turned to leave. He saw Jetta standing a few feet away with an all too familiar look of hostility. He frowned and hurried past her to the roof door. Jetta approached Bishop and offered a tiny, pleased smile.

"I'm assuming you won that argument," Jetta teased.

"You heard that, huh?"

"It would have been hard not to."

Bishop appeared unusually tense then looked over the half wall to the resort grounds and the town beyond it. "As you can see, we have our work cut out for us."

Jetta looked across town as well. As many as one hundred zombies milled about the hotel grounds and throughout town. There were larger pockets closer to the hotel and around several of the buildings, indicating where survivors were probably stranded. The hanger was nearly a mile away with the helicopter sitting in plain sight.

"Nothing like a challenge, huh?" Jetta teased.

"Yeah."

There was an awkward moment of silence. Several thoughts were now racing through Jetta's mind. Carter's comments about Bishop's feelings for her were a close second to something else Carter had said.

"So you don't actually work for Carter?"

"Heard that too, huh?" he asked then snorted a laugh. "Have you heard of Harlan Rafkin?"

"He's that eccentric millionaire recluse who owns a dozen beach resorts. A real bastard, I hear," she casually replied.

She'd actually heard her father mention Rafkin once as well. Something about a mission in Rio followed by a party at one of Rafkin's hotels that ended with an embarrassing mishap. Her father never elaborated, and she wasn't sure she wanted to know the details. With the admiral's team, the term *embarrassing* took on a whole other meaning, and *mishap* usually referred to something being blown up.

"Well, he's also my boss."

Jetta couldn't help feeling surprised yet somehow not too surprised. "At least now I know where you get your sunny disposition."

He chuckled softly and casually leaned on the wall. "Nine months ago, Rafkin bought controlling interest in Winter Harbor

Hotel," Bishop informed her. "Carter didn't want anyone to know he was on the verge of bankruptcy."

"Carter is having financial problems?" she asked then suddenly turned hostile. "That little bastard!" She was now angry with Carter all over again. She shouldn't have been surprised that he lied to her. "He offered to pay for Hunter's surgery if I agreed to be his *girlfriend* for a couple of months."

Bishop appeared slightly uncomfortable while straightening. "I hope you turned him down--considering he's broke."

"I never considered it for a minute," she replied with a soft laugh. If she intended to sleep with any man in this hotel, it would be Bishop, but she certainly wasn't going to tell him that. "I have zero tolerance for rich men."

"Yes, so I've heard." Bishop offered a teasing grin. "Want me to beat him up?"

"You'd do that, wouldn't you?" she asked with a laugh.

"I have to amuse myself somehow," Bishop teased and smiled at her longer than he should have.

Jetta couldn't help but smile back in response. It wasn't for his own amusement. She realized Hunter had been right. Bishop did like her.

"I appreciate the offer, but I'll get even with him later." She offered a devious grin. "So--which car is his?"

Chapter Twenty-three

$\mathcal{T}$he lights were on within the tavern, but it was deathly quiet. Nearly sixty zombies roamed the parking lot and pushed against the doors and windows. A lucky few were eating the remains of some unlucky person. The fifty men and women quietly sat in the tavern with glasses of beer or something stronger before them. The windows were crudely boarded, and the shattered jukebox was barricaded against the main door. Fei Yen sat at one of the back tables and drew pictures on the waitress's tablet. Ming sat close to her and remained worried as she listened to the sounds of zombies groaning and thumping against the doors and windows. It was unsettling and a cruel reminder of their desperate situation. Sheriff Palmer appeared from the back with Daniels and two other men, Kyle and Dirk. They carried a rifle, a shotgun, a baseball bat, and a tire iron. They placed the items on the bar alongside the six pool sticks. This represented their arsenal of weapons. It wasn't exactly impressive.

"Okay, so this is what we have for weapons," Palmer announced then appeared disgusted. "Anyone else carrying?"

Edwin and Wayne approached and revealed their concealed revolvers. Each weapon held six rounds with no extra bullets. It wouldn't be much of a last stand, if it came to that. Palmer wasn't overly confident.

"I suppose every single one of those trucks outside has a rifle in it," Palmer remarked with frustration.

"Yeah, mine too, but I'm not volunteering to go out there and get it," Dirk scoffed lowly while counting the remaining shells for the shotgun.

Shelly appeared from the kitchen and approached them. "We have enough food to last us a couple of days."

"Hopefully that'll be enough," Palmer replied.

Shelly frowned and appeared uncomfortable while rubbing her chilled arms. "Sheriff, there's no response from Wes locked in the pantry."

"He's almost certainly one of them by now," Daniels bluntly informed them.

"Your compassion in commendable," Palmer muttered.

"When we don't report in, it'll be at least a day or two before someone comes to check on us," Daniels announced. "If I hadn't given Anderson my cell phone--"

"I suppose us hicks are a dime a dozen, huh?" Palmer demanded and allowed his temper to again rise. "If they lose control over this infection, they can just blow the entire island off the map, isn't that right, Daniels?"

Daniels appeared uncomfortable with Palmer's rising temper. "Drastic measures would only be used as a last resort."

"I'll take that as a 'yes'," Palmer remarked then looked back at Shelly. "Any luck with the radio?"

"It was trashed when those things broke into the back," Shelly informed him.

Palmer appeared humored and snorted a laugh. The stress was clearly getting to him. "I suppose every one of those damned trucks outside has a radio too? Not that it'll do us any good in here." He looked at Daniels while casually placing his hand on his gun holster like some western day gunslinger. "This is your party, Daniels. I elect you to take a little stroll into the parking lot and call someone up on one of those radios."

Daniels glared his disapproval at Palmer's tasteless joke. Of course, with Palmer, it was hard to tell if he was joking or not. Shelly remained tense and watched the exchange between Palmer and Daniels.

"What about Wes?" Shelly asked with a more determined tone. She was obviously bothered about Wes' fate.

Palmer looked at Shelly, shifted with discomfort, and reluctantly removed his revolver from his holster. "Yeah, I'll check on him." As he headed toward the kitchen in the back, he was heard mumbling, "Where the hell is that damned deputy when you really need him?"

Sheriff Palmer entered the kitchen and approached the bolted pantry door. He stared at the door a moment while clutching his gun, took a deep breath, and pounded on the door.

"Yo, Wes, you in there?"

There was no response. Palmer waited a moment longer, frowned, and reached for the bolt on the door. Shelly suddenly appeared behind him. He turned with surprise and aimed his gun at her. She screamed and jumped back. He lowered his gun while groaning.

"Jesus, don't do that," Palmer scoffed. He looked at her then indicated the door while taking a step back and aiming his gun. "Open the door."

"Are you out of your mind? What if he's one of them?"

"Then I shoot him in the head," Palmer informed her. "You'll be safe behind the door. He'll come after me."

"You're not exactly making your case," she remarked. "What if he gets you?"

"Then we're all screwed," Palmer snapped, realized how he sounded, and then attempted to sound more reassuring. "It'll be okay. Just open the door. I won't let anything happen to you. Trust me."

Shelly uncertainly nodded. She moved in front of the door, grasped the handle, and reached for the bolt. She looked back at Palmer. He took a wide stance, aimed his gun at the door, and nodded to Shelly. She pulled the bolt free and threw open the door while seeking shelter behind it. Palmer aimed his gun at the empty pantry then appeared surprised.

"What the hell--?"

Shelly uncertainly peeked around the door. Palmer slowly approached the open pantry and looked inside. Wes lie moderately spread out against the back corner with his eyes closed. He appeared to be dead. Palmer uncertainly approached the motionless man with his gun aimed and his finger tight on the trigger. He paused before him and gently kicked his foot.

"Yo, Wes," Palmer announced. "Last call."

Wes didn't move. Shelly now stood in the pantry doorway and stared as well.

"Is he dead?" she asked softly. "I mean *dead* dead?"

Palmer frowned and shook his head. "That bastard Daniels doesn't know his ass from a hole in the ground. Wait until I get my hands on him."

He returned his gun to his holster, turned within the pantry, and approached Shelly by the open door. Shelly suddenly appeared horrified and screamed. Palmer quickly turned. Zombie Wes was already on his feet and charging for Sheriff Palmer. Palmer reached for his weapon as Wes plowed into him and knocked him against the nearby shelf. His gun flew across the pantry floor. Palmer held Wes back with his forearm against his throat. Zombie Wes snapped at Palmer's face while snarling viciously. Palmer reached behind him, grabbed a can, and repeatedly struck Wes in the head with it. As Wes fell to the floor, Palmer delivered the final blow, crushing his skull. The can opened and coffee grounds flew across the pantry floor. Wes no longer moved. Palmer slowly straightened and looked at the coffee can in his hand. He snorted a laugh.

"Look at that," he announced and appeared almost humored while indicating the coffee can. "Saved by coffee. There's a little bit of irony to that."

"Yeah," Shelly said and appeared relieved. "That was our last can of coffee too."

Sheriff Palmer looked at the empty can in his hand then to the coffee grounds scattered across Wes and the floor. He rolled his eyes and tossed the can over his shoulder.

"Irony is cruel," he muttered.

The faint sound of loud, rock music vibrated the kitchen walls. Palmer and Shelly exchanged bewildered looks then appeared surprised, if not encouraged by the sound. They ran from the pantry, across the cluttered kitchen, and into the bar area with the other startled patrons. The pulsating rock music grew louder along with the sound of a car. Everyone ran to the windows and peered out through the cracks in the boards.

A black sports car with flames on the side flew past the tavern. The loud, rock music blared from the car's speakers and vibrated the entire area. The screeching of tires was heard as the car skidded into a turn. The car burned out with a cloud of smoke and raced back past the tavern. The zombies turned away from the tavern and headed across the parking lot toward the car and the loud music it produced. The sports car again spun around and made another pass, this time flying into the parking lot as it skidded in a circle, and struck several zombies. The car peeled out in the gravel, drove back to the road, and spun again. Hunter appeared from the sunroof with an assault rifle. He wore black swat gear and clenched a cigar between his teeth while grinning. He rapidly fired with precise headshots at the zombies in the parking lot. The car spun and sped back down the road with Hunter continuing to fire. He pounded the roof of the car. The car again spun and returned for another pass. He was obviously having a little too much fun.

Sheriff Palmer appeared horrified and turned toward the others while frantically waving his arms. "Everyone down!" Palmer shouted. "It's that crazy, son-of-a-bitch, Hunter!"

Everyone screamed and dove to the floor. Palmer returned to the barricaded window and watched.

The car skidded to a stop near the tavern. Hunter no longer had the assault rifle in his hands. He casually held his cigar and maintained his enthusiastic grin.

"Hey, maggot bait!" he called out. "Fresh meat! Come and get me!" His chuckle could be heard above the blaring music.

The zombies made their way closer to the car. Desmond sat behind the wheel and watched their approach with a concerned look on his face.

"They're getting closer, Hunter!"

Hunter chuckled lowly and puffed on his cigar in a most sinister manner. He was definitely off fighting the war this time. "Crazy is the new sexy, Desmond! Enjoy the rush!"

The zombies got closer to the car. Desmond revved the engine and stared out the window with a paranoid expression.

"Don't get twitchy on me!" Hunter yelled to him.

The zombies were nearly upon the car. Hunter produced a stick of dynamite, lit it from his cigar, and handed it to the closest zombie. The zombie grabbed for him and took the dynamite. Hunter hit the car roof. Desmond burned out and raced down the road as Hunter disappeared into the car. The zombie looked quizzically at the dynamite in his hand. The fuse ran out. It exploded and took at least ten zombies with it. Zombie parts rained down upon the parking lot in a bloody, fleshy mess.

"Jesus Christ!" Palmer was heard shouting from within the tavern.

The sports car sped down the road in reverse then spun around in front of the tavern. Hunter shot more zombies from the sunroof. The sports car pulled into the parking lot and up to the front door. While Hunter continued to shoot from the sunroof, Desmond jumped out of the car and hurried to the trunk. He slammed his palm against the tavern door then opened the trunk. Loud movement of the jukebox being dragged across the floor was heard from inside. The door opened to reveal Palmer with a stunned look. Desmond tossed him an assault rifle. The trunk was filled with weapons and ammunition. Hunter climbed through the sunroof, stood on the hood of the car, and continued to shoot approaching zombies. Palmer turned to the tavern and yelled inside.

"Get these weapons! Let's go!" Palmer cried out.

Several people hurried outside to the car. Palmer and Desmond handed out the arsenal of weapons.

"May I make a suggestion?" Hunter casually announced between shots from the car's hood.

"What?" Desmond asked.

"Turn off that fucking music!"

Desmond groaned and shut off the car. Zombies continued their approach but from further away. Desmond passed out the last of the ammo and shut the trunk.

"Done!" Desmond cried out.

"Is there access to the roof from inside?" Hunter asked the small crowd of patrons collecting outside.

"There's a crawl space in the attic, but it's blocked with shelves in the supply closet," Shelly informed him.

"Well, open it up," Hunter announced then looked at Desmond and grinned. "I'll be on the roof. I'll meet you inside when I'm bored."

"How the hell do you intend--?" Palmer asked then fell silent while watching Hunter.

Hunter slung his weapon over his shoulder, easily leaped to the porch roof, and swung up onto the tavern roof. Palmer stared with amazement at Hunter's agility and shook his head.

Desmond offered a tiny, nervous smile. "He's in commando mode. Be afraid."

He hurried Palmer inside and shut the door behind them. Desmond and Palmer approached the bar where all the weapons were laid out. Dirk set a bottle of whiskey on the bar near Desmond. Desmond took a quick swig and immediately grimaced. Gunshots were heard from the roof.

"We heard some radio chatter from a crashed truck on our way here," Desmond informed the group surrounding him. "People are trapped in the school and at the hotel. We'll wait until morning to make our move."

"How many people?" Palmer asked.

"Unknown," he replied. "We didn't exactly hang around for the entire conversation." Desmond clapped his hands together and looked around the tavern. "Listen up!" All eyes were on him. "Hunter is off fighting the war. No one is to mention Jetta! If he thinks she's in any danger, he's going to lose it, and we can't afford that. Got it!"

Everyone nodded. A few minutes passed. Hunter appeared in the tavern and approached Desmond at the bar. His rugged swat team appearance and the assault rifle in his arms caused tension among everyone. Hunter propped the rifle against the bar, sat on the stool, and reached for the whiskey bottle. Desmond tensed and stopped him.

"We need you frosty, Hunter," Desmond said gently while attempting to sound calm despite his concerns. "How about a cup of tea instead?"

"Tea?" Hunter asked gruffly and appeared almost offended by the suggestion.

Desmond and Palmer tensed.

Hunter suddenly smiled. "I'd love some tea."

"I'll be right back," Desmond announced then eyed Palmer and indicated the pool table in the back.

Palmer nodded as Desmond hurried for the kitchen. He looked at Hunter and attempted a casual smile.

"Care to play some pool?"

"Don't mind if I do," Hunter replied cheerfully.

Chapter Twenty-four

*E*veryone within the hotel remained in the lounge at the bar or at tables with drinks before them. It was getting late and everyone was exhausted.

"We should probably get some rest; maybe sleep in shifts," Carter announced. "We can take turns guarding the kitchen and lobby."

"If there's an emergency, we can pull the fire alarm," Styles remarked.

"The place seems pretty secure," Jetta said while standing wearily. "We could use rooms on the second floor and pair up. That way no one is alone, and we're still close enough to one another. I think we could all use some sleep."

"I'm never sleeping again," Stacy muttered.

Rafael looked at Bishop. "Guess it's you and me, dude. Hope you don't snore."

"I'm staying with Jetta," Bishop casually replied.

Jetta suddenly glared at him and appeared surprised if not shocked. "Excuse me?"

She didn't know what he was up to, but she wasn't humored. Bishop remained casually reclined in his chair and stared at her. Jetta stared back at him.

"Yeah, right, that will be the day," Carter said with a throaty chuckle.

Jetta and Bishop maintained their locked stares, almost as if waiting to see who blinked first. For a second, she thought she read his mind, and his reasoning suddenly dawned on her. Jetta finally looked away.

"Okay," Jetta casually replied.

A tiny smile crossed Bishop's face. Carter appeared surprised then instantly annoyed.

"Wait--so I'm alone?" Rafael suddenly asked.

"You can stay with my father," Lee informed him. "I'll take a room with a connecting door. We can leave the connecting door open."

"Oh, okay," Rafael replied and appeared relieved.

Elise glanced at Stacy. Stacy seemed painfully aware that she was about to be stuck in a room with her monster of a boss. Life was suddenly even less fair. It couldn't be allowed. Stacy sheepishly glanced at Lee.

"Is there room for one more in your room?" Stacy asked Lee while attempting not to sound desperate but failed.

"Absolutely," Lee replied while understanding Stacy's concerned look. "Elise can pair up with Colleen."

Elise looked at Colleen, who sat at the bar in a drunken stupor and babbled incoherently. Her mental state was clearly questionable after seeing her husband turn into a zombie, nearly kill her, and then being shot in the head.

"I'll get key cards for everyone," Elise said without enthusiasm and left the room.

Jetta avoided looking at Bishop, who continued to watch her with a grin on his face. She caught Carter's cold stare. He was obviously upset that she agreed to stay in a room with Bishop over him, though she couldn't understand why he seemed so surprised. She wanted him to get the wrong idea. He tried to play her feelings for Hunter to get her into his bed and didn't even have the means to uphold his end of the bargain. If she had fallen for it, there would be a good chance she would have seriously hurt him.

✝

*N*early everyone within the tavern attempted to sleep in chairs or on the floor using anything they could find for a pillow. Random gunshots were heard coming from the roof, but they were fewer and far between. One or two armed men remained awake in chairs by random windows and watched outside. Hunter slept reclined in one of the chairs with his feet propped on a nearby table and his hat over his face. His assault rifle lie across his lap with the heat-seeking device alongside it. A tiny hand touched the rifle.

"That's not a toy," Hunter said softly without looking.

Fei Yen jumped back with surprise. Hunter raised his cap and looked at the little girl standing alongside his chair.

"I wanted to play with your game," Fei Yen said softly while indicating the heat-seeking device on his lap.

Hunter looked at the device then handed it to her. "It's not a game, but you can see body heat with it."

He showed her how it worked. She aimed it at the people around the room and watched to see their body heat. She looked at him with great curiosity.

"Are you the crazy Army guy?" she asked.

He suddenly grinned at her question. "No, I'm the crazy Navy guy."

"My daddy was in the Army. Did you know him?"

He found her notion that all military men must know one another endearing. "I don't think so," he replied with a tiny smile. "I've been retired a long time."

"My daddy died," she said without hesitation. "A car blew up."

Hunter stared at her a long moment with a shattered look. He twitched slightly at the grim reminder. Sounds from the past of men yelling and guns firing echoed through his mind. He returned to his version of reality and stared at the little girl.

"I'm so sorry, Fei Yen."

"Mommy says you got blown up too."

Hunter again sank into his own thoughts while staring at her. Ming hurried toward them with mild alarm and placed her hands on Fei Yen's shoulders.

"Fei Yen, don't disturb people while they're trying to sleep." She looked at Hunter and smiled timidly. "I'm sorry."

"It's okay," he replied. "Believe it or not, I'm actually very good with children. I helped build a treehouse for Jetta when she was--" Hunter suddenly looked around and appeared concerned. Something was wrong. "Where is Jetta?"

Ming stared at Hunter with some concern then indicated the device Fei Yen held. "What is that?"

"It's a heat seeking tracker," he said.

"I'll show you, Mommy."

Fei Yen aimed the device around the tavern. As she passed the outside wall, it revealed dark movement.

"What's that?" Ming asked.

"That's *them*," Hunter replied. "It has a range of fifty feet or so. There must be more approaching."

There was the sound of gunfire. Hunter offered a smile and pointed to the roof. "They're on top of it."

Ming returned the device. "We'll let you get some sleep." She looked at her daughter. "Say good night to Hunter."

"Good night, Hunter."

"Good night, dear."

†

*T*wenty or more zombies piled against the entranceways on both sides of the hotel. More aimlessly wandered the grounds. The hotel appeared peaceful despite the groans of the zombie horde. A small group of zombies knelt over a dead man and picked him apart. As they feasted on his flesh, the man twitched and sat up. Most of the flesh on his face was missing, revealing his jawbone, cheekbone, and left eye socket. His right arm was torn off, and most of the flesh was missing from his left thigh. As he stood, his insides spilled out onto the ground. The group of zombies surrounding him suddenly lost interest in this one as their snack. They stood and roamed around aimlessly with the others.

†

*J*etta and Bishop entered the well-appointed guestroom with two queen beds and a view of the ocean. Jetta turned on the light and looked around while Bishop shut and locked the door behind them. She had never been inside the guestrooms before. The guestrooms were actually rather stunning with expensive bedding, tasteful furniture, and exquisite artwork. Of course, for what they charged for the rooms, Jetta assumed they should be stunning.

"You have to admit, the look on Carter's face was priceless," Bishop said with a devious grin.

"I can imagine mine wasn't far from his," she replied. "I appreciate your assistance in sticking it to Carter, but a little heads up would have been nice."

"So you're assuming my offer was just to annoy Carter?" he asked.

She cast a glare at him and sharply raised her brows. "I suggest you stick with that story, if you know what's good for you," she replied with a tiny smile on her face.

"After the day I've had, you'd actually inflict bodily pain on me for wanting a little sympathy sex?" Bishop remarked then shook his head.

"Tread lightly, Bishop. I've had a bad day too."

Bishop sighed and removed his jacket and shoulder holster. "On that note, I guess I'll settle for a couple hours sleep before our guard duty shift." He carelessly tossed his jacket and shoulder holster onto the foot end of the bed.

Jetta approached the first bed and collapsed on it with exhaustion. Bishop removed his shirt then opened his pants. Jetta suddenly glared at him.

"What are you doing?"

Bishop gave her a serious look. "This is how I sleep," he informed her and allowed his pants to fall to the floor. "You don't scare me."

Jetta couldn't help but catch an eyeful of his sexy, black boxer briefs, which resembled a sexier, cotton version of bicycle shorts. Bishop had an athletic build with broad shoulders and just enough chest hair to hold her interest. There was no denying it; he was stunning! She looked away in what she hoped came off as casual disinterest, but the image was already burned into her mind. In all her encounters with her father's men feeling liberated to strut around the house in their boxer shorts during visits, she didn't remember any of them looking quite like that. Although most were muscular in build, their floppy, no-frills boxer shorts held no appeal. Bishop slipped under the covers, propped himself on his elbow, and eyed her with a sly smile. She hoped he hadn't noticed her quick, once over of him in his underwear. She'd never be able to live that one down, not after the other day in the helicopter.

"Is that how you intend to sleep?" he asked with a little too much enthusiasm.

"Unlike you, I don't want to be caught with my pants down," she remarked.

"And unlike you, I'm confident we're safe here." Bishop patted the bed alongside him with a devious grin on his face. "But if it makes you feel better, you can snuggle against me. I'll keep you safe."

"You're just begging to be hit."

"Just trying to be nice," he replied.

"I seriously doubt that."

He maintained his smile. "If you need me, you know where to find me," he teased.

Bishop then turned onto his side facing away from her. Jetta stared at him a moment longer and considered his invite. It actually sounded pretty good. Cuddling with a man while she slept was something she wanted to do, but it always seemed to come with certain strings attached. One of her father's buddies pulled that stunt on her a few years back. Apparently, 'cuddle' actually meant 'sex', even if he swore it didn't. Their 'cuddling' didn't end well for him. The wrath of the admiral was nothing compared to the wrath of Jetta. Perhaps that was military men, but Bishop did seem a lot like them in many aspects. She dismissed her overtly sexual thoughts and opted to get some sleep instead. The image of Bishop in his black, boxer briefs kept flashing through her mind, almost taunting her to join him. She groaned softly, turned on her side, and buried her head in the pillow.

Chapter Twenty-five

*T*he tavern appeared peaceful as everyone attempted to sleep in chairs and on the floor. One of the men sat before the window on guard duty with an assault rifle across his lap. He nodded off in the chair several times while attempting to stay awake. The sounds of gunshots coming from the roof had ceased. All was quiet. Hunter slept in his chair twenty feet from the door. He twitched in his sleep to the sounds of explosions, screaming, and gunfire. He was once again fighting the war and sacrificing himself for his team. The nightmare was never-ending. It was a battle he lost every night; one he never meant to survive. A strange slurping sound was heard as a breeze blew past him. He jerked awake from his nightmare, clutched his rifle, and stared into the dead eyes of a gruesome zombie only inches from his face. In a split second, he had the zombie by the throat and his pistol drawn. Without hesitation, he pulled the trigger and shot the zombie in the head.

The sound of his gun firing in close quarters woke everyone. Their frightened gasps turned to horrified screams. Two zombies were already devouring two others who had been asleep, which was the slurping sound he'd heard in his sleep. Hunter jumped to his feet with his assault rifle grasped firmly in his hands and looked at the open door. He should have heard it being opened, but he hadn't. The sound of rock music suddenly blared from the sports car just outside. More zombies filtered into the tavern. People screamed as others grabbed their weapons. Hunter rammed the butt of his assault rifle into the face of a zombie eating one of the men near the door. As the zombie fell to the floor, he shot it in the head. It seemed as if his gunshot started a chain reaction among the others. Several men began firing and bullets appeared to fly randomly around the crowded room. Chaos erupted as people screamed and ran in every direction. Hunter watched in horror as a few fleeing people were struck by stray bullets. A zombie pounced on one of the women, who fell to the floor after being shot, and tore into her face as she attempted to fight it off.

"Cease fire! Cease fire!" Hunter yelled, but no one heard him over the screaming and gunfire.

A zombie jumped on one of the men near Ming and her daughter. As the zombie knocked the man across the pool table, Fei Yen watched it tear into the man's forearm. Fei Yen screamed and ran across the room.

"Fei Yen!" Ming cried out and ran after her.

A stray bullet whizzed past Fei Yen's head. She ducked while continuing to scream. Another stray bullet struck Ming and forcibly knocked her against the wall. A zombie grabbed Fei Yen's hair as she ran past. A small tuft of hair, ripped from her scalp, was all the zombie got from the fast moving little girl. Fei Yen ran for the open door and darted out of the tavern. Ming straightened while clutching her bleeding arm and saw Fei Yen running from the tavern. Ming appeared horrified, screamed for her, and ran out the door after her daughter.

As Ming emerged from the tavern, the sports car burned out in the parking lot and nearly struck her. She dove out of the path of the car and rolled across the gravel parking lot. She painfully moved to her knees while clutching her arm and saw Daniels behind the wheel. The car spun out from the excessive pressure on the gas pedal, jetted forward, and struck a truck. The car burned out in the gravel but appeared stuck against the truck. Ming saw her daughter running across the parking lot and ran after her. Fei Yen dodged several zombies before stopping by a pick-up truck to cry. Ming ran for her and was almost to her when zombie Brian grabbed Fei Yen and pulled her off her feet. Ming attempted to pull her daughter from the zombie's grip. Fei Yen and Ming both screamed as zombie Brian's mouth neared the back of Fei Yen's neck.

The muzzle of an assault rifle was rammed into Brian's mouth, forcing his head back and away from the little girl. Hunter fired a shot through Brian's mouth, exploding the back of his head. Ming pulled Fei Yen from the falling zombie's hands and fell with her to the ground. Two more zombies were suddenly hovering over them, preparing to pounce. Ming screamed and clutched her daughter, shielding her where they half lie on the ground. Hunter spun into a high, roundhouse kick above Ming's head and struck the first zombie in the face. He spun toward the second one almost on top of Ming, tossed his rifle aside, and broke the zombie's neck with one motion. As the first zombie attempted to move back to its feet, Hunter threw himself to the ground, grabbed his discarded rifle, and aimed it at the first zombie. Ming saw the rifle close to them and again shielded Fei Yen. Hunter shot the zombie twice in the head from his position on the ground.

Once the firing ceased, Ming uncertainly looked at Hunter on the ground near her. Their eyes met only briefly. Her gratitude was almost overshadowed by her shock of the impressiveness of his combat skills. Hunter stood and pulled Ming to her feet.

"Get her inside."

Ming grabbed Fei Yen and rushed her back into the tavern. The man on the roof finally woke and began shooting random zombies. Hunter looked up, shook his head with disgust, and muttered a curse. The sports cars engine was still heard revving. Hunter casually walked toward the car attempting to pull free from the pick-up truck. Daniels looked out the window and appeared to panic as Hunter approached. The sports car broke free and flew backwards into another parked car. It then burned out and jetted past Hunter. Hunter removed a grenade from his pocket, pulled the pin, and casually tossed it through the sunroof as the car raced past him. Hunter walked back to the tavern while lighting his cigar. He paused, puffed on his cigar, and blew out smoke. The sports car spun onto the paved road and exploded. Hunter smirked and continued into the tavern.

†

*T*he tavern door was crudely sealed. Several people lie dead and others were injured either from friendly fire or from zombie attacks. Eight zombies lie mangled on the floor. Hunter sat in a chair across from Ming, who clung to her daughter, and patched Ming's injured arm. Despite their situation, Hunter was unusually peaceful. Palmer, on the other hand, was a raging bull. Sheriff Palmer paced the tavern while shaking his head and gesturing wildly at several men standing before him. Each man kept his head down and appeared ashamed.

"Idiots!" Palmer cried out. "Who the hell fires a weapon in a crowded room with innocent people running every damned direction? If I have my way, I'll see to it that none of you yahoos ever gets a damned hunting license again!" He threw his hands around while gesturing wildly. "Let's get these rotten bastards out of here before they stink up the place!"

Palmer was playing bad cop enough for everyone, so Desmond went the direction of good cop and attempted to keep the remaining patrons calm.

"If you've been hurt, see the field medic," Desmond announced between Sheriff Palmer's continual outbursts.

Hunter looked over his shoulder and eyed Desmond with a curious look. "We have a field medic?" He wondered why no one told him.

"Yeah--you."

Hunter smirked and shook his head. Palmer continued his pacing and ranting with no letup in sight. Perhaps if there had been coffee for the good sheriff, he wouldn't have lectured as long as he had. Hunter looked at Ming across from him and offered a tiny, pleasant smile.

"You're very lucky the bullet only grazed your arm," he informed her. "You should probably have stitches, but scars build character."

Something clicked in Hunter's mind. He uncertainly looked around the room. He was sure he was forgetting something. He looked back into Ming's big, brown eyes as she stared helplessly at him. Those eyes of hers melted him.

"Thank you for saving my daughter," Ming said timidly. "I don't know how I'll ever repay you."

A thousand thoughts flooded Hunter's mind. He entertained one or two of the less appropriate ones, but her innocent beauty chased them away.

"Invite me for dinner, and we'll call it even," he said with a warm smile.

"I'd be honored," she replied warmly then blushed with embarrassment.

He was captivated by everything about this woman. She was too beautiful for words. He was sure they had met before, but he was having a hard time remembering where. Hunter took her hand, suavely kissed it, and excused himself. He needed to get away from her before he forgot they were in a combat situation. Beautiful women were distracting to soldiers, and he'd seen too many men die because they allowed themselves to be distracted. Ming could *easily* distract him. He walked toward Desmond and several others who were injured. Desmond appeared tense and pulled Hunter away from the injured people and closer to Palmer, who reloaded his gun. His rant had apparently exhausted him.

"Four of the injured were bitten," Desmond said softly. "We have maybe an hour before they turn."

Palmer groaned and rolled his eyes. "Well, this just keeps getting better and better," the sheriff snapped while slinging the gun's cylinder closed. He immediately fidgeted, stared at Desmond, and attempted to keep his voice down. "What do we do now?"

"There's the radical solution," Hunter replied.

Desmond and Palmer eyed Hunter with shared looks of horror. Hunter stared back at them and wondered why they were looking at him like that.

"No way," Palmer growled lowly. "We don't shoot our own citizens." He paused and appeared to reflect the last twenty-four hours. "At least not the live ones."

"Then we need to isolate them, wait for them to turn, and then humanely put them down," Hunter informed him.

"Show some respect," Palmer snapped. "These people are my neighbors."

"In less than an hour, your neighbors are going to bite you in the ass," Hunter remarked casually.

"He's right," Desmond replied with a defeated sigh. "We need to isolate them and deal with them when they turn."

Palmer subconsciously rubbed the day's growth of stubble on his face with the barrel of his revolver. "I'm really starting to hate my job."

Shelly approached them while clutching her bleeding arm. "Sheriff," she said gently.

Palmer turned, looked at Shelly's bleeding bite wound, and groaned softly while looking away. He fought his sorrow, replaced his gun to its holster, and then looked back at her while putting on a false look of hope.

"How's the arm, Shelly?" he asked gently.

"It feels like it's on fire," she replied. "I'm going to become like Wes--like those outside, aren't I?"

"It's not an exact science," Palmer fumbled over his words and attempted not to cringe from his lie.

"You're a terrible liar, Sheriff," she remarked gently then drew a deep, shaken breath. "If it's all the same, I'd rather you didn't wait until I turned."

Palmer appeared horrified at the suggestion then turned stern with her and shook his head. "No, that's not happening. We're going to wait."

"Sheriff--" she protested.

"We don't know for sure," he insisted.

"Sheriff, please," she begged. Shelly took a deep breath and fought her emotions. "Then give me a gun."

"No, I'm not doing that either," Palmer informed her. "We'll isolate you and the others and wait. Someone may come along and rescue us. There could be a cure."

"You know better," she remarked. "You heard what Daniels said. There is no cure."

Palmer shook his head defiantly. "No, I'm sorry," he announced firmly. "We're waiting."

Shelly frowned then turned to Desmond. He stared at her with the same horrified expression then lowered his head and looked away. She appeared frustrated then glanced at Hunter, who watched her closely. His expression was hard to read.

"Will you give me a gun?" she asked.

There was no hesitation. Hunter removed the semiautomatic from his shoulder holster, checked the click, and cocked it. Desmond and Palmer jumped with surprise and attempted to protest as he handed Shelly the gun. She took the gun, offered him a tiny, grateful smile, and headed for the kitchen. The three others who were bitten solemnly followed her. Desmond stared at Hunter with his mouth hanging open while Palmer began another rant.

"I can't believe you did that!" Palmer shouted. "You may as well have pulled the trigger yourself! What the hell is wrong with you?" He suddenly shook his head and threw his arms around. "Scratch that, I know what's wrong with you!"

"She's dead either way, Sargent," Hunter informed him firmly. He outranked this soldier. He didn't know why he felt the need to justify his actions to his subordinate. "She should be allowed to die with a little bit of dignity. It is, after all, her decision, and I commend her for living and dying on her own terms."

Palmer glared at Hunter and appeared unable to come up with a response. There was a moment of eerie silence throughout the entire tavern. The semiautomatic was heard firing from the kitchen. Everyone flinched. Three more shots followed. Everyone stared at the kitchen with the horror evident on their faces. Palmer and Desmond sadly looked down. The silence that followed was deafening. Hunter stared at the guilt-ridden looks on Palmer and Desmond's faces.

"There was nothing you could have done," Hunter remarked gently. "It was already too late for them. Our focus needs to be on those we can still save. We'll strike the school just after dawn. They're the ones you need to focus on. Those are the people you *can* save."

Chapter Twenty-six

Lee and Carter sat quietly in chairs strategically placed by the locked out elevator. Rafael stood near the driveway side doors and watched the zombies paw at the glass while trying to get to him. There were now a few dozen zombies at both the beachside and driveway side doors. The next zombie was more gruesome in appearance then the last.

"I wish you wouldn't stand so close to the glass," Carter remarked from across the lobby. "They're just dying to sink their teeth into you."

"Nah, they don't want me, dude," Rafael informed him without bothering to look back. "Too grisly. They want, like, a lean jogger or a tender, young swimmer." He suddenly appeared surprised by something outside. "Oh, look, a live one!"

Carter and Lee sprang to their feet.

Rafael suddenly frowned. "Oh, dude, they got him. Poor bastard." His grimace described the gruesome feeding that must surely have followed.

The second elevator opened to reveal Jetta and Bishop, who were loudly bickering.

"Oh, please, you're one twister away from having a house fall on you," Bishop snarled as he briskly walked ahead of her and out of the elevator.

"So now you're calling me a witch?" Jetta demanded while glaring at his back as she followed him.

"If the broomstick fits--"

167

Carter, Lee, and Rafael eyed Jetta and Bishop as they stepped off the elevator with their fight in progress.

"Somehow I don't think that room sharing went the way he'd hoped," Carter remarked with a humored laugh. He appeared to be having the last laugh now.

"There's a reason why some people shouldn't breed," Bishop announced firmly to Carter. "This one would undoubtedly eat her young."

Carter laughed softly and guided Lee toward the elevator. "You two enjoy guard duty for the next two hours."

Lee looked at Jetta as she passed them and appeared sympathetic. "Did you want me to stay with Bishop on guard duty?"

"No, that's okay. We'll be fine," she replied and smiled her appreciation. "He's just cranky because he hasn't gotten laid--" Jetta sneered at Bishop. "--in over a year."

"And now we know why you're still a virgin," Bishop snapped and cast his back against the desk.

Lee cringed, appeared sympathetic to Jetta, and entered the elevator with her father. Rafael walked past them while heading for the elevator to join Carter and Lee and gave Bishop a firm, scolding look.

"Dude," Rafael said to Bishop, "you really need to stop with the hostility."

"She's the one--"

"You know it's you," Rafael interrupted then firmly motioned at them. "You two--kiss and make up. Seriously."

Rafael entered the elevator. The doors closed. Jetta approached the front desk and easily jumped on it in a sitting position. Bishop stared at both doors crowded with zombies and appeared to reconsider.

"We do have bigger problems," he remarked with less enthusiasm for fighting. "We shouldn't be arguing."

"We don't argue, we banter," she replied simply. "People who argue don't get along. We enjoy annoying the hell out of each other. It's just what we do."

Bishop studied her a moment then appeared humored and grinned. "Oh, so you enjoy my company?" he teased.

"Of course I do. Does that surprise you?"

His teasing smile faded into a look of surprise. "Actually, it does. I always thought you had little use for me," he remarked then placed his hand on her thigh.

Jetta casually removed his hand from her leg. "I'm used to dealing with all sorts of attitudes. My father's men are pretty over-the-top," she informed him. "Besides, you're not without your charm."

Bishop appeared humored and moved even closer to her. "Are you hitting on me?"

Jetta rolled her eyes and jumped off the front desk while groaning with disgust. "Oh, please--"

"That wasn't a denial."

Jetta walked past him, cast herself onto the nearby sofa, and appeared tense.

"No, I wasn't hitting on you." At least she hoped she wasn't. Maybe she was. It had been a confusing sort of day. She wished she could shake the image of him in those black, boxer briefs. "I was just--" She hesitated to collect her thoughts, so she wouldn't say something stupid. "I don't want you to think I don't care about you."

Bishop sat next to her on the sofa and stared at her with genuine surprise. "Oh, my God, you are hitting on me." He suddenly grinned. "This is nice for a change." He placed his arm around her shoulder while looking at her lustfully.

Jetta rolled her eyes, pulled away from him with a groan, and stood. "I don't know why I bother."

Bishop grabbed Jetta around the waist and pulled her off her feet and onto his lap. She gasped with surprise then glared at him as he held her.

"You know this won't end well for you."

"I've seen you sit on Desmond's lap plenty of times at the tavern."

"That's different," she remarked. "There was limited seating. You're just scratching an itch."

"No, I actually just want you to sit on my lap," he announced. "I think I'm entitled to one, last cheap thrill before you get me killed."

There was a moment of silence. Jetta stared at him and considered his comment. There was the distinct chance she might get him killed on her suicide mission. She didn't want that to happen. As she stared into his eyes, she couldn't deny that she was attracted to him any longer. If life ended tomorrow, she wanted a night of pleasure with this man.

"You're right," she replied softly and uncertainly touched his chest while avoiding looking into his eyes. "We could both use one, last cheap thrill."

Bishop groaned softly, pulled her against him, and kissed her passionately. She uncertainly returned the kiss, which seemed to encourage his aggression. Then a thought occurred to her. If life didn't end tomorrow, he would undoubtedly torment her endlessly if she slept with him. She couldn't let this go any further and broke off the kiss. Bishop was reluctant to end the kiss but managed a smile all the same.

"I was actually hoping for a longer, one, last cheap thrill," he teased.

"I'd love to accommodate you, Bishop," she remarked then grinned slyly. "But I'm afraid our odds of survival are a little too good for me."

"Oh? And what are our odds?"

She considered it a moment. "I'm giving us a forty percent chance of survival."

He appeared stunned. "That's it? Seriously?" he demanded. "I gave us seventy percent, and I thought that was deserving of 'our last night on earth' sex."

Jetta laughed and touched his face. "You're cute."

As he stared into her eyes, his look turned serious. He gently took her hand from his face and warmly kissed it. Jetta couldn't look away as her heart pounded with anticipation. It didn't seem possible, but somehow she'd fallen in love with him. This wasn't like the childhood crushes she'd had on every man in her father's unit while growing up. This was love. Bishop gently caressed her chin while brushing his lips past hers. The look in his eyes and the firmness of his lap conveyed his intentions. She knew she should stop him, so he wouldn't get the wrong idea--even if it was what she really wanted. Certainly, she was entitled to one night of regret just like anyone else. He kissed her gently on the lips.

"Bishop," she heard herself softly protest.

She immediately wondered what was wrong with her. It was just one night. Lots of women did that sort of thing all the time. Why couldn't she? She cursed herself for being such a prude, and at the same time, praised herself for being so virtuous. As she wrestled with her emotions, Bishop looked into her eyes and offered a warm, sincere smile. She'd never seen that smile on him before.

"It's okay, Jetta," he said softly. "I'm not looking to seduce you."

She appeared surprised.

He seemed to hesitate then grinned timidly with an afterthought. "Well, maybe I am a little," he remarked with boyish charm then reestablished his seriousness. "I haven't been in a relationship for, well, a long time." He appeared to tense. "And when I say relationship; that includes all sexual activity. In fact, I haven't even asked anyone out in the nine months I've been in Winter Harbor. But I guess that's mostly because I figured you'd say no." There was a moment of silence, as he appeared to consider something. "Jetta, will you have dinner with me some evening?" he asked with a sincere smile on his face.

Jetta stared into his eyes a moment with surprise then smiled and nodded. "Yes, I'd love to."

Bishop appeared almost surprised then chuckled softly. "That was easier than I thought. Oh, and for the record," he indicated her on his lap. "I intend to keep you right where you are until the end of our shift."

She slipped her arms around his neck and laughed softly. "I'm actually quite comfortable," she replied simply. She allowed her hand to slide along his shoulder and to his chest. As she stared into his eyes, she couldn't deny her feelings any longer. "And as long as we're being honest with each other," Jetta said softly. "I'd like to reconsider that offer of sympathy sex."

Bishop appeared stunned, shifted sharply beneath her, and attempted to hide his lustful grin while acting casual. "Would it be wrong for me to throw you down on the sofa and rip your clothes off?"

Jetta casually indicated the zombies pressing against the doors. "I'd prefer someplace a little less crowded. I recommend waiting until after our shift."

"I suppose you're right," he replied while caressing her back and thigh. He could no longer control his grin. "I'd be willing to hold off on the ripping off of the clothing part, if you'd agree to me throwing you down on the sofa."

She looked at him with some surprise. A devious smile then crossed her face. "Okay."

Bishop suddenly groaned and tackled her to the sofa. She let out a playful scream as he landed on top of her.

Chapter Twenty-seven

It was just before dawn. The parking lot outside the tavern looked like a war zone with smashed cars, scattered zombie body parts, and several zombies lying on the ground attempting to pull themselves along with severely mangled legs. What was left of the sports car smoldered in several pieces on Millers Road with the remnants of a charbroiled man melted into the seat and steering wheel. The remaining survivors within the tavern stood near the back wall and stared at the bar with concerned looks on their weary faces. Hunter sat at the bar with a grenade and a cup of tea in front of him. Everyone watched and held their breath as he carelessly spun the grenade. It made a distinctive sound as it rolled around the top of the bar.

"Should we be concerned?" Palmer softly asked Desmond while closely watching the spinning grenade.

Desmond's eyes were wide with fear. "Oh, yeah--"

He patted Palmer's shoulder, gathered his courage, and approached Hunter while he spun the grenade and casually sipped his tea.

"Hunter--"

Hunter's mood was cold, and he didn't bother looking at Desmond. He just stared at the grenade. "Where's Jetta?" he demanded to know in a low tone.

"We're going to find her, Hunter," Desmond insisted and attempted to sound reassuring. "Remember our mission? We're going to liberate the school and then the hotel. That's where we'll find Jetta."

"You don't know where she is, do you?"

Desmond uncertainly eyed the grenade then looked back at Hunter. "She took Deputy Styles to the hotel. She's there. We need you, Hunter. We need you to hold on to every shred of reality you have for Jetta's sake."

"Is she dead?" he asked calmly.

"No, she's not dead."

"She is!" Hunter suddenly lashed out while glaring at Desmond with the look of a demon in his eyes. He appeared wildly unpredictable. "You're lying to me!"

"Oh, crap--" Palmer muttered.

Fei Yen looked at Sheriff Palmer then tugged on Ming's pants leg. "Mommy, he said a bad word."

Ming clung to Fei Yen, who stood by her legs, and continued to stare at Hunter along with everyone else.

"If he loses it, we're all screwed," Palmer said softly although more to himself.

Ming appeared to consider the situation then picked up Fei Yen and handed her to Palmer. Palmer took the child with some surprise and watched Ming head toward the bar. She paused behind Desmond.

"Hunter--"

Hunter looked at Ming just past Desmond and his charming smile suddenly returned. He wondered why such a beautiful woman looked so distressed. He'd get to the bottom of that as soon as he was finished interrogating Desmond.

"Good morning, Ming. How's your arm?"

"A little sore," she replied then indicated the grenade. "May I have that?"

Hunter uncertainly glanced at the grenade in his hand then looked back at Ming. It was the strangest request he'd ever gotten from an attractive woman.

"Why do you want it?"

"Because you're scaring me."

Hunter stared at Ming with some surprise. He uncertainly looked at the grenade in his hand then back at Ming. He was the reason she looked so concerned? How was that even possible? He'd never hurt her. Surely she knew that.

"You don't need to be afraid of me," he said gently and smiled at her. "I've never blown up anything without purposeful intent--not even myself."

She appeared surprised by his comment. "You blew up yourself on purpose?"

"Someone had to manually detonate the bomb, and since it was my bomb--" Hunter smiled gently. "It was the only way to save my men." Hunter placed the grenade in his pocket, showed her his empty hands, and smiled. "Better?"

"Yes, thank you," Ming said.

Everyone relaxed. Palmer approached Desmond while still holding Fei Yen, who played with the sheriff's badge on his bloodstained uniform. Hunter spoke Chinese to Ming. She appeared surprised, smiled her delight, and responded back in Chinese. Both laughed.

"He speaks Chinese?" Palmer asked Desmond with apparent surprise.

"He may seem borderline, Sheriff, but he's smarter than you and me put together," Desmond informed him.

"Of course he is," Palmer muttered. "Why wouldn't he be?" Sheriff Palmer eyed Fei Yen in his arms and appeared curious. "Do you know what they're saying?"

"He likes her hair," she replied.

"Great, he's hooking up," Palmer scoffed then looked at Desmond. "Get the Casanova to share the plan. It's going to be light soon."

"He seems to be enjoying himself," Desmond remarked gently. "Maybe we shouldn't interrupt them."

"Ming!" Palmer called out with a devious look on his face. "Fei Yen needs to use the potty!"

"No, I don't," she protested.

Ming and Hunter exchanged a few more words in Chinese while smiling. Ming said something, kissed his cheek, and then returned to Palmer and Fei Yen.

"Mommy, the sheriff told a lie," Fei Yen firmly said to her mother.

Palmer handed Fei Yen to Ming. "No one likes a tattle tale, kid."

"It's nearly sunup, Hunter," Desmond informed him. "What's our plan of attack for the school?"

Hunter shrugged with little interest and shook his head. "That's your department. I just blow up things. You're in charge, remember?"

Desmond and Palmer exchanged looks and groaned. Palmer's disgust was quickly returning. Perhaps it was just from lack of caffeine.

"Yes, of course I'm in charge," Desmond muttered. "Why wouldn't I be?" He studied Hunter and took a more firm stance. "What was the plan I'd told you?"

"You said we needed trucks with radios, drivers, and shooters. Our best shooters, you, me, Palmer, Wayne, Edwin, Kyle, and Dirk, will be on the front lines."

"Yes, that's the plan," Desmond replied with a sigh of relief. "Why don't you relay that to the men for me?"

Hunter stared at Desmond with disappointment and slowly shook his head. "How on earth did you become an admiral?"

"I honestly have no clue."

"College boys," Hunter scoffed then casually sipped his tea.

✝

*P*redawn light entered the guestroom through a part in the heavy curtains, providing dim lighting within the room. Bishop and Jetta kissed passionately and aggressively while firmly groping each other beneath the covers. Jetta clung to Bishop as he firmly and rhythmically moved against her. She moaned her pleasure. He was panting heavily between kisses then moved more aggressively against her. He gasped then groaned lowly as his body relaxed on top of hers beneath the sheets. He attempted to control his heavy breathing then looked into her eyes while grinning.

"You lied," he teased softly while panting. "There's no way you're a virgin."

"Well, not anymore," she replied with a soft laugh.

Bishop chuckled, moved off her, and collapsed on the bed alongside her. He pulled her into his arms, and she rested her head against his chest. She was pleasantly mussed. Bishop was nearly exhausted and still breathed heavily. He looked at her as she lie against his chest and remained curious.

"You weren't, were you?"

She lifted her head, met his gaze, and remained bewildered. "Weren't what?"

He smiled timidly and fidgeted. "You know--a virgin."

Jetta lifted herself onto her elbow and looked into his eyes with all seriousness. "There have been a couple of minor indiscretions with a few overzealous Navy Seals over the years, but my virginity was never compromised."

Bishop appeared surprised then looked oddly puzzled. "Okay, I'm going to lead with 'holy shit, my first virgin' then follow-up with

175

'can you elaborate on minor indiscretions'," he teased with a devious grin on his face.

"Call me old-fashioned, but maybe we should save something for our first date," she remarked while grinning and returned her head to his chest.

He gently caressed her shoulder and hid his smile. "Never mind. I'll just leave it to my imagination."

Jetta laughed softly and nuzzled his chest.

"I had a crazy thought," Bishop announced.

"Crazier than running through a parking lot full of zombies?" she teased.

"Why don't we stay in bed the entire day and roll around naked instead of that *other* thing we intended to do?"

"Or--we could take a shower and then follow through with the original plan," Jetta said simply.

Bishop playfully grinned. "You mean the one where I knock you up, so you're stuck with me forever?"

"I don't recall that particular plan."

"Yeah, I was sort of saving that one in case you ever got drunk at the tavern again," Bishop teased.

"Let's stick with the one where we wipe out every last zombie without getting ourselves killed. Afterwards, you can do whatever you want to me for as long as you want. Deal?"

Bishop appeared interested and looked at her in his arms. "Can I get that in writing?"

Chapter Twenty-eight

The sunrise was warm and inviting throughout the town of Winter Harbor. It was a beautiful fall day and the birds were singing. A gentle breeze blew warmly past--the hundreds of zombies surrounding the high school. They pounded on doors and windows while attempting to get inside. Hanson and Dixon stood in the alcove and watched more than fifty zombies attempting to get in through the front doors. The zombies looked less human now as their flesh continued to decompose.

"Decomposition is a bitch, eh?" Dixon remarked while grimacing at the zombies outside the doors.

"Found a few bodies working NYPD over the years," Hanson informed Dixon. "I thought they were gruesome, but even they didn't look quite this bad."

"Maybe because they weren't walking around trying to bite your ass," Dixon teased and studied the horde of zombies outside the doors. He suddenly appeared interested. "Hey, I think I know that woman."

"Unfortunately, you probably know most of them," Hanson said sadly.

"How many do you suppose--you know?"

Hanson shrugged. "Hard to say. There's probably two hundred or more surrounding the school. Who knows how many others are around town and elsewhere."

Dixon moved closer to the gate across the doors and studied the glass. A small crack was noticeable. He frowned and shook his head with disgust.

"I think we overestimated the strength of the glass," Dixon muttered.

"It's only a small crack," Hanson remarked. "It'll hold."

"I hope so." Dixon looked past the zombies and into the parking lot. Something caught his attention. "Son-of-a-bitch! I don't believe it."

"What?" Hanson asked and strained to see past the crowd of zombies.

"There are survivors on the school bus in the parking lot!" He suddenly laughed. "I'll be damned. Look, they're waving at me." Dixon grinned and waved back.

Nearly thirty or more zombies crowded the school bus near the far end of the lot and attempted to get inside. The survivors on the bus attempted to stay away from the windows.

"I don't think they can get inside the bus, but those people won't last very long without water," Hanson announced. "We have to think of a way to get to them."

"Might be a problem," Dixon informed him. "Maybe you haven't noticed the wall of zombies outside the door."

"If we could find the science labs, maybe there's enough chemicals--"

Remy hurried into the alcove and appeared excited. "I just got word over the radio. They're coming!"

Both men looked at her with bewilderment.

"Who's coming?" Dixon asked.

"Sheriff Palmer," she said while excitedly running for the gate before the glass doors. "All he said was 'it's going to get really loud'."

The sounds of approaching pick-up trucks could be heard speeding through the parking lot. All three pressed up against the metal gate despite the hungry zombies attempting to break through the glass to reach them. An explosion rocked the building, rattled the windows, and vibrated the metal gate. Several zombies were blown apart while being thrown through the air on fire. It rained down flaming zombie parts. Remy looked at both men and grinned with enthusiasm.

"Boys, the Cavalry has arrived."

One of the zombies pounded on the crack in the glass. The glass shattered, leaving a large, twelve-inch hole. Both men jumped, and Remy let out a startled scream. They moved away from the metal gate and watched as the zombies reached through the hole in the glass for them. Their decaying flesh was shredded against the jagged glass, but it didn't deter them. All three appeared alarmed. As the trucks continued to race through the parking lot, the sound of gunfire was heard. A majority of the zombies left the alcove doors and opted for the moving trucks. Remy, Hanson, and Dixon appeared relieved.

✝

*S*tyles and Doc stood on the terrace on the third floor of the hotel and looked at the parking lot below. A dozen or more zombies aimlessly roamed the lot. They seemed clueless and without purpose. A box filled with crudely made explosives in glass bottles sat on the floor alongside Styles and Doc. Styles painfully leaned against the wall and indicated several cars throughout the lot.

"I think I can make the first two cars Bishop has on the list, but I don't know about the third."

"Tyler has a good throwing arm," Doc announced. "They also have a better position from the sunroom. We'll just take out what we can."

"They seem to be everywhere," Styles said softly. "How many people do you think were infected?"

"I'm afraid to even guess," he replied. "I prefer being up here to do this. I won't have to see their faces. I don't want to personalize it in any way."

"I know what you mean," Styles said with a sigh. "I haven't lived here long enough to know everyone personally, but I saw a lot of familiar faces outside those doors. People I've said hello to." He appeared tense. "I'm scared to death the next one I see will be Sheriff Palmer. I know he's a real pain in the ass, but he's the closest thing to a friend I've got in this town."

"Then you also know him well enough to know he can handle himself in just about any situation," Doc informed him. "Sort of like you."

"Me?" Styles said then laughed. "I was benched before the first down. If I'd been of any use, I wouldn't be laid up here; I'd be out there stopping these things."

"You are stopping these things," Doc protested. "This is an important thing we're doing today. And you may have been benched, but you survived an attack before you even knew there was a threat. It was your quick response that saved your life." Doc studied him a moment and appeared curious. "Did you know that Sheriff Palmer had over two hundred applicants applying for your position? Out of two hundred applicants, he chose you. That should tell you something."

"Yeah, my application was on the top of the pile, and he hadn't had his morning coffee yet," Styles teased.

"Hiring deputies isn't something he'd take lightly. There was a local boy among those who'd applied," Doc informed him. "Anyone else in town would have gone with the local boy. In fact, a lot of folks were pissed with Sheriff Palmer when they found out he didn't hire the local boy, but he stuck with his decision. People in town have accepted you as one of us. Typically, that takes years with hardheads like us."

"You really think people in town like me?"

"Of course they do," he replied then sank into thought. "Although, I'm sure there are a lot of fathers out there wishing their teenage daughters didn't like you quite so much."

Styles hid his smile and laughed softly. Bishop's voice was heard over the handheld radio alongside them.

"You in position?" Bishop asked over the radio.

Styles picked up the handheld radio and spoke into it. "Yeah, Bishop. Doc and I are in position. Over."

†

*A*t the same time in the sunroom, Rafael, Tyler, and Carter stood before the large windows on the second floor. They stared at the parking lot below. Rafael and Tyler exchanged bewildered looks. Rafael appeared concerned and spoke into his handheld radio.

"Yo, dude, these windows don't open," Rafael announced to Bishop.

"So? Open them," came Bishop's response.

Rafael and Tyler eyed each other, casually shrugged, and then approached a heavy wall table. Carter jumped into their path and stopped them.

"Don't you dare!"

Neither man was impressed.

"Dude, either move out of the way or go out the window," Rafael remarked with a serious look in his eyes. "Your choice."

Carter stared at them a moment, realized they were serious, and moved out of the way. Rafael and Tyler threw the heavy table through the large window. Carter cringed as the table shattered the glass and crashed to the parking lot below.

"Window is open," Rafael cheerfully announced into the hand radio while grinning. "We're in position."

Tyler looked out the large opening in the broken window. A male zombie writhed beneath the heavy table, which had successfully crushed him from the waist down.

"Nice shot," Tyler announced with an approving nod. "That's one down."

"Yeah, about a million to go," Rafael remarked then looked out the window as well.

The zombie clawed at the pavement while pinned beneath the table. His upper half tore free, and he inched his way along the pavement by his fingers. Rafael and Tyler made faces and exchanged looks.

"I could have lived the rest of my life without seeing that," Rafael remarked.

"Yeah, but you have to admire his determination," Tyler replied with all seriousness.

Carter and Rafael looked at Tyler with their mouths hanging open. Tyler grinned and chuckled.

†

*W*ithin the kitchen, Jetta and Bishop stood by the back door with Lee and Stacy. Neither woman looked particularly enthusiastic. Jetta wore Deputy Styles' gun holster in preparation to their zombie run. Stacy stared out the small window to the parking lot and what she saw clearly stressed her. Lee handed Jetta the keys to her car dangling on a pink keychain in the shape of a shoe.

"My car is out of the fire zone," Lee announced.

"There are about a dozen zombies outside the door," Stacy informed them.

"We need a diversion," Jetta announced. She was now feeling nervous and apprehensive about confronting the zombies on their home field.

"Got you covered," Lee replied and held up a second set of keys. "When I push this button, my father's car alarm will go off. If it's true that sound attracts them, it should lead them right to his car. My car is in the opposite direction of his."

Jetta nervously nodded then looked at Bishop. He offered a reassuring smile and removed the gun from his shoulder holster beneath his jacket.

"On your mark--"

Jetta removed the gun from her holster, returned the smile, and nodded. Lee pressed the car alarm button.

The expensive car's lights flashed as the horn loudly sounded. Zombies were quickly alerted to the sound, left the kitchen door, and headed toward the beckoning car. Styles and Doc looked over the wall with their bombs and watched the parking lot below. Several zombies collected around Carter's car while pawing and pounding on the windows.

"We're ready to deploy--now!" Doc said into his radio.

Styles and Doc lit the cloth wicks on the homemade bombs and cast them into the lot below. Bombs from both locations shattered against predetermined cars, including Carter's, causing them to ignite and then explode. Several zombies were blown up along with the cars and scattered across the parking lot.

"My car!" Carter was heard shouting.

Two more sets of bombs flew from the building and struck other cars with explosions that took out more zombies. Jetta and Bishop ran from the kitchen and shot at the remaining zombies while running for Lee's car. The parking lot was littered with exploded car and zombie parts. Jetta and Bishop reached Lee's tiny, pink car. As Jetta opened the passenger side door, a zombie suddenly appeared from behind the car and grabbed Bishop's arm. Bishop shot it in the head as it bit his arm. As the zombie collapsed, Bishop appeared stunned while staring at his arm. Jetta grabbed him and pulled him into the car with her. The car started and drove away at high speeds, plowing down a few zombies on the way through.

†

*T*he tiny, pink car raced toward the hanger at high speeds and skidded to a stop near the helicopter. A zombie lunged for the car. Jetta threw open the car door, striking the zombie with force, and casting it to the ground. Jetta jumped out of the car, shot the zombie in the head, and hurried for the helicopter. Bishop jumped out of the passenger side with his radio and gun and scanned the area while Jetta prepped the helicopter.

"Zombie, ten o'clock, Bishop," Rafael's voice was heard over the radio.

Bishop immediately turned, saw the zombie approaching the helicopter, and shot it in the head. The helicopter revved and the rotors spun. Bishop quickly jumped inside the helicopter and subconsciously rubbed his arm. Jetta was about to lift off when she saw his torn jacket and noticed him rubbing his forearm. Horror suddenly swept over her.

"Were you bit?"

Bishop snorted a soft laugh and removed his hand from his lower arm. His jacket was torn, but there was no damage to his shirt beneath.

"No, but they ruined a perfectly good jacket," he replied then shook his head with a soft groan. "That was way too close for my comfort."

Jetta appeared relieved. Both laughed softly. As the helicopter lifted from the pad, distant explosions were heard from across town. Both appeared surprised and looked outside the helicopter. There weren't any visible sign of explosions near them.

"Did you hear that?" Jetta asked.

"It sounded like it came from the school," he replied.

Chapter Twenty-nine

Cars exploded throughout the nearly filled high school parking lot. Several pick-up trucks raced through the parking lot with men firing out the back and through windows. The zombies abandoned the entrances and attempted to reach the speeding trucks. More zombies appeared from other areas of the building and throughout the parking lot. Desmond drove the red pick-up truck while Palmer shot from the passenger side window. Hunter sat in the back and fired from the tailgate. Jetta's helicopter could be heard approaching in the near distance. All three looked to the sky. Hunter grinned and chuckled. He knew that sound and what it meant. His little girl was coming for him. The helicopter flew across town at top speeds.

"It's Jetta!" Desmond cried out excitedly and grabbed the truck's radio. "Jetta! Jetta! You there?"

"Desmond, you bastard! Where are you?" came Jetta's enthusiastic reply over the radio.

"The red truck with Hunter in the back--" Desmond eyed Hunter in the back of the truck. "--waving at you."

The red truck abruptly stopped in the parking lot. Hunter sprang onto the roof of the truck and slung his rifle over his shoulder as the helicopter lowered above them. He jumped onto the rung and quickly climbed into the helicopter. The helicopter lifted and the truck raced across the parking lot. Hunter grabbed Jetta from behind while she concentrated on flying and kissed her. Jetta smiled and was overjoyed to see him. She somehow knew he'd survive. His look turned serious.

"Next time I tell you I see zombies, you may want to believe me," Hunter firmly lectured her.

"Rub it in all you want, I'm just happy you're alive," she replied while chuckling.

"Of course I'm alive," he remarked simply. "Hell rejected me once already. They certainly don't want me back."

"We're breaking off and running an assault on the hotel," Desmond was heard over the radio. "The rest of you finish this here."

†

*T*he helicopter flew across town while heading toward the hotel. Winter Harbor residents flocked onto rooftops and waved at the passing helicopter, signaling their location for possible rescue, and indicating where they were trapped since the attack. Hunter mowed down several zombies on Main Street with a barrage of bullets. The red and silver trucks raced down Main Street behind the helicopter and shooters within the trucks took out several more zombies. Residents waved from second story windows and cheered as they passed. The helicopter approached the hotel with the red and silver trucks following in the distance along the resort's road. The helicopter lowered to a van a safe distance from the lobby parking lot entrance, where a massive number of zombies had collected and attempted to get inside. Hunter jumped onto the van roof with a rope tied to the helicopter. He shot out the sunroof as the helicopter hovered then stomped on the roof to attract attention. He had already gotten the attention of several zombies.

"Fresh meat! Come and get it!"

The zombies began their approach. Hunter casually lit his cigar and sat on the van roof. As the zombies approached the van, the lobby door was left nearly vacant. Elise was visible on the other side of the doors while watching the battle. When the horde of zombies were just about on top of the van, Hunter casually stood, placed his foot in a loop in the rope, and signaled to Jetta in the helicopter. As the helicopter lifted him from the van, he dropped a grenade through the broken sunroof. The helicopter flew away with Hunter lazily dangling from the rope. The van exploded and took a dozen zombies with it. The red truck was speeding in Hunter's direction toward the hotel. Desmond and Palmer looked out the windshield at Hunter hanging from his rope directly in front of them. Hunter grinned and waved at them as he just barely cleared the truck. The silver truck

185

broke formation, picked up speed near the lobby entrance, and plowed through three zombies. All three zombies were thrown across the truck's hood. One crashed through the windshield.

Zombie Herb, who was sticking through the windshield, grabbed Dirk and bit him in the face. Dirk cried out while attempting to stop the zombie from tearing into his flesh and slammed on the brakes. Kyle, sitting next to him in the passenger seat, tossed his rifle aside and grabbed his handgun. As Dirk struggled against the zombie attached to his face, his foot slipped off the brake and onto the gas. The truck picked up speed. Elise stood before the lobby doors and watched with horror as the silver truck rocketed toward her and the doors with a zombie stuck through the windshield and another clinging to the hood. Gunshots were heard from inside the truck. Elise screamed and ran from the entrance as the truck plowed through several zombies and crashed through the glass doors into the lobby.

The helicopter hovered just outside the hotel. From their position within the helicopter, Jetta and Bishop stared at the shattered lobby entrance in horror. Hunter climbed the rope and joined them. He too had seen the catastrophe unfold.

"The lobby has been compromised," Bishop shouted into the hand radio to alert those inside the hotel. "Get everyone to second. Seal the stairs!"

"Stacy and I are going to get the others," Lee was heard over the radio. "We'll take the locked out elevator"

"Copy!" Doc was heard yelling into the radio. "We're locking the stairs!"

"Desmond," Bishop said into the radio, "we're going in from the roof. Do what you can to secure that opening."

"Copy."

"Take me down," Hunter ordered. "I'm going in."

"What? No!" Jetta protested.

"Those are my men down there! You need to trust me!" Hunter yelled back then appeared serious and calm. "For once, Jetta, have a little faith in me."

Jetta hesitated a moment, cursed softly, and lowered the helicopter near the driveway entrance. Hunter kissed her and jumped out the side and to the ground. Hunter ran for the silver truck in the shattered lobby opening. The red truck skidded to a halt near Hunter. Desmond and Palmer joined him. They shot several zombies between them and the opening created by the truck in the hotel lobby. There was no telling how many zombies had already gotten in through the massive opening. Within the hotel, Lee, Stacy, Colleen, and seven others ran for the elevator then stopped to stare at the smashed truck within the lobby. Elise appeared seemingly out of nowhere and ran past them. She entered the locked out elevator and pressed the button. The elevator doors closed as Stacy watched in horror.

"The elevator!" Stacy cried out.

The silver truck door suddenly opened. Kyle jumped out while holding his bleeding neck, stumbled several feet, and fell to the floor. Zombie Herb fell out of the truck behind him. Kyle seized and thrashed a moment, became still, and then moved to his feet with the same dead look in his eyes. Two zombies crawled out from beneath the truck and stumbled to their feet. Both appeared mangled but managed to walk. Dirk, now a zombie, fell out of the truck as well. Despite the encouraging sound of gunfire just beyond the shattered lobby doors, it was unlikely they'd make it in time to stop the approaching zombies. Lee pushed the others toward the elevator and frantically pressed the button. The elevator wasn't returning, and soon it would be too late. She hurried them away from the elevators.

"The stairs! Go!" Lee cried out.

Lee, Stacy, Colleen, and two other guests ran for the stairs. The other five remained by the elevator in hopes it would soon arrive. As several zombies approached them, the five screamed and ran down the hall. More zombies headed for the stairs toward Lee's group. Lee attempted to open the door. It was locked!

"Guys!" Lee shouted into the radio. "We're trapped! Unlock the beach stairs!"

"We're on our way! Hold tight!" came Rafael's response.

They watched in horror as the zombies approached. There was no place left to run. Colleen attempted to run from the area by the stairs and collided with zombie Herb in the hallway. She screamed as she was tackled to the floor. She thrashed against the zombie as he bit her hands then lunged for her face. She screamed as he tore into her cheek. The remaining zombies closed in on Lee and the others by the stairwell door. All four appeared horrified, realizing they had nowhere to run and stared helplessly as zombie Herb tore into the screaming Colleen. Lee suddenly backed against the door and stared with horror as zombie Glenn approached them. In her mind, it was almost as if karma was getting even with her. For the way she'd treated them, all of them, perhaps this was her punishment. The sound of gunfire was heard loudly from close by. Hunter suddenly appeared and shot zombie Herb while he ate Colleen's face. Palmer and Desmond charged for the zombies nearly upon the four women by the stairwell door.

"Watch your fire!" Palmer yelled.

Zombie Glenn was nearly upon Lee. She stared at him and held back her scream as he snarled and lunged for her. Desmond suddenly struck zombie Glenn with his rifle, surprising Lee, and then safely shot him in the head when he had a clean shot. A zombie grabbed Desmond from behind and attempted to bite his shoulder. Lee screamed with horror. Desmond rammed his rifle backwards into the zombie's midsection then turned and struck it in the face with the rifle. He shot the zombie in the head as it fell. Palmer struck one repeatedly with his rifle before shooting it as it writhed on the floor. Hunter spun into a high, roundhouse kick and struck the remaining zombie in the head. Lee watched in amazement as the zombie was thrown to the floor. Without missing a beat, Hunter straightened from his spinning kick, skillfully flipped the assault rifle in his hands, and shot the zombie in the head.

Lee stared at Hunter with her mouth hanging open. "My God," she gasped softly to herself. "He is a hero."

The fire door suddenly opened to reveal Rafael. All four women dived into the safety of the stairway. Palmer and Desmond ran after the other zombies. Colleen lie on the floor with half her face torn away. She twitched slightly. Hunter followed the others and casually shot Colleen in the head as he passed. The elevator door shut as the three men approached. They looked at one another with shared concern.

"What are the chances one of them hitched a ride?" Palmer asked.

"It stopped on second. I've got it!" Desmond informed them and ran for the stairs.

"Guard that opening, Sargent," Hunter ordered to Palmer. "I'll go after the other two."

Palmer nodded and returned to the lobby entrance.

†

Lee, Stacy, and the two other women ran out of the stairway door and hurried along the second floor hallway toward the sunroom. Stacy was nearly down to tears and fell behind. Lee saw her stop and hurried back for her. The other two women stopped and looked back at them. Lee motioned them on.

"The sunroom is just down the hall," Lee informed them then looked back at Stacy. "Stacy, we're okay now. Let's get to the sunroom. You'll feel safer there."

Stacy uncertainly nodded and collected herself. Lee pulled her along the hallway several feet behind the two other women. As the other women passed the elevator, it dinged, and the doors opened. Lee suddenly stopped Stacy. Zombie Dirk lunged from the elevator and tackled one of the women to the hall floor. The second woman screamed and ran down the hall for the sunroom. Lee pushed Stacy against the wall and grabbed the nearby fire extinguisher. She ran for zombie Dirk, preparing to strike him on the head as he tore into the woman's throat, when zombie Kyle appeared from the elevator and tackled her into the wall. Lee's head struck the wall, dazing her. Kyle lunged for her throat. Lee opened her eyes in time to see zombie Kyle's teeth coming at her. She was about to scream when the handheld radio was shoved into his mouth. Kyle released Lee and struggled to remove the radio. Stacy grabbed Lee's hand and pulled her back down the hall toward the stairwell.

Chapter Thirty

*J*etta and Bishop ran down the stairs with both duffel bags filled with weapons. As they neared the second floor, groaning was heard. Both stopped, raised their guns, and waited. Rafael appeared on the steps while panting. He saw them, suddenly gasped, and held his hands up.

"Don't shoot! I'm out of shape--not a zombie!"

They relaxed and lowered their weapons.

"The others are on second," Rafael panted while leaning heavily on the railing. He appeared unable to continue. "The guys are rounding up the rest on first."

Thundering footfalls were heard on the stairs. Jetta and Bishop again raised their weapons. Desmond appeared on the stairs, cried out, and aimed his assault rifle at them. All three appeared relieved and relaxed.

"One may have gotten on the elevator," he informed them with concern.

All four hurried into the second floor hallway with Rafael bringing up the rear from further behind. Lee and Stacy collided with Jetta, knocking her into Bishop, and taking all four to the floor. Zombie Kyle appeared around the corner and lunged for them. Desmond cried out with alarm and fired several shots into Kyle. He was thrown back into the opposing wall from the body shots then straightened, snarled, and again lunged for them.

"Sorry, buddy," Desmond said gently and pulled the trigger.

The bullet struck zombie Kyle in the forehead and exploded out the back, taking most of his head with it.

"There's another," Stacy gasped as she helped Jetta pull Lee to her feet.

They hurried along the hall toward the elevator to see zombie Dirk, with most of his face eaten, tearing flesh from the still thrashing woman's face. She continued to struggle despite the large amount of her blood spilling onto the floor.

"Dirk!" Desmond cried out.

Zombie Dirk turned to reveal blood down his fleshless face. He released the squirming woman and moved to his feet while facing them and snarling. Desmond frowned with disgust and shot Dirk in the head. He dropped to the floor. Rafael finally appeared in the hallway behind them as they approached the gasping and groaning woman. Jetta showed little emotion as she shot her in the head. Rafael jumped with surprise.

"Dude--"

They hurried past the scene of carnage and entered the sunroom. Doc, Styles, Tyler, and Carter approached them from their position at the broken window. Stacy helped Lee to one of the sofas in the area where Elise and four other guests quietly sat. Lee held her head and still appeared slightly dazed from a possible concussion. Stacy glared at Elise, who refused to look at them. Bishop and Jetta tossed their bags onto a coffee table.

"Hand these out," Jetta said to Desmond then looked at Bishop. "We need to add air assault at the school and try to take out as many as possible."

"Do you want me to come along?" Desmond asked while passing out assault rifles and ammunition.

"No, you stay here, Desmond. I'll take Hunter," Jetta quickly informed him. "He's amazingly accurate firing out of moving helicopters."

Bishop grabbed a rifle and some extra clips for himself.

Desmond rummaged through the bag and removed the rocket launcher. "Better take this," he said while tossing Jetta the rocket launcher then smiled deviously. "Hunter will want that."

Jetta grinned her response. She was sure he would. She nudged Bishop, and both ran from the sunroom. Desmond showed Doc, Styles, and Carter how to load the assault rifles. Tyler seemed to figure it out on his own with minimal instruction. While they loaded the weapons, Stacy could be heard shouting. All five looked across the room. Stacy was on her feet and stood before Elise, who just stared at her with a dumbfounded look.

"It's your fault those women died!" Stacy shouted in anger. "You cowardly bitch! You left us there!"

"I'm still your boss," Elise remarked lowly, but she didn't appear to have much fight left in her.

"I don't give a shit who you are," Stacy continued her rant. "You nearly got Lee killed when you stole our only escape route! How many friends do you think I have? I can't afford to lose any! You're lucky I don't punch your teeth down your throat!"

"Stacy," Lee said softly. "Let it go. It's not worth it."

Stacy attempted to relax then turned and approached Desmond. She indicated the arsenal of weapons.

"Can I have one of those?"

"If you promise to only shoot zombies with it," Desmond remarked with a look of distrust to the once meek woman.

She snorted a soft laugh and extended her hand. It wasn't really a promise. He uncertainly handed her a semiautomatic. She cocked the gun without instruction, causing all five men to jump, and walked across the sunroom. They held their breath as she approached Elise on the sofa. Stacy continued past her and toward the broken sunroom window. There were several relieved sighs.

"Damn," Tyler said softly. "I was sort of hoping she'd shoot Elise's ass."

"Normally I'd agree with you," Desmond replied, "but I think we've had enough of that. We need to concentrate on killing just the zombies."

✝

*T*he lounge appeared quiet. Dirty glasses and empty bottles remained on top of the bar and on several tables throughout the room. Zombie Pam and a male zombie stumbled around the room. They sniffed the air and looked around as if attempting to find something. Three of the five women who had scattered from the elevator crouched behind the bar and listened to the zombies walking into tables, bumping into chairs, and knocking over empty glasses. The first woman removed a fancy corkscrew and clung to it. She indicated the lounge entrance to the others with her eyes. They uncertainly nodded. She moved to the opening behind the bar closest to the entrance while remaining close to the floor and looked across the lounge. She watched the two zombies fumbling around with no particular purpose. She motioned for the other women to make their run. All three darted out from behind the bar and ran for the entrance.

A third zombie, zombie Dennis, suddenly appeared in the doorway. The first woman screamed and ducked as he grabbed for her. The second woman ran from the lounge. As the third woman attempted to follow, Dennis lunged for her and knocked her backward onto one of the tables. She screamed while attempting to keep him from biting her. The first woman saw the other two zombies closing in. Instead of running while she still had a chance to escape, she ran for zombie Dennis on top of the third woman and stabbed him in the head with the corkscrew. The woman beneath the zombie screamed. Dennis straightened with the corkscrew still in his head and spun toward the first woman. The third woman ran for the entrance as zombie Pam and the other zombie charged the first woman. Zombie Dennis, with the corkscrew in his head, snarled and grabbed her shoulders.

The butt of an assault rifle was rammed into the corkscrew, driving it deep into the zombie's head. Dennis' eyes rolled back as he released the woman and fell to the floor. She spun to see Hunter holding the assault rifle. His gaze was fixated on the two quickly approaching zombies.

"You should probably leave," Hunter informed her. "This could get a little messy."

The woman gave him a bewildered look, appeared alarmed, and ran from the lounge. As the zombies approached Hunter, he raised his assault rifle and pulled the trigger. It clicked. Nothing happened. That was impossible! He knew his ammunition count. How could he be empty? Zombie Pam and the male zombie were nearly on top of him now. He removed his Bowie knife from his boot, spun into a roundhouse kick, and kicked the male zombie in the chest. The zombie was knocked back several feet. Hunter went for the return kick and struck Pam in the head. As the male zombie regained his balance and came for him, Hunter threw the knife. The knife was impaled through the zombie's eye, stopping him in his tracks. He dropped to the floor. Zombie Pam lunged for Hunter. He grabbed her by the head and swiftly broke her neck. He reclaimed his Bowie knife and grimaced at the zombie's eye dangling from the blade. He wished he could say that was the most gruesome thing he'd ever seen, but sadly, he'd seen worse. He wiped the gooey remnants onto the dead zombie's shirt and replaced the knife to his boot. He removed his cigar and casually lit it.

t

*P*almer stood by the back of the smashed silver truck within the lobby and kept watch out the opening with his assault rifle aimed. Several zombies lie dead in the opening not far from him, indicating he'd done a good job at keeping the lobby opening secure. A mangled zombie crawled out from under the truck several feet behind him. One of its legs was missing and its torso was only held on by its intestines. Palmer fired at a zombie several feet outside the hotel and appeared unaware of the zombie crawling toward him. The zombie reached for Palmer's cowboy boot. Palmer casually turned with his revolver now in his hand and shot the zombie in the head. He holstered his revolver and resumed shooting zombies outside with the assault rifle. The elevator doors opened to reveal Jetta and Bishop carrying several weapons. Palmer eyed them then shot an approaching zombie.

"You okay here?" Jetta asked.

"Got it under control," he replied.

"Have you seen Hunter?"

"Nope, but I heard a commotion in the lounge," Palmer replied then grinned. "The damned bastard's enjoying himself a little too much."

Jetta and Bishop ran down the corridor and approached the lounge. They cautiously entered with their rifles raised. Hunter casually sat on the bar with the two dead zombies by his feet and puffed on his cigar. He eyed Jetta and grinned.

"Did I tell you I have a date?" Hunter asked.

"A date, huh?" Jetta said with a smile. She wondered if it was a real date or an imagined one. "I'm jealous. You can tell me all about it once we're airborne."

Hunter suddenly appeared excited and jumped off the bar. "Can I fly?" he asked while grinning.

"Not even on your best day," she grumbled.

Hunter appeared to pout while approaching them and the doorway. "I was flying before you were even born," he said firmly. "I'm an excellent pilot."

"Is that so? I heard you crashed three out of four times," Jetta remarked.

"It was only two times," he stated flatly while following them from the lounge, then muttered, "--out of three."

t

*D*esmond, Tyler, Styles, Rafael, and Stacy fired their weapons from the broken sunroom window while Doc and Carter kept watch on the hallway entrance. Stacy was surprisingly accurate with her shots. Tyler glanced at her several times between his own shots and grinned.

"I never knew you could be such a badass," Tyler remarked while grinning.

Stacy glanced at him, considered the comment, and smiled in response.

"Would you ever consider going out with me?" he asked.

She looked at him and attempted to hide her surprise. She flashed a smile and shrugged. "I may be interested."

Tyler grinned and resumed shooting from the window. Stacy smiled to herself. She'd finally gotten her date with a handsome, somewhat decent guy. Lee sat on the sofa not far from Elise, who slept in the corner. Lee held her aching head and watched the four men and Stacy firing out the window then looked at the four guests. They clung to one another while sitting on two other sofas not far from her. The four guests looked worried but more relaxed now that they felt safe for the moment. Lee glanced at Elise. It seemed odd that she could sleep with all the gunfire coming from the nearby window. She studied her a moment longer then uncertainly moved closer to her on the sofa.

"Elise?"

Lee gently nudged her shoulder. She saw a small amount of blood on Elise's hand. Almost everyone had blood on them by this point. Even Lee had blood on her arms, hands, and pink sneakers. Lee appeared curious and gently turned Elise's hand over. The bite mark glared back at her. It was small, but a bite all the same. Lee gasped and jumped up from the sofa as Elise turned her head to reveal dead eyes. She snarled at Lee and lunged for her. Lee screamed as zombie Elise tackled her to the floor. Desmond turned away from the window, saw them on the floor together, and ran for Lee. Zombie Elise had her teeth close to Lee's face. Desmond kicked Elise off her. Elise fell to the floor then sprang to her feet while snarling at Desmond. Desmond raised his rifle and shot her through her eye. As zombie Elise dropped to the floor, Desmond knelt alongside Lee and checked her for injuries.

"Are you okay?" he asked with concern in his voice. "Did she bite you?"

Lee stared at Desmond a moment as if unable to speak then slowly shook her head. He appeared relieved and rubbed her shoulders.

"That's a relief--"

Lee suddenly threw her arms around his neck, startling him, and kissed him passionately on the mouth. She pulled away before he had a chance to react. As he stared into her eyes, she smiled at him in a way she had never smiled at him before.

He stared back at her and remained stunned. "Uh, you're welcome."

Chapter Thirty-one

*J*etta's helicopter hovered over the school parking lot as Bishop and Hunter rained bullets down upon the zombies. Men from the trucks now sat parked by the school and shot the remaining zombies. Wayne drove the white pick-up truck toward the school bus. Edwin jumped out the back while Wayne continued to shoot the few approaching zombies. The school bus doors opened. Edwin ushered the weary survivors out and into the back of the pick-up truck. Once they were loaded, the truck raced across the lot and to the front of the school where Dixon, Hanson, and Remy stood just outside the open doors while shooting zombies. Edwin helped the ten survivors from the bus off the back of the truck. Dixon hurried them inside.

More than a dozen brave survivors from the gym gathered in the alcove to watch the ensuing battle with the undead. It was a welcomed relief to know someone was doing something to ensure their survival. Tanner held the little girl in his arms as the survivors from the bus ran inside.

The little girl's face lit up as she screamed, "Mommy!"

One of the women from the bus looked across the alcove and saw Tanner holding her little girl. She was overjoyed while running for them.

"Lily!"

Tanner set the little girl down. She ran into her mother's awaiting arms. Her mother hugged her to the point of suffocating her. Tanner approached and smiled with satisfaction.

"Mommy, this is Tanner," she said. "He saved me from the bad people."

The little girl's mother looked at Tanner, sobbed softly, and hugged him. "Thank you, thank you so much."

"She's been very brave," Tanner informed the girl's mother then looked at the little girl. "Isn't that right, sunflower?"

The little girl smiled and nodded.

The battle ensued outside in the parking lot. A small herd of zombie football players, cheerleaders, and band members aggressively charged Wayne's truck. Wayne and Edwin shot as many as they could, but they kept coming at a rapid pace. Wayne attempted to start the truck, but it wouldn't turn over. Hunter disappeared from the back door of the helicopter then reappeared with the rocket launcher in his hands. A rocket whizzed from the helicopter and into the approaching zombies. The horde of zombies were blown to bits and body parts scattered across the parking lot, leaving a large crater in the pavement. Wayne and Edwin cried out with surprise and shielded themselves from the charred, fleshy body parts raining down upon them.

"Oh, yeah! I've got to get me one of these!" Hunter cried out with enthusiasm.

As Jetta's helicopter turned, it nearly collided with a military helicopter. Jetta veered her helicopter away from the massive, intimidating military helicopter and landed in the parking lot. Hunter, Bishop, and Jetta jumped out as the military helicopter lowered. Eight fully armed men leaped from the helicopter, stormed the parking lot, and immediately fired on the remaining zombies. The last man, Admiral Quinn Cross, stepped out and smiled at Jetta. The admiral was tall and built like a tank. His shaved head added to his intimidating appearance. Jetta stared at her father with surprise then became excited.

"Dad!"

Jetta ran to Quinn and jumped into his arms. He held her in his arms and appeared reluctant to release her. Jetta pulled away and stared at her father. How did he know to come and rescue her? He had his ways, but this was too amazing.

"But how--? The lines were down," she announced. "How did you know we were in trouble?"

"I got your message about a problem," he replied while grinning. "When I couldn't reach you, I poked around, learned a thing or two, and deployed the men."

"That call was before the real problem even began," she said then laughed. "But I'm glad you're a man of action."

Hunter approached Quinn, grinned with the cigar between his teeth, and saluted him. Quinn stared at Hunter with a cheerful grin, but the look in his eyes conveyed his concern about the condition of his friend.

"Oh, wow, he's really fighting the war this time," Quinn said softly to Jetta then gave a return salute to Hunter. He indicated the nearby crater from the rocket launcher. "Captain, I'd recognize your work anywhere. As always, I'm glad you're on our side."

"Thank you, Sir."

Quinn hugged Hunter, who returned the manly hug. Quinn pulled away and indicated the Navy Seals storming the parking lot.

"There's your team," Quinn announced then made the familiar motion indicating 'rear assault and take no prisoners'.

Hunter grinned and joined the other eight Navy Seals. Most were former comrades and had fought alongside him years ago. They cheerfully patted him on the back as he approached, but their reunion was brief. They returned to shooting stray zombies with Hunter by their side. Bishop approached Quinn and Jetta, attempting not to interrupt their joyful reunion. Jetta saw him approach and grinned at her father.

"You've been gone a while, Dad," Jetta remarked. "I don't think you've met--"

Quinn grinned and proudly extended his hand to Bishop. "Harlan Rafkin, it's a pleasure to meet you again."

Jetta's expression dropped. Harlan Rafkin? It couldn't be true! How could he keep something like that from her? Why had he lied to her? Bishop and Quinn shook hands. Her father looked at her and grinned while chuckling.

"Mr. Rafkin put the team up for free in one of his luxury hotels last year after we finished a little mission outside Rio," Quinn informed her then grinned at Bishop. "Again, sorry about the mishap in room 5010."

Bishop avoided looking at Jetta. He suddenly appeared to recall the incident and uncertainly nodded. "Oh, yeah, I remember now," he muttered. "The flamethrower thing."

Jetta stared at Bishop, although he still avoided looking at her. "Harlan Rafkin?" she growled lowly.

He finally looked at her and appeared apologetic. "Jetta, I can explain," Bishop gently announced.

"Yeah? Well, don't bother."

Jetta hurried back to her helicopter and jumped inside. Quinn appeared surprised and watched the helicopter lift and fly away. He eyed Bishop while maintaining his grin and placed his hand firmly on his shoulder to the point of causing him physical pain.

"Please tell me you didn't screw my little girl."

Chapter Thirty-two

*T*wo days had passed since Winter Harbor was a zombie war zone. Jetta and Hunter stood before the hanger and hugged the men from her father's team as the military helicopter prepped for departure. It was a long, tear-filled good-bye for everyone. She had two wonderful days with her father and his rowdy team. It was exhausting but exhilarating being able to fight alongside her father, and, for the first time in her life, be a part of his world. It was an amazing experience, which she hoped she would never have to repeat. The prospect of mind numbing helicopter tours with the rich and pampered never sounded so good. Quinn shook Hunter's hand then gave him a manly hug.

"Look after my little girl until I get back."

"I always do, Admiral."

Hunter once again returned from fighting the war both real and in his mind. It was the longest he'd ever been lost in his own mind since he came out of the coma seven years ago. His three-day siege proved one thing to him. No matter how lost he became; no matter what he thought he saw; he still knew enough not to take innocent lives. He no longer feared becoming an unstoppable monster. He also discovered he was still a damned fine soldier. Despite all that he lost the day he nearly died, he'd actually lost nothing that really mattered. Quinn approached Jetta, grinned, and held her firmly in his arms. She returned the hug and didn't want to let go.

As he held her against him, he whispered in her ear, "Keep Hunter away from anything that explodes, okay?"

Jetta laughed then nodded and kissed him on the cheek. Quinn pulled away, smiled at her, and then turned while secretly wiping a tear from his eye. He hurried for the helicopter and jumped inside before anyone would notice. Hunter moved alongside Jetta and placed his arm over her shoulder as they watched the helicopter lift off. She rested her head on his shoulder and sadly watched as the helicopter slowly vanished, once again whisking her father far from her. She was grateful she would always have Hunter. He was the one constant in her life the last seven years. And every time her father had to leave, she knew her second father would always be there with her. He gave her a knowing squeeze, as if he'd read her thoughts. She was almost sure he had, because he was probably thinking the same thing. Both stared at the empty sky and appeared reluctant to look away. There was a long moment of silence between them.

"Thanks for not telling on me," Hunter said gently.

Jetta grinned and laughed softly while clinging to him. "What's one rocket launcher between friends?" she teased.

Hunter chuckled and kissed her forehead.

†

*P*iles of charred zombie bodies, exploded cars, and demolished buildings were everywhere throughout town. Army vehicles still flooded every street in Winter Harbor. Despite the destruction, a majority of the town seemed to have survived. This was indicated by the number of survivors milling about the sidewalks in front of their homes and other places they had sought shelter during the zombie rampage. Sheriff Palmer walked along the sidewalk with Deputy Styles on crutches alongside him. Both cheerfully greeted townsfolk as they passed. Spirits were high despite all they had suffered. The residents of Winter Harbor were survivors. Perhaps it was instilled in them from enduring their long, harsh winters, or maybe it was because they were direct descendants from Mainers just a short trip across the ocean.

Sheriff Palmer had his own, distinctive theory to their survival as he approached the diner. He watched his neighbors helping the cook remove boards from the diner window. He grinned and proudly patted the heavy door to the diner. The door had deep scratches down the front stained with blood and several torn fingernails embedded in the wood. It was his opinion that old-fashioned country craftsmanship kept the good people of Winter Harbor alive. If their homes could survive Maine winters, they could most certainly withstand a zombie outbreak.

Stella hurried out from the diner and handed Sheriff Palmer his usual extra-large cup of coffee-to-go. He grinned and, without warning, hugged her. She smiled, returned the embrace with delight, and nodded him inside. He placed his arm around her and held her affectionately to his side as he walked with her into the diner. She wasn't sure if it was the coffee or her that he missed, but he'd never displayed affection toward her like that before. It didn't matter; she'd take it either way. Styles watched them enter the dinner, grinned, and shook his head. It was a defining moment for the good sheriff. *Everyone* in town knew Stella made the worst coffee, yet Sheriff Palmer continually bragged about it. If that wasn't love, nothing was. Styles proudly looked around at his town and took a deep, cleansing breath. As he looked down the sidewalk, his smile suddenly faded. Several teenage girls were watching him and chattering softly among themselves. They hurried toward him while fussing over his injuries. Deputy Styles appeared alarmed and quickly hobbled away from them and into the diner after Sheriff Palmer.

†

*T*he hotel looked like a war zone. Nearly every door and window on the first floor of the hotel was boarded up after shattering from the force of the improvised explosives. The parking lot had charred, wrecked vehicles sticking out of crater-sized holes in the blacktop. Scores of military men collected the remains of exploded zombie parts and bagged them for *whatever* their reason. A large bonfire burned nearly one hundred zombies as more were being tossed on. Carter walked the parking lot with a solemn look while shaking his head. Recovering from the devastation seemed a long way off, and he didn't have the energy for it. Bishop walked the parking lot with his clipboard and documented the damage. Carter frowned and uncertainly approached him.

"What's the damage?" Carter reluctantly asked while looking around his once luxurious resort. "Do you think the insurance will cover this?"

Bishop snorted a laugh while busily writing on his clipboard. "Our insurance doesn't cover biohazard contamination, willful property destruction, and damage sustained from a zombie apocalypse. But, on the bright side, Harlan Rafkin agreed to pay for the damages I orchestrated. I just need to submit a bill of damage for the parking lot and first floor windows."

"What about the rest?" Carter asked.

"You can't exactly sue a zombie," Bishop replied. "You and he will have to assess the remaining damage and come to an agreement. I was only responsible for the damage done by our homemade explosives."

Carter groaned and shook his head with disgust. "The next time you speak to Mr. Rafkin, tell him I'd like to reconsider his buyout offer."

"I think the buyout amount dropped drastically, but I'll mention it to him."

Carter nodded and walked away.

The parking lot entrance to the hotel lobby was crudely boarded with a makeshift door in the middle. Despite the fact that a pick-up truck had been sitting in the middle of the lobby just two days ago, the lobby appeared almost tidy. The debris from the door and wall was already cleaned and removed. The salvageable remaining furniture was neatly organized to restore some sense of normalcy even if the hotel wouldn't be reopened until the following summer after all necessary repairs had been made. Several bloodstains remained as a grisly reminder of recent events. Desmond held Lee in his arms as they stood before the front desk. She smiled while clinging to him and played with the buttons on his shirt. Desmond grinned and indicated the pink high heels she wore.

"Those are my favorite," he informed her. "Maybe you could wear those on our trip to the mainland."

"Maybe I will," Lee teased.

"How many pink shoes do you actually own?" he finally asked.

"Twenty-three," she said sheepishly. "I know; that's too many pink shoes."

"Actually, I was remembering a pair of pink slippers I saw at that mall on the mainland. You'd look adorable in them."

Lee laughed and kissed him warmly. Desmond returned the kiss with a little more passion and some added aggression. Rafael approached, saw them in their compromising embrace, and cleared his throat while attempting to hide his smile. They quickly jumped apart and appeared flustered.

"Dude, you should hear the word around town," Rafael informed Desmond. "You and Hunter are heroes."

"I'm no hero," Desmond remarked with a humored chuckle. "Hunter pointed a gun at me and made me help. He's the hero."

"According to him, you gave the orders."

"Not exactly how I remember it," Desmond replied with a laugh.

"You'll always be a hero to me," Lee cooed with a grin.

"Well, hero worship does have its rewards," Desmond teased and quickly kissed her.

"Get a room," Rafael teased.

"Hmm, excellent idea," Lee replied without taking her eyes off Desmond.

Hunter and Ming entered the lobby through the beachside doors. She kissed him warmly on the lips then headed down the corridor toward the kitchen. Hunter watched her with a grin until she was gone then waltzed toward the front desk. He cast his back against the desk and sighed dreamily.

"She kissed me. Did you see that?"

"Yeah, dude, we saw. I'm happy for you," Rafael replied cheerfully. "And when the hotel reopens next summer, I heard Ming will have Elise's job."

"I didn't hear about that," Lee remarked.

"Oh, that's right, it's supposed to be a secret," Rafael muttered. "I probably shouldn't have said anything."

"Why would my father be keeping secrets from me," Lee asked and appeared curious.

"If I'm not mistaken, he's been keeping a few secrets from you," Rafael replied then hesitated. "Oh, I wasn't supposed to mention that either. Maybe I should return to the kitchen, before I say something else I'm not supposed to."

"Did my father tell you he intended to sell the hotel?" she asked. "I heard he got an offer last year from that mogul, Harlan Rafkin."

"Uh, well, that might have something to do with it," Rafael replied then immediately cursed himself for speaking.

"You do know something," Lee announced with surprise. "How do you know so much?"

"Well, I, uh," Rafael fumbled then shrugged. "I'm sort of tight with Harlan Rafkin."

"Oh, my God," Lee suddenly gasped. "You're a mole!"

"No, just a chef," Rafael replied.

Hunter rolled his eyes and shook his head. He was already way ahead of this conversation, and it no longer held his attention. Bishop entered the lobby through the makeshift parking lot door. Hunter saw him and straightened with a groan.

"If you'll excuse me, I'm feeling a walk on the beach," Hunter announced and headed across the lobby toward the beachside doors.

Bishop saw him, changed direction, and hurried after him. "Hunter, wait."

Hunter stopped halfway to the beachside doors and turned. He grinned deviously at Bishop. "Mr. Rafkin, I presume."

"Stop calling me that. Someone might hear," Bishop muttered, appeared tense, and looked around. "I had a very good reason for not telling anyone who I was."

"I'm sure you did," Hunter replied casually and smirked. "If Jetta knew you were a playboy millionaire, she never would have slept with you."

Bishop suddenly appeared tense while staring at Hunter. "Oh, she told you about what happened," he said softly then turned defensive. "And for the record, I'm not a playboy. That lifestyle never agreed with me." He again turned timid. "I just want to talk to Jetta. She's been avoiding me for two days. Can't you talk to her?"

"Of course I can talk to her," he replied. "I talk to her every day."

"You know what I mean."

"Yes, I know what you mean," Hunter retorted. "Why would I want to come to your defense?"

"Because you know how I feel about her," Bishop said then considered. "And I can get you a rocket launcher."

"Thanks, I already have one."

"Just tell her I want to talk to her," he said. "I want a chance to apologize."

The helicopter was heard just outside the lobby beyond the beachside doors. Bishop was suddenly alerted to the sound and hurried for the beachside doors. Jetta entered and nearly collided with him. There was an awkward tension between them. Hunter casually approached.

"Want me to handle this?" Hunter asked while indicating Bishop with a slight nod.

"It's okay, Hunter."

Hunter frowned and shook his head. "At least pretend to put up a fight before letting him have his way with you," he remarked. "I'll be right outside. Call if you need backup."

Jetta nodded her response. Hunter glared at Bishop through piercing eyes then left the lobby. Bishop watched Hunter leave then turned to Jetta.

"Please let me explain--"

"Explain what? Girls like me are a dime a dozen to guys like you," Jetta remarked.

"It's not like that, and you know it," he insisted. "No matter what name I use, it doesn't change the fact that I'm crazy about you, and I have been since the day we'd met. You know there hasn't been anyone else."

"Why didn't you tell me you were Harlan Rafkin?"

"Because Harlan Rafkin is an unfeeling prick. When I came here as Bishop Kane, a no body, people treated me like a no body, and I liked that. I don't want people kissing my ass because of who I am and what I have. That's what turned me into a prick in the first place. And let's be honest, if you knew I was a mega millionaire, you wouldn't have wanted anything to do with me." He then appeared to consider something he hadn't before. "And Lee would have suddenly found me interesting."

"You're right," Jetta remarked firmly with a sigh. "I don't fit into the world of the rich and pampered. I like military men, men like Hunter, men like my father--men like Bishop Kane."

Bishop suddenly appeared encouraged and gently pulled her into his arms. "You'll never have to meet Harlan Rafkin, I promise."

Jetta reluctantly ran her hands along his chest. "Good, because I doubt I'd like him, and I really wasn't ready to give up Bishop just yet," she said gently then met his gaze with a slightly embarrassed grin. "And I certainly didn't want what we had to be a one-night stand."

He stared at her with some surprise then grinned his humor. "You intended to forgive me no matter what I said, didn't you?"

"I wouldn't go that far," she said firmly. Her mood immediately softened. "Besides, I sort of had to avoid you until my father left anyway." She hid her smile. "It'd be too easy for him to write you off as collateral damage."

"I don't want to hide our relationship from your father."

"Oh, we're in a relationship now?"

"I assume we are," he replied. "If we're not, it's going to make sleepovers a little awkward."

"Can you honestly tell me you're interested in a commando's daughter?" she asked. "I come with a lot of baggage--and he's extremely protective over me."

"I accept that Hunter's part of the package deal," he said while holding her against him. "And if the time comes that he wants that surgery, it'll be Harlan Rafkin's pleasure to fund it."

"That's up to Hunter," Jetta announced but appeared pleased by the offer.

He stared into her eyes and smiled warmly. "So about your father?"

She reluctantly sighed then smiled. "I'll tell him about us when I talk to him next week," she said gently. "That'll give him a couple of months to get it out of his system and blow up a lot of stuff before he sees you again."

"You do love me. I knew it."

"Don't read too much into it," she teased while running her hands along his chest. "I'm just here to make good that promise I made to you."

Bishop groaned then kissed her passionately. He broke off the kiss, took her hand, and led her toward the elevator. Rafael, Lee, and Desmond applauded them as they passed. Bishop and Jetta appeared embarrassed by the applause, hid their smiles, and slipped into the elevator.

Lee smiled and shook her head. "I finally get it."

The End

Town Darling
(Coming Soon!)

Preview Excerpt

After surviving a brutal attack that claims the lives of those she loves, a young woman seeks revenge on a corrupt town.

Going back home is never easy, but for Casey, it means returning to her corrupt hometown where she barely survived a brutal attack. Accompanied by two *family friends*, she seeks justice for the night that destroyed her life. Her physical scars are nothing compared to her emotional ones, forcing the local sheriff to believe that the town darling is back for revenge. As the conspiracy for her revenge appears to be leading up to the coveted town fair, the sheriff is determined to stop her from fulfilling her vengeful scheme...but guilt over his role on that fateful night continues to haunt him. His desperate need for Casey's forgiveness could be his undoing.

The Battle for Andrea Maria
(Available Now!)

Preview Excerpt

A cruise ship attack turns six survivors into overnight celebrities after they take credit for the heroic act of a stowaway who died saving them.

The cruise is just what Jess needed--a bit of harmless fun far from her daily grind. But what begins as a relaxing vacation turns into a desperate fight for her life when terrorists take over the ship and start piling up bodies. Teaming up with a mysterious stowaway, Jess attempts to send out a distress call but knows they cannot wait for help to come. If she or the few remaining passengers have any hope for survival, Jess must act now. The papers dub it "The Battle for *Andrea Maria*," but to Jess it is the moment she fought side-by-side with her enigmatic Romeo, saving the ship--and losing him. She thinks the story ends there, but really, the nightmare is just beginning...

ABOUT THE AUTHOR

Holly Copella has been writing since the age of twelve when her frustration at a book's poor plot drove her to author her own story. Over the last decade, she's written a number of screenplays, some of which she's now adapting into novels. Her fascination with zombies and other darker material lends an edge to her writing, which tends to lean toward horror. As a fan of Agatha Christie, she appreciates the craft of a good plot and the importance of creating significant characters.

Hailing from Pennsylvania, Copella lives in the Endless Mountains on a farm with her rescue horses and other animals. In addition to writing and reading fiction, she enjoys riding horses and traveling to Las Vegas and Disney World.

www.ingramcontent.com/pod-product-compliance
Lightning Source LLC
Chambersburg PA
CBHW072227190626
46809CB00017B/1055